CRUSH

CRUSH

edited by
Simone Corletto
Amy T. Matthews
Jess M. Miller
&
Lynette Washington

First published 2017 by MidnightSun Publishing Pty Ltd
PO Box 3647, Rundle Mall, SA 5000, Australia.
www.midnightsunpublishing.com

Cataloguing-in-Publication entry is available from the
National Library of Australia.
http://catalogue.nla.gov.au

Edited by Simone Corletto, Amy T. Matthews, Jess M. Miller and Lynette Washington
Cover design by Kim Lock
Internal design by Zena Shapter

Printed and bound in Australia by Griffin Press. The papers used by MidnightSun in the manufacture of this book are natural, recyclable products made from wood grown in sustainable plantation forests.

CONTENTS

*For our crushes
and for all those who have been crushed.*

INTRODUCTION

This anthology is a creative response to the ideas and conversations generated over four days at the Romance Writers of Australia's 25th anniversary national conference, 'Ain't Love Grand', which included two academic streams hosted by Flinders University. In *Crush* there is intimacy and isolation, comfort and connection, hurt and heartbreak, longing and disappointment; there is love that lasts beyond death, love that never speaks itself aloud, and love that ends in all manner of ways: good and bad. Love is not simple; it is as unique as the people who feel it—who *suffer* it. Love changes us; it makes us grow and bloom, but it can also wound us, sometimes irreparably. Love is crushing on people, and being crushed by them. Love is transcendent and love is mundane; it is a fundamental part of being human.

The authors in this collection face the burning beauty of love and write of both the blaze and the ashes left behind. They write about the *crush*. For many people, a crush is our first experience of love. It's an instant attraction. A fascination. An obsession. From here, there are at least two paths these emotions can take: if the crush is returned, it can lead to romance, to love; if the crush is unrequited, it can lead to heartbreak, to longing, to breaking into the Dean's office to rifle through medical records.

For others, the crush is influenced by the presence of others—parents who don't approve, friends who are searching for something different or similar, and sometimes complete strangers, whose brief presences in our lives can be akin to magic. These are stories that are bursting with people: loves non-monogamous, loves which curl from the crevices of confined spaces, difficult situations, online dating apps, and bustling cities; loves which are never simple, often humorous, and always remarkable.

The perspectives on romance within *Crush* are boldly non-traditional, heroically heartfelt and full of imperfection and vice, just as love is. We do hope that you will be swept away.

The Editors
Simone Corletto, Amy T. Matthews, Jess M. Miller and Lynette Washington

PERSPECTIVES ON LOVE

SUSAN MIDALIA

1. Definitions

An academic: In ancient Greek myth, sexual or passionate love (Eros) was conceptualised as a form of madness, the consequence of being struck by one of Cupid's arrows and rendered blind to reason. The idea of love's blindness also underpins the more recent concept of Eros as a life force, akin to the philosopher Schopenhauer's notion of will, a fundamentally unthinking or instinctual striving for survival and reproduction.

A misogynist: Love is having the sensitivity not to tell your wife she's getting fat. It's not complaining when she wants yet another pointless night out with the girls. It's resisting the urge to root the girl in the office who's virtually giving it out for free, in those tight short skirts she's always wearing.

A Marxist feminist: Heterosexual love in general, and heterosexual marriage in particular, are indisputably the products of patriarchal ideology, designed to ensure the continuing subordination of women as a group. See Engels, *The Communist Manifesto*, Chapter 2.

A humanist: Love means treating the loved one with kindness and respect. And it *does* mean having to say you're sorry.

2. The love song 'Cry me a River'

'Cry me a River' was first recorded by Eileen Barton in 1955. It has since been recorded and re-interpreted by over sixty artists, including Shirley Bassey, Ella Fitzgerald, Sam Cooke, Barbra Streisand, Sammy Davis Jr, Ray Charles, Joe Cocker, Joan Baez, Etta James, Jeff Beck, Frank Sinatra and Nina Simone.

An historical approach: 'Cry me a River' has been recorded in many different musical forms, including country and western, blues, hard rock, jazz, big band, and even as the theme to the 2010 Vancouver Winter Olympics. The continuing appeal of the song for both artists and audiences is arguably the singer's refusal to cry in the face of a lover's abandonment. It seems to speak of the universal need for inner strength and dignity. The only recorded criticism of the much-loved 'Cry me a River' is that of the chief of Columbia Records, Mitch Miller, whose objection to the word 'plebeian' in the lyrics was the basis for his refusing to allow his artist Peggy King to record it. Since Miller did not elaborate on the reason for his objection, one can only assume that he found the word 'plebeian' unappealingly unromantic.

As an interesting side-note, research also reveals that the writer of 'Cry me a River,' Arthur Hamilton, feared that the words would be mis-heard as 'Crimea River'. There is no record, however, of such a misunderstanding.

A Marxist literary critical response: The use of the word 'plebeian' in this song to evoke the lover's disdain for romantic love reinforces the inescapably ideological nature of all art forms, including music. Further, since the goal of Marxism is to reduce human suffering by building a world of democracy and hope in which everybody has food, shelter, education, healthcare and the other benefits of civilisation, it could be argued that such suffering would be substantially reduced by prohibiting the further dissemination of the self-indulgently bourgeois song 'Cry me a River'.

A popular culture approach: Arthur Hamilton's version of 'Cry me a River' is not to be confused with the version released in 2002 by the contemporary musical phenomenon Justin Timberlake. Critically acclaimed and commercially successful, indeed spectacularly so, Timberlake's version has been described as 'an acidic, filthy little song teeming with spite and retribution'.

'Cry me a River' also generated a video clip, claimed by many critics to be Timberlake's act of revenge on his unfaithful girlfriend at the time, the singer Britney Spears. The production and distribution of the video has been described by the editor of *Billboard* as a deliberate attempt by Timberlake to court controversy, and, because of its depiction of his raunchy sexuality, 'to make its star seem more grown-up".[1]

A feminist music fan's response: Grow up, Justin.

---

1 Justin Lipshutz, 2013. It has also been suggested, by an anonymous source who appreciates good music, that Timberlake should do what the editor's surname decrees.

3. The longest love song title ever recorded

'How could you believe me when I said I loved you when you know I've been a liar all my life?' (sung by Jane Powell and Fred Astaire in the 1951 movie 'Royal Wedding').

An academic interpretation: For all its playful sense of wit, the title also raises a philosophical conundrum. For if the speaker's claim to be a liar is true—and in the context of the title this in itself is radically un-decidable—it must logically follow that her or his declaration of love could be either true or not true, hence reinforcing the ultimately irresolvable nature of the question.

The response of a writer of literary fiction: Heck, that song title is even longer than the famously long title of Raymond Carver's relatively short short story 'What we talk about when we talk about love.' Anyone interested in love should read this story for its conceptual complexity and brooding sense of bleakness. And if you're not into bleakness because you like your love stories to be all vacuous sweetness and light and stereotyped characters and simplistic clichéd happy endings, then just fuck off to the section in the bookshop labelled Chick Lit.

4. The (possibly) most misogynistic love song title of all time

The Country and Western song 'It's Hard to Kiss the Lips at Night That Chew Your Ass Out All Day Long'.

A feminist academic's analysis: While the song title perpetuates the misogynistic stereotype of the nagging woman or shrew, it is important to move beyond the binary model of power that conceptualises men as oppressors and women as victims by recognising the ways in which women in the context of heterosexual romance can also be self-victimising. A notable example of this self-victimisation is evident in another Country and Western song, 'Stand by your Man,' first recorded by Tammy Wynette in 1968. The song unwittingly, and dismayingly, confuses feminine loyalty with subservience to the patriarchal order. Indeed, the singer's very name is a symbol of her distressingly subjugated status: 'Tammy' is distinctively infantilising, while 'Whine-ette' clearly speaks for itself.

A feminist comedian's response: My favourite version of 'Stand by your Man' is a song called 'Stand by your Can', performed on Sesame Street by the singer Hammy Swinette, in which the porcine gal urges us to put our trash in the trash can.

5. How many lovers does it take to change a light bulb? An older conservative member of society replies: Before I answer that question, I must insist on replacing the word 'lover' with 'husband,' because changing a light bulb implies domesticity and hence marriage, a union sanctioned by God and in which it is the responsibility of the husband to perform any activity requiring initiative and dexterity (such as changing a light bulb).

A young, progressive member of society replies: Hey, it can take as many lovers as you like to change a light bulb. And the lover can be male, female, transgendered, whatever, because what the hell does it matter who puts what where as long as it's consensual and doesn't hurt anyone and might even be goddamned pleasurable. To be honest, I just don't get this obsession with anatomy and chromosomes and dangly bits and holes, as though any of that stuff defines a person. What matters is in your heart and in your head, not the physical body we use to carry our heart and head around in.

So, yeah, we need to create a society that embraces not just diversity but ambiguity, ambivalence, a wonderful mess of contradictions and confusions. We need to shout out loud that it's OK to love whoever we want, to marry whoever we want, or not marry, if that's our choice, because it's never a matter of anatomy or sexuality but of basic and inalienable human rights.

And hey, don't forget to use an energy-efficient light bulb.

crush

noun

1. an intense infatuation, especially for someone unattainable

    'He had a crush on Dr Reynolds.'

THIS ONE TIME...

LAUREN FOLEY

We saw each other. We smiled. We moved near. Nearer, nearer, nearer, near. We put our stuff down in-between us, in front and behind us and all around us. We moved the stuff and rearranged it, unpacked it and restacked it. We sat up straight, we sat down heavy, we leaned left, we tilted right. We laughed and teased those onstage with ease. We brushed arms so hairs might meet and greet. We laughed. We joked. We shared a Coke. We perspired. We sweated. In our minds, we heavy petted. We laughed, we breathed, we fantasised with need. We sat up straight, we sat down heavy, she leaned left, I tilted right. We sighed. We groaned. We looked ahead. We moaned.

We took a break. She went for Coke. I very nearly stole a smoke even though I thought I'd quit two years ago. There's no hope. There's no hope. She came back. I got wet. We sat. We dreamt. And dreamed. And dreamt. Dreamt and dreamed about how we felt. About another world. Where we could. Just do it. Out in the woods. Just do it. Screw it. Her sexuality. My instability. The logistic inability. We sighed. She groaned. We looked ahead. I moaned. We sat erect. We reclined. We leant on borrowed time.

She looked at me. I looked at her. She gave her number. I heard her purr. I looked ahead. She looked at me. We talked of coffee while I got clammy. No hands. No cigarettes. We performed like fucking majorettes. I thought of God and penance for inverted sexual dilemmas. I thought if I wasn't married this might be my one chance for a lesbian dalliance. We looked together. We looked at each other. If only I could be another. Another woman with another face, not subscribed to the matrimonial race. I want a baby. I love my spouse. We are saving for a pretty house. Full of nice things and *Happy Days*, filled with neat sex, neat kids, neat toys. Filled with neat girls who love neat boys.

I looked at her. She looked at me. Heat radiated between my knees. She looked at me. I looked at her. I could feel my body quiver and purr. Desire blossomed. Desire remains. Desire etched her body's outline into my brain. How much I wanted to say 'Yes. Where's your car? Let's run. Let's have sex.' I've never done it with a woman. I might like to. Imagine coming. Over and over. Again and again. No need to explain how it feels, where the pressure must go. I imagine lesbian sex must flow – together, two tributaries of the one stream, over a waterfall headed downstream.

No—this is me naked. No—my nipples don't look like you think they should from that porno book you grew up with in your neighbourhood when all the guys were constructing body shapes for girls so we could look like Barbie toys, and when guys see us with no clothes on they look like '*hmmm*' that's not the same pussy I was imagining all these years under my duvet, or how our armpits smell like theirs if we won't wash and talcum powder to smell like schoolgirls while men get harder. Is it not easier? To have sex. With one who knows your boobs can hang down to your toes, and that it's ok, it doesn't matter, you can still go at it nail, tongs and hammer. And that after your vagina is stretched into oblivion for a procreation act, that it's ok, it doesn't matter, you've done your Kegels, you'll take the wham-bam-thankyou-mama.

We moved together. We moved apart, skipped a beat, thump-thumping hearts. We moved together, we slid apart, slipped and slid, our knees apart. We moved. We sighed. We moved. We groaned. We moved. We looked. We moved. We moaned. We moved. We laughed. We moved. We teased those up there on the stage with ease. We moved together. We moved apart. Shuffled in seats, a reckless start. Thump-thump bumping knees. Thump-thump pumping hearts. We moved together. We played our parts. Slipped and slid our lips apart. Sitting there. Under the trees. Under blue skies. Her and me. I thought of her. I thought of you. I thought: 'I really, really want a screw.'

It's been so long. Such a long, long time since I didn't have to wear lace panties. A matching bra. Since I could scratch that itch. We've come so far. It's just a glitch. In our marriage. Just a half-term miscarriage.

I look at her. She looks at me. I think I really, really need to leave. She gives her number, says I should call her. Fucking hell — I adore her. I look at her. She looks at me. I think I really, really need to leave. I say I will. I'll give her a bell. We'll meet for coffee. But she can tell. By my diamond, my wedding ring. We can never ever be a thing. I have a husband. He has a wife. And we love each other, almost every night. It gets difficult, relationships do. But I can't give it all up for a fast screw. I want a baby. I love my spouse. We are saving for a pretty house. Full of nice things, and sunny days, filled with great sex, great kids, gender non-specific toys. Filled with girls who love boys who love girls who love boys who love girls who love...

I look at her. She looks at me. We see each other. We have no need. To go any further. It's as they say, the best sex is fantasy. I look at her. She looks at me. I say 'I think we'd better leave.' I look at her. She looks at me. We kiss goodbye.

Breasts meet. Bodies hug.

I think, fuck it, fuck it, fuck it—we'll do it right here—under a picnic rug. I look at her. She looks at me.

I come. She leaves.

I never call her. I never will. That one-time-hour, time stood still.

SMALL WORLD

REBECCA HANDLER

He looked like Winona Ryder in *Girl Interrupted*, small with short black hair and brown eyes that were both affectionate and frightened, like a deer. He even wore a corduroy jacket two sizes too big. I met him at my co-worker's birthday party, an ironic affair at an ice skating rink off the highway. She was turning twenty-five and gave out goodie bags filled with smelly erasers and strawberry lip gloss.

He was behind me in line for face painting, and tapped me on the shoulder. 'What are you getting?'

'Maybe a rainbow. Not sure.'

'You could get your whole face done as a cat.'

I snorted. 'I don't like cats. Why don't *you* get your whole face done as a cat?' He did, and later that night, when we fucked after watching *The Simpsons*, his whiskers smeared all over my couch.

I outweighed him by eighteen kilos. I had never been intimate with someone so small. At first I was self-conscious about my thighs and felt like a nutcracker, but soon I loved how delicate his body seemed, and how I could cup his shoulder blades with my palms as he pushed in and out of me. He was always cold. I wanted to protect him. I wondered if this is what it feels like to be a man.

He was peculiar about food, and spent hours thinking about where we should eat and what he should order. He'd send me texts in the middle of the day. 'The Indian place on Hampden has a vegan curry,' and then two minutes later, 'We could get the chicken dish without cream.' Of course when we ended up at whatever restaurant, in this case the Indian place, he would nibble on half a samosa and scoot the rice around on his plate. He had always had a big lunch.

He belonged to a gym. He was an early riser, said it was the birds, and met a trainer there five days a week. The trainer knew that he was focused on weight loss, and developed a strict regimen for him that he kept on his phone. Now that I think about it, I'd like to kill that Orlando Bloom lookalike asshole trainer. Those people are paid to keep obsessives obsessed.

According to the medical establishment I was, and still am, considered mildly obese, but he never once criticized me about my body, my eating habits, or my lack of interest in the gym. He told me he loved my size, and I think he did. He liked how I ate what I wanted and bought form-fitting clothes. Once, after fucking, with his head resting on my chest and his fingers playing with my nipple, he whispered, 'Are you really 77?' He sounded jealous.

I loved him. I loved everything about him, except for this. I tried to understand, to get him help, but his preoccupation with being thin became the other girlfriend who was always stealing him away. I started hating his skinny body and resented being bigger and stronger. I didn't want to protect him anymore. I wanted to expose him to the world and have him get frightened and then get better. I fantasised about force-feeding him, and begged him to change. But of course there are things that will never change, things that are as central to a person as a heartbeat.

I am only bringing all this up because I ran into him just now, on the way to meet you. He was with someone. They had groceries and a dog. He introduced me to the girl and I shook her hand. It was tiny and cold.

FETTUCCANCÉ

[fett-*uh*-chance-ay]
Noun: a woman to whom a woman is
engaged to be married, a proposal that
takes place while straining fettuccine

MICHELE FAIRBAIRN

I

Two things of significance have taken place over the past two
weeks.

They may or may not be related.

Number one—

My entire left hand side has become numb. Post-dental-
visit numb. I can't feel a prickle or the coolness of jelly, numb.

There is a line drawn precisely and intimately straight
down the middle of me.

How very strange.

Number two—

Whilst draining fettuccine for our meal last Friday
evening, I was asked for my hand in something resembling
marriage.

It went as follows—
Her: Would you like to go shopping?
Me: Is it in the budget?
Her: For rings.
Me: That's not in the budget.
Her: Engagement rings.
Me: (A sudden fascination with the ability of fettuccine to speed dry and grip to the edge of a colander.)

At the risk of sounding ungrateful when clearly all the world needs now is love sweet love…*while straining fettuccine?*

I'm a modern gal. I'm not a traditionalist. I'm jumping all over Kinsey's scale, even on a decisive day. Never, never, did my imagination ever indulge in fantasies of delirious engagement announcements, icy clear diamond rock on finger and white, white wedding.

But of all the ways and places available to woo and beguile…while straining fettuccine?

It's hard to swallow. Like dry butterless toast on waking in the morning. Mouth and throat tender with dream speak and soft snores. It is hard to swallow but also feels like butterflies on a birthday morning.

So.

I am engaged it seems.

We're going to a baby shower today.

We'll eat blue or pink cupcakes if the gender of the unborn is known.

We'll eat fluffy white if it's a delicious secret.

I love babies. I'm officially clucky.

And I'm a little bit bitter, bordering on narky too.

Maybe it's the relative *ease* with which these things happen for the heterosexual couple. It is the happy concept that a baby may be created at the moment of orgasm with a lover. The vagina drawing in, drawing in the lover's seed, cervix dipping and searching. Wetness, stiffness, longing, joining, thrusting, breathlessness, demanding, surrendering, dying a little death, creating a little life.

Synthesis. A whole from two parts.

God, I am so green with envy.

We will never have this.

This mind-bending, every day, recurrent ability to bring ourselves together in such an intimate and astonishing way that is beyond the symbolic and biologically pleasurable. An act of love that will one day wear loafers or crocs or stilettos and bleed us dry financially.

Instead, as a balm of sorts, she shares with me the theory of the etheric on the drive there—

Me: I wish I had a penis.

She: You do my darling.

Me: To be inside you.

She: You are.

Me: Deep inside you.

She: You are.

Me: To feel you grip me, pull me into you.

She: You can.

Me: What?

She: I have felt your etheric penis in me. Moving. Thrusting.

Me:

She: Mmmm.

Me:

She: Aaahhhh.

Me: Am I...sizely?

She: Ooohh yes. You're sooo big.

Me: (smug) Mmm hmm.

Tonight, for a few hours, I am not engaged. She and I are not what we were and not what we may be. We are all things that are kept in attics, dungeons and rusty old sheds. We are at war.

So, I just sit. Skew-whiff and pissing blood, bleeding bile.

Tonight we are not engaged.

A little knowledge can be devastating in the wrong hands. What was love is fear. What was connection is hatred. What was security is despair.

In these moments, straining fettuccine feels eons away. Another planet. Another galaxy.

She wanted to take me shopping for a ring.

She asked me while I was straining fettuccine.

She's in bed now. In the next room. I can hear her snoring. That has been the most communicative she has been today. She is the calm in a storm. English stiff upper lip. Frustratingly, clinically, dead calm.

It keeps her safe she says. It drives me fucking mad, I say.

She says:

Nothing.

She is in bed now. Through that flimsy wall. Right there.

And I can't bring myself to go in.

To lie in bed with a grand canyon of space between us.

To lose her to her dreams.

Right now.

Through that flimsy fucking wall to the snore-filled, sleep-filled room.

Beyond that wall there is no space for me. No air.

So.

I watch porn.

I get on my dodgy dial-up internet and spend an hour watching my staccato way through a three-minute porn clip. A straight porn clip. A woman riding her husband.

I'm smug for the first fifty-seven minutes, imagining her finding me fantasising about hetero sex. Craving a dick.

Mrs Smith riding Mr Smith silently.

Mrs Smith looking like she's astride an old hack gelding.

She's been on this ride before.

She's seen the sights. Sniffed the smells. Knows every pothole and slippery pebble on the way.

And I'm watching and I want her to know I'm watching and imagining being Mrs Smith. Imagining being anything but her fettuccancé.

He's pig rooting now. Things are warming up.

Hah! If only she could see us now.

Just through that thin wall. Just through there. She's still snoring.

Winter is coming.

It stole like a whisper into a crowded room full of noise. It snuck up. Surprised me. It is only just autumn but in the new house it feels like winter. I have only lived here for four months. This will be the third winter in a different home. Fettuccancé would want me to interject here and state that this is *our* home. Plans have been made. Pains have been taken.

Two weekends ago she carved out a wardrobe space for herself in my—*our* bedroom. Inside hang new clothes we bought for her. A purple-striped shirt. Pin striped pants. Fluffy pink striped socks I bought her for Easter. None of these smell like her. None of these have her sweat or skin flakes like invisible snow on them. None of these stripes when stripped back are anything but generic shop smelling cloth.

This is our place and she is rarely here.

Every moment with her feels like the last rites.

Every Sunday afternoon becomes infused with the desperation of a terminally ill person gasping and grasping at every moment.

I am tired of being bookended by her arrival and departure.

We are framed by impermanence. She haunts the home like a ghost summoned on stolen nights when the veil between our worlds is thinnest, to dance and pass through me.

Sometimes I invite friends when she stays so that they may witness the trick of my summoning her.

So they know she's real. So I know she's real. So they stop asking me if she is real. We do not grocery shop together. We do not decide on toilet paper together.

Yet, we are engaged.

I have taken to sleeping with pillows piled around me like a wall. I make love to the night air and shadows calling her name. When she comes home to me I must acclimatise like a climber approaching the peak of Everest. The oxygen around her is too pure, too light, rarefied.

Then.

She's gone.

Again.

I breathe easier.

I feel heavier. Hungover.

Clock-watching for the next climb.

I say: Read to me.

She says: What shall I read?

I say: Words.

I say: Constructed into sentences.

I say: Just read to me.

We made love last night after many weeks of fighting.

Her head is turned away from me towards my cunt, staring beyond it into the fathomless darkness at the foot of the bed.

Her hand moves as I guide it marionette-style towards the places that are now foreign to her.

She is with me. She is beyond me. These are the moments I wonder at.

She has built a strong fortress and now I find her in a prison of her own making.

I, her fiancé, have to navigate subterranean demons to reach her.

There is no hint. When I cry out for the loss of the present moment to a fear I cannot fathom, the blueprint she refers to constantly to sooth and calm is lost to me.

I don't want to miss a minute.

If it were not for the burning and bubbling of our skin, muscle, sinew, bone, we could almost be happy.

II

There's a new cafe in town, employing only the fresh and funky: they smile you to your seat, take your order with the intensity of a nurse reading vital signs, they deliver plates of aromatic, home grown, homemade stews with crusty bread to your rickety retro table.

The cafe slopes down, pouring me and my friends into a dimly lit room, past the tables, past the hoi polloi, past the out of work jazz band the owner felt pity for. The dimly lit room makes us feel like we are intruding on someone's '60s lounge room tableau without an invite.

We drape ourselves over the orange and brown seats, forty-eight year-old springs creaking and groaning. The faint whiff of Nag Champa lingers with mothballs in the fabric of the couches and velvety psychedelic prints on the wall.

This is good.

And then.

She comes descending into the room. She swoops smoothly into the room.

She takes up the room. She briefly takes up the breath from our lungs. The straight boys. The straight girls. The gay boys and me.

Especially and potently...me.

I am confounded.

Gladly, desperately, fanny gagging on its own juices, heart-space turned into a pulsing discotheque, confounded.

Have I *ever* seen anything like her?

It's my turn to order—

She: What can I get you?

Me:

She: (looks up quizzically)

Me: (She's used to this. Look at her. How could she not be? She's fucking perfect. How can someone be so perfect? Can I paint you...draw you...write great odes to you...fashion your likeness from cool marble...can I...could I...touch you?)

She: Would you like to order? (She grins) We're a bit busy tonight.

Me: Uh, (dumbly) a drink.

She: Wine, cocktail?

Me:

She: Alrightee. Berry Tango with a twist coming up. Sound OK to you?

Me: (Nods vigorously, pathetically.)

I ooh and ahh in all the right conversational places as the friends enthusiastically applaud the space, the decor, the smell and the sexy waitress.

We are all most impressed thank you.

Most impressed indeed.

The night flies by.

No part of the conversation adheres.

Nothing is interesting or diverting enough.

An effort must be made to peer around her to see or hear any of the social intercourse.

I will not leave until I make an impression on her. I have consumed enough Berry Tangos to be convinced that she must know my intentions. Or, if nothing else, she must know my phone number.

She: Can I take your glass now?

Me: Can I have you phone number?

She:

Me: You see. I need to see you again.

She: I'll go get a pen and paper.

Text afterwards:

Me: *thank you. it was so good to meet you...to watch you.* (Too creepy? Don't care.)

Her: *np's. u have nothing to thank me for yet. c me again soon and i'll give u a 100 reasons x*

I walk in and see her, the waitress, sitting, reading a book.

Glass raised to her lips, forgotten, as she reads her book.

She is androgyny. Head shaved, number one. Eyes blue, large, undressing me at a glance. Delicious lips. Blue blood lines carve symmetrical poetry. Her top, turned up at the collar, unbuttoned to her sternum.

Lines and lines and curves and shadows and undulations.

It's poetry. This girl is fucking poetry.

We sit in a bar. Each sprawled on a bench seat torn whole from a 1950s car wreck. Sitting opposite each other.

I was late. She has bought a platter with ripe cheeses, oily sweet olives and a glass of wine, ruby red in hue and dangerous with alcohol.

I begin to drink. Drinking in the aged ripe red and the young firm her.

I can feel guilt erecting a city of tents inside me one by one because I know, just *know* that I have to touch this woman.

And fettuccancé knows this too.

How she knows this, I do not know, but I find as I leave the bar a trail of notes left by her on my car, in my letterbox, on my bed.

First—

Just finished at the accountant...thought I would drop in. Saw ur car. Luv u x

Then—

Have been waiting for u outside of your house. ur still not home. ring me when u get in.

Then—

I hope she's worth it.

I don't know why, but I must do it and it must be worth it.

She will help me build a bridge over that which drifts you and me further apart.

The waitress stands in front of me. She is dressed.

She: Begin.

It is so, so easy. It is criminal. It is trawling the sea bottom with a wide, wide net with impossibly tight woven squares.

The pleasure is intolerable. The waiting is bliss.

The view. The view is extraordinary.

She is turning down her collar.

She moans and laughs at the game.

She knows I know she is mine.

The passion is in the having of this one. Not in the resistance.

She stands.

There is a river surfacing. Pushing apart the lips of her sex. She is flowing, flowing like a natural well.

I am so thirsty for her.

This is not love.

There have been lovers. Circus tents of lovers, crowds, so many, I do not remember half of their names.

This is new.

As I lean in, as I move my hands gently either side of her boyish hips to hold her closer to me, as I feel my tongue nudge apart the temple gates and enter the musky sacred space of her, as I taste her salt, her sweetness, her seemingly endless river of desire, as she drips and pours herself into the goblet of my mouth, I am giddy.

I have never felt clearer or more confused. So melded and so alone.

There are no rules here but: Don't. Get. Caught.

No rules, no boundaries.

The land is too boggy with wet and lust to erect a fence line.

Pleasure exists intensely on the periphery of emptiness. I think of fettuccancé. While I fuck this beautiful two-dimensional woman.

This woman who gives her body to me.

Who asks no questions. Who joins me in a fire that burns and leaves us shivering with cold. I fuck her as hard as my tiring fist and arm gushing with the pulp of her can fuck. It is never enough. I can never get deep enough, for long enough. She is too wide and long. My body longs for her, my ego swells with her nearness and desire for me.

My heart and my divinity is withering and screaming for home.

My shower has a panoramic view of the stars.

Tonight I bathe in what is left of their glow as they push through light years of space, city light smog, trees and glass to reach me.

Water, light, heat.

A fire within baptising me.

Bringing me to new understandings that some part of me—a part that is wiser and older than my conscious mind—is being born to itself. This part that understands… no…*knows*…that the places full of sex with the siren waitress are feeding and making monsters of a primal wound so deep, so elusive as to not have a name. Once awakened, it devours and guzzles body, blood and the essence of all it meets. It has fed on perky breasts, oily cocks, tendrils of dark pubic hair, hungry looks, warm engulfing cunts, sweat laden lashes, throw away compliments, dripping neck hollows, fucking and more fucking.

Still wet from the fucking, still wet from my shower I put on my oversized Little Miss Naughty pyjamas and wonder how I got from straining fettuccine to here.

III

This reckless quest is for home.

This search is for a steady core under the fragmented plates that move and seismically shift constantly. I have been caught in lava. Moulded in the foetal position assumed when overwhelmed by heat or imminent death. The final pose of defiance. The painfully useless and desperate act to fend off extinction.

I seek home. I seek to dive beneath the layers. To be burned by my own fury for life. I seek the primal spaces. The places of messy birth, death, funerals and descending coffins.

Into fire, into the earth, into the self.

Into the spaces and places that consume ego and return us to our rawest form.

To be naked. To allow surrender. To allow love through

the barriers guarded by sharp tooth and jagged nail, barriers mossy with resistance. To set free the tears betraying the depth of fear. To fling free the carnival masks. To allow the air movement through sinew, rain through bone, light through soul and relax.

Relax into the beauty.

And yet…

The merry-go-round slows to a stop.

My fettuccancé has left her seat. She leaves the ride. And I am left holding her crumpled, stained admission ticket in one hand and a scruff of merry-go-round steed's mane in the other as the music starts up again and the ride jolts back to life without her on it.

And this time, I am numb on both sides.

BIG RED LOVE

CARLA CARUSO

It had been love at first sight when Tia clapped eyes on Monty. Everything else—the industrial surrounds and look-at-me fluoro sales signs—had faded away. It was like she'd zoomed in on a phone picture, hypnotised by his good looks, defined contours and raw sex appeal.

She had to have him.

So, despite her trembling knees and normally reticent nature, she'd sidled up alongside and dared to run a hand over his rear. She'd lost her dignity and a sizeable chunk of cash that day. But it had been worth it: they'd been together ever since. Ridden the ups and downs of life as one.

She and her 2004 Holden Monaro CV8-R in 'Pulse Red'—or fire engine red for the Holden-clueless—the pulse-racing colour of passion.

Tia's love of cars had been fostered as a kid, as she helped her single dad with his restoration projects on weekends. But Monty—because she always nicknamed her cars—was special. Automatic, with a sunroof, shiny alloy wheels and a throbbing V8 engine. The fact he was preloved wasn't a problem. Everyone, after all, had a history.

Even her blind date that night, Jed. And as with Monty, she wouldn't hold it against the guy. It'd be a clean slate for all involved.

Tia stood back to assess her handiwork in the afternoon's fading light. She'd spent the past few hours lovingly tending to Monty on her driveway before her hot date. Earlier, she'd texted Jed, prearranging to pick him up. If it was unusual for a woman to drive first time, she didn't care; she wasn't your average girl.

Getting Monty scrubbed up had been the usual workout. First, she'd hosed him down, arcs of water purifying every inch of him, then she'd got him all sudsy with the help of a microfibre mitt. Again, she'd rinsed him before polishing his angles and planes to perfection with her chamois. She'd followed this up by cleaning and conditioning his leather interior. The pièce de résistance was blacking his lush tyres.

Tia placed her hands on her boyish hips and gave a little shake of her head. 'If Jed doesn't fall head over heels too, he's an idiot.'

All she knew about Jed, from Debbie at the call centre where she worked, was that he liked the Adelaide Crows football team (Tia couldn't date a Port supporter), techno music and cars. Plus, he worked in mobile phone sales. Which really could have depicted any number of male Adelaide twenty-somethings. Unfortunately, Debbie hadn't known if Jed favoured Holdens or Fords, but Tia had a good feeling regardless. And she'd at least seen a Facebook profile pic of him, even if half his face had been obscured by mirrored sunglasses. At any rate, a blind date had to be better than Tinder.

Tia reached to open the passenger door, carefully so as not to leave fingerprints, and leant in to squint at the digital clock. *Holy Monaro.* She had just half an hour to get showered and changed. Her own appearance had been the last thing on her mind. Lucky Jed only lived a few suburbs away.

Plus, she knew Monty would create a striking first impression anyway. He looked particularly handsome at dusk, gleaming in the glow of the setting sun and the amber streetlights.

Tia imagined parking him on the street and Jed peeking through the curtains, his mouth agape. Then Jed's gaze would swing to her climbing out in her flippy dress, which matched Monty in colour and brought out her long, dark curls. (Nature had given her a permanent spiral perm.) She'd feel like Christie Brinkley playing 'Ferrari Girl' in *National Lampoon's Vacation.*

It'd be a history-making day, just like when Tia first spotted Monty at that used car yard all those years ago.

Things weren't quite going to plan later that evening. Tia had had to circle the block a few times before a parking space was vacated diagonally down the road from Jed's share house. Who knew the guy would live on such a busy street? Her hope of him seeing her disembark her chariot had been dashed.

By the time she landed on his doorstep, she felt pink-faced and messy. The beginnings of a blister also stung her left little toe. Yet she was determined to think positively. Jed would see Monty soon enough, plus she'd be sitting for most of their restaurant date. Maybe later there'd even come time to kick off her heels. She wasn't easy but it'd been a while between Midoris and attraction couldn't be denied.

With shaky fingers, she pressed the rusty brass doorbell, hearing it chime through the semi-detached abode. Momentarily drowning out the canned TV laughter floating through a window. Then a male voice boomed, 'Door, motherfucker!'

Tia swallowed. Hard. Okay, so the date's start wasn't living up to a scene from Corey Haim's *License to Drive*. But she hadn't wasted half a ton of her favourite car-cleaning detergent, and almost given herself tennis elbow using it, to give in to negativities now.

Several long minutes later, footsteps sounded indoors. Then the scratched wood door pulled back and she stared into her date's peepers—an attractive denim-blue, she discovered, and framed by heavy brows.

Jed's tanned, skinny frame was encased in a charcoal T-shirt as faded as his jeans and his stubble indicated at least a few days between shaves. Immediately, she felt like she'd tried too hard. 'Disheveled' was the new cool and Jed was good-looking enough to pull it off.

He flicked his light brown hair off his forehead like he'd only recently departed One Direction and quirked up a side of his mouth. 'Lady in red! You must be Tia.'

'Yeah ... h-hi.'

As she gave an awkward wave, he leant in to kiss her cheek, smelling of zesty cologne, and her heart lifted. Jed pulled back. 'Gotta admit, I almost forgot our date was tonight.' He patted his non-existent stomach. 'But good thing we made plans; I'm starving.'

Tia's heart sank to the vicinity of her near-blistered foot, but she covered it up with a weak laugh. 'Ha, yeah. Well, the Italian restaurant I chose is meant to be super-generous with its serving sizes.'

Not that she was sure where he'd put any pasta, he was more of a waif than her.

'Cool.' Jed looked past her shoulder. 'So where's your wheels?'

A smile returned to Tia's lips as she turned and pointed down the street. The familiar sight gave her a little thrill and a sense of calm all at once. She girlishly giggled. 'Over there. Why match your dress with your nails when you can do it with your car?'

'Oh ... huh. Daddy's wheels?'

Tia's head jerked back. 'No, he's mine. All mine.'

Jed's forehead wrinkled like a bedsheet. 'You call your car a "he"?'

Tia shrugged. 'Yeah.'

Jed smirked again. 'It's a little *Christine*, but cute. I've never dated a girl with a red Monaro before. Wanna get going?'

'Please.'

On the road, Monty displayed better behaviour than Jed, smooth in everything from idling to taking off and changing gears. Meanwhile, Tia flinched but bit her tongue when Jed's Converse sneakers trailed dirt on her tailor-made car mats and when he failed to notice a plastic wrapper from his pocket falling to the floor. But Jed did give Monty a few vague compliments; perhaps he was just overawed.

Things improved once they arrived at the popular candle-lit restaurant on the city fringe. Tia got a rock-star park right out the front and their table by the window meant she could also keep an eye on Monty, awash in the streetlights, throughout.

She ordered the ravioli with tomato sauce, figuring it safe. Any splashes would barely show up on her dress or the red-and-white chequered tablecloth. Jed went for the veal sirloin medallions, which was a shame for the young cows. But freedom of choice and all. Jed redeemed himself by ordering a bottle of the most expensive shiraz. Even if she was partial to a beer, it showed he wasn't cheap.

A balding, bowtie-adorned waiter buzzed around them like a blowfly at first, filling their bulbous glasses and laying starched white napkins in their laps. Then they were alone again. Or as alone as two people in a busy restaurant could be.

Tia took a sip of liquid courage. It fizzed on her tongue and slipped down her throat like velvet. 'So, uh, have you been on many blind dates?'

Jed reached for a roll from the bread basket and ripped it in half. She wondered if he'd ever done the same to another girl's heart. 'Nup, but I *was* curious.'

Tia half-smiled. 'About blind dates, or me?'

'You, actually.' Jed's eyes twinkled in the candlelight. 'I mean, you sounded too good to be true. A dream girl. Debbie told me you like cars, football and beer. In that order. It's not the norm. I'm not being sexist, that's just a fact.'

Tia straightened in her seat, not keen to be perceived as some sort of freakish curiosity. 'I also like *Offspring*, Beyoncé and dresses.'

Jed smiled. 'See, you're an enigma. And I saw you sneak a look out the window at your Monaro just then too.'

Tia couldn't help grinning as she reached for a bread roll of her own. 'Speaking of cars, what do you drive?'

She'd been waiting for seemingly eons for the right time to pose the question.

Jed flipped back his fringe once more. 'Nothing right now actually. I had an old Mazda RX-7 but I bloody wrote it off. Good thing you offered to pick me up. Still, I've since found out public transport's pretty good in my area. Which is why I'm actually thinking of going without a car for as long as I can and saving the dosh. As much as I appreciate a good set of wheels, it means zero chance of write-offs or speeding fines, you know?'

Tia almost dropped her bread roll. Not only did Jed *not* have a car, nor a desire to get a new one, he preferred rotary engines. For a final mark against him, he shoved a hunk of bread in his gob and chewed open-mouthed. The fact that his teeth were professionally whitened was neither here nor there.

Their meals arrived and Tia found the ravioli much more appetising than the Jed-centric banter that followed. Every now and then, she checked on Monty as the parked cars, passers-by and colours shifted around him like an ever-changing kaleidoscope pattern. When the waiter returned to ask if they wanted dessert or coffees, Tia was relieved when they both shook their heads. Seconds later, a little leather folder, containing the bill, was placed on their table with a flourish.

Jed appeared to have ants in his pants as he patted down

his pockets. 'Shit, sorry, man, I left my darn wallet at home. You okay to cover it?'

Tia's eyes rounded. Jed wasn't just cheap, he was a filthy liar. The expensive *vino* no doubt had been on her all along. It was a wonder he hadn't chosen to dine on the eye fillet steak.

But rather than make a scene, Tia gritted her teeth and plucked her credit card from her bag. Wordlessly, she slid the shiny plastic inside the bill folder.

After the waiter had her sign the receipt, Tia jumped to her feet, blisters be damned. Jed followed suit, waggling dark eyebrows. 'So what now? Wanna go for a drive or something?'

Tia saw red. Pulsating Monaro-red.

She wasn't Jed's dream girl; clearly just a desperate, dateless, easy ride, in his eyes. She never should have trusted Debbie's taste. The woman drove a Hyundai and teamed ratty cardis with shower-wet hair at work.

Tia forced a smile at Jed. 'Sorry but I have other plans. However, I saw a bus stop outside the shop next door. Lucky you're adept at public transport.' Feigning a doe-eyed expression, Tia tipped some coins from her wallet into her palm. 'Would this cover your trip?'

Jed was the one to resemble a wide-eyed puffer fish this time. 'Er, maybe a bit more gold, if you wouldn't mind, so I can get a slushie for the way home.' He cleared his throat. 'Bit parched.'

Tia's shoulders only relaxed when, minutes later, she sank into Monty's front seat, alone. For a moment, she just sat there, breathing in his heady combo of leather, petrol and pine, the latter owing to a dangly tree-shaped air freshener.

She stroked his steering wheel. 'Sorry about that jerk

before. Where do you want to go?'

Naturally, Monty couldn't respond in words. She knew he was a machine. But he spoke to her in his own way, seeming to take the lead in driving her through the suburban streets and up winding roads before sliding into a tree-shaded spot at their final destination: a clifftop lookout at Skye. A discreet distance away from the other cars.

The city stretched out before them, its multi-coloured lights twinkling like a pinball machine in the velvety darkness. Who needed candles?

After losing her heels, Tia queued up her CD of The Flamingos' 'I Only Have Eyes For You'. Then she climbed out, leaving Monty idling in park and his windows wound down.

Barefoot, she picked through the dry grass, then perched on Monty's shiny hood, her hem lifting a little at the movement. Through her frock's flimsy fabric, she felt the radiant heat and gutsy throb of Monty's engine. And, intermixed with the occasional scent of cigarette smoke and low hum of conversations on the breeze, the scent of jasmine wafted.

Tia patted the sleek metal beneath her fingertips, whispering, 'Apart from a sagging middle, I have to say, tonight's been perfect.'

She could have sworn Monty responded with an uneven rev, fluttering beneath her. And seeing as there was no one to tell her otherwise, she allowed herself a happy sigh. *This* was what made splashing out on a new frock and carwash worth it. The perfect end to her evening; one she might not have thought to indulge in if things had played out differently. All that had led up to this moment felt like foreplay.

Nothing—*nothing*—could have been more romantic.

A ROUGHIE IN THE FOURTH

With a nod to W.H. Auden and his poem
'As I Walked Out One Evening'.

SUE ROBERTSON

It is still hours until sunset when the dinner bell sounds. Doors open. A hodgepodge of Zimmer-frames and walking aids spew into the hallway pushed by owners on the scent of roast meat and three veg.

Tonight's dinner is just one more activity to tick off in the mind numbing routine that gets the residents of the Sunnyside Retirement Home out of bed in the morning and back to bed at night. Dinner, showers, pyjamas, television. Tonight it's *Family Feud, Getaway*, then either hot cocoa, or peppermint tea, and bed. The residents grunt and nod as they gain momentum, muttering noisily to themselves or to those they manage to overtake, or who overtake them, all of them moving one foot in front of the other. Like the Eloi in *The Time Machine*. Not relevant, but the midday movie on Channel Seven today, so fresh in the minds of some, and one of Jack's all-time favourites. The muzak switches tempo. *The*

Sound of Music takes over from the sounds of whales, waves and seagulls.

Jack registers it all—the bell, the music, his peers on the move—but he stays put, refusing tonight to abandon his post in the main reception area. He stands in the shadows, his body tucked as far back as he can manage it, his subterfuge aided by a cumbersome leadlight-fronted cabinet, and a large ceramic pot of hydrangeas in purple, pink and mauve. His body, all six foot two of it, curves into his walking stick, his plans for dinner restricted to the contents of a small sterling silver flask. He lifts it to his lips and whisky streams into his gut. The trail of embers left in its wake necessitates a second swig. He tucks the flask back into his hip pocket, rotates his shoulders to relieve the ache in his neck, and resumes his watch on a door midway along the corridor. Olivia's room. Inside it, he knows, fellow resident Olivia is in earnest conversation with her son Max. He knows just how earnest because not that many minutes ago, he stood outside her door, his hand poised, withdrawing it when he heard the low frustration in Max's voice.

The residents in general have been timely in their response tonight, and are making reasonable headway. It is remarkable what can be achieved when a roast is on the menu. Steamed cod, of course, will never result in anything near comparable. There are quite a few already halfway down the hallway when Olivia's door opens and Max steps out. Jack's heart lurches so violently he's knocked sideways into the foliage of the *ficus elastica*. He pushes out of its rubbery hold and bites down on his tongue because lately his internal voice has, without warning, begun to force itself through his teeth and insinuate itself on the external world. An unattractive trait in the elderly, chattering to oneself, and not at all the image Jack is aiming for on this vitally important day.

His surveillance of the hallway resumes just as Max hesitates to check the phone cupped in his palm. Despite himself, Jack gasps. Mobile phones are considered the enemies of pacemakers, even though they are not, or every second resident in the place would be in the morgue by now. Still, rules are rules and Jack harbours an enduring envy for anyone who can ignore rules, any rules, and so blatantly. He takes off his glasses and rubs them on the front of his jacket, puts them back on.

The able-bodied Dolly and three of her cronies draw level with Max just as Julie Andrews, having listed all her favourite things, is replaced by a symphony of rubber stoppers on wooden floorboards, the thud and shuffle of soft-soled shoes, the click of heels and chatter. While most residents are normally eager to acknowledge Max's presence, any visitor's presence in fact, they pass him tonight without faltering. If they do glance back it is not to acknowledge him, but rather to check on the progress of those behind.

Jack watches as they jostle like jockeys in the straight, squeezing up as they overtake, expanding again when the space in front is free. Except for Dolly. She's dropped way back and now has her arm tucked into Max's, dragging him back to her pace. She holds on like a python.

Is it possible Jack has misread the signals? In going down this track, is he setting himself up for disappointment? The heavy card, bearing his declaration of love, secreted deep inside his pocket, sizzles like steak on a barbecue. He takes another slug from his flask but struggles to embrace the whisky's volatility and accept the slight buzz in his head. He fingers the card again.

It is entirely possible he misinterpreted completely when Max pulled him aside to say hello, when he dug into his briefcase and presented Jack with a copy of his latest book inscribed with *Be true to yourself* ✪ *Maxwell V. Alexander*.

...or when Max held his pen over the dedication page and their gazes locked, when Max quoted from W.H. Auden, '*O plunge your hands in water,/Plunge them in up to the wrist;/Stare, stare in the basin/and wonder what you've missed*'? The same poem Jack sought out, and has painstakingly copied onto the card.

What about when Max touched him on the arm, brushed the back of his hand, laughed with him when he signed the book? And last month, when Jack was feeling faint at the TAB, how Max came to his rescue, had insisted on escorting Jack back to Sunnyside. It was only a ten-minute walk but time enough for Max to ask if Jack had 'checked out' his book. Small-talk probably; tongue-tied, the best Jack could manage was a brief nod, but he'd never forget Max's parting words that day.

'Listen to me, my friend. You are never too old to take a risk.'

And take a risk is exactly what Jack plans to do but for the moment, he is in limbo, mesmerised and impatient at the same time. Mesmerised by the way Max, now free of Dolly, walks, the creases in his trousers barely disrupted by the evenness of his step, or the pressure of his knees as they make contact with each step forward, or the release as the contact is lost momentarily. Impatient as he counts the seconds Max takes to chat to the residents who invite it and rallying when Max skirts around those who stare bleakly ahead of them, seeing nothing but their seat at the table.

Antsy, Jack guzzles from his flask. His legs cramp through lack of movement and his bladder niggles. His arm aches from its extended reliance on his walking stick. The whisky does continue to warm his stomach, but the slight buzz it delivers brings with it a litany of questions that bombard him like magpies in spring.

The poem? He pats again at his pocket. Auden's carefully transcribed poem. '*I'll love you till the ocean…*'

Jack may not be able to '*conquer time*', and he could, in all likelihood after this effort, wake up in the locked ward. But how much time has he got left to take risks? He knows he can't spend what little time there is thinking lustfully about his past life pitching jam jingles to Coles, pretending to be content and whole, retiring each evening to a pristine apartment for one.

Max has reached the lobby. Jack's heart is racing, and without him realising it the palpitations have reached almost dangerous proportions. A quick self-check tells him 120 beats a minute at least…and rising. That is not good. He leans heavily on his stick, ignoring, this one time, the way the feet of its tripod support make indents in the antique Persian carpet. He breathes deeply, slow and steady, just as his cardiologist recommends.

If that fails he's to bear down, or drink endless glasses of iced water, anything to return his heart to its normal rhythm. But the water cooler is in the Residents Lounge at the other end of the hall and, at his age, to bear down is prone to result in an unpleasantness not worth thinking about. This development is both difficult and untimely, and probably more than a little due to the whisky he's been pouring down. Giddy, he reaches out to the wooden stand, which houses the day's newspapers and where even the Racing Guide and Green Guide for the television warrant their own wooden spine.

His stomach is closing in on itself but at least his pulse is slowing. *Stay calm*, he warns. *Stay calm.* But how can he stay calm? He's fifteen years old again. And what fifteen-year-old placed before the object of his desire is going to stay calm? What to say if Max does acknowledge him? And there's his breath, what about that? Damn the whisky. He should have resisted but that race was run the minute he spotted Max's silver BMW pull into the car park, earlier this evening.

Passion ricochets through Jack's body like a ball bearing in a pinball machine. At this very moment, with Max so close, pressure is building in Jack's gut like homemade ginger beer kept for too long in a hot garage.

For years now, he's listened to stories about gay rights, marriage equality, gay couples adopting babies, having families, even something called gaydar. Things his generation never dared acknowledge, let alone speak about. He's spent his life denying it and now, at seventy-nine, it really is almost too late.

Max is in reception, his butt resting on the Director's faux Louis XIV desk. The functional oak veneer desk for admissions, rejections and payments, is neatly secreted behind a chest-high screen. The new girl behind it is young, too young, and Max's voice is low and his tone flirtatious.

Jack's resolve falters. Again he forces oxygen into his lungs. The racing guide he's plucked from the rack offers little in the way of comfort. He hadn't made it to the TAB this evening. Max's arrival put paid to that, sent his routine out of kilter. He had a hot tip on a roughie in the fourth at Randwick, and another in the second at Sandown, but no win could justify letting this opportunity pass.

He takes another sip. The flask is almost empty. His toes curl in his good shoes, and his left calf aches.

On the other side of the room, Max's left foot taps in time with the muzak, the material on the seat of his pants stretches and pulls first on one buttock and then the other, tightening and bunching to accommodate the bulk of his thighs. Sweat seeps through Jack's pores, on his palms, on his back between his shoulder blades and behind his knees. His privates twitch.

Shy and sensitive, his mother was fond of saying, as she had him paint seam lines up the back of her naked legs when he was a kid, when stockings were impossible to get. And he had a good steady hand. Fragile, when the Sisters belted him at school, and over-cautious when he didn't make the team, any team.

Well, not today, not anymore. As Max steps away from the desk and turns, Jack, taking a risk like never before, lurches out. His body is taut and his arm extended. He wields the apricot pages of the racing guide on its spine, like a starter's flag at the Grand Prix.

The mind is willing but the body way too slow. He has been standing still for too long and his legs fail him, so with his apricot flag flapping, he falls into Max's path. He lands heavily on the side of his head and crunches his shoulder on the carpet. He sees the shine of Max's shoes at the exact moment he hoped to see the shine in his eyes. There is a scuff near the toe of the left shoe. The paper lies on the floor next to it. Drool seeps from the corner of Jack's mouth, runs along his cheek and onto the floor. Max's face is there, beside his, cocked on one side, peering into his. 'Climb Every Mountain' blasts from every speaker in the place.

'Jack,' he hears. 'Jack. Can you hear me?'

Hear you?

'Do you know what happened? Do you know who I am?'

Know you, Max? You need to ask?

Jack breathes slowly, he lets the world slow down, '*The clocks had ceased their chiming,/And the deep river ran on*', he recites, huddling into the warmth of Max's body. He opens his mouth to devour a gutful of Max's after-shave, Armani, a fragrance as familiar to Jack as his own. How many hours has he spent sitting with Olivia, making small talk, after Max's visits? The suffocating smell of her cheap perfume, the stale taint of her last illicit cigarette, the smell of stewed cabbage that seems to dwell longer in her room than anywhere else, all worth it just to catch the occasional whiff of what is closing in on him now.

He feels Max's arms under his body. His hand on his elbow, his lean muscles urging, his voice soft and comforting—*Get a footing, old fellow.* Jack settles back, his head and shoulders melting into his paramour's chest. He's writing his own story, gathering up every shred of detail to the closing stanza of 'Climb Every Mountain'. Another voice breaks in, young and female, wanting to know if he's going to be all right.

She finishes her question on a pronounced up-stroke. Jack opens his eyes. The receptionist is staring down at him. Her eyelashes are false. The left one is coming adrift in the corner. Her brown eyes are moist and teary, her smile uncertain. Her skirt is tartan, reds and greens, and too short. The hemming stitches are uneven and in the wrong shade. She has a tiny pull in her right stocking just above the knee, and Max has his hand on it.

Fingers circle Jack's wrist; fingertips cover his pulse. 130, someone says. We're going to need that gurney. We don't want any broken bones. Brittle bones. Brittle bones. Gurney. Gurney. 130 bpm. Jack. Jack. Breathe for us, old fella.

Brittle bones, that's a new one.

Jack? Can you tell me where you are? What day it is? Your birthday?

Sunnyside. Tuesday. Born 13 September at 4:14 in the afternoon. Breech. Forceps delivery. Mother needed twenty-seven stitches. She was a sharer. Left her scarred for life.

The Prime Minister?

Are you kidding?

Max's breath is warm and smells like Cadbury Milk Chocolate. Jack wills his body to move the way Max wants him to but it's limp like a rag doll. It must be the whisky. Dutch courage. Too much flipping Dutch courage.

There are more around him now, two, three, four, all groping at him, squabbling among themselves.

His head flops back. He can see the hydrangeas. They're on the floor. Must have gone down with him. He chortles. He rarely allows himself to become the focus of attention but this evening he is happy to take the stage, and he knows the residents will be at a standstill by now, watching, ogling, considering their own inevitable demise and the possibility of a vacant room and a new resident.

He leans into Max and lets his eyelids flutter. The rattle of cutlery on crockery, chairs scraping on wooden floors brings the next disappointment. Nobody's watching. They've all moved on without him.

His disappointment builds as he feels the vibration of a mobile phone near his shoulder. He hopes Max will ignore it but he doesn't, and when he shifts to answer it, he disrupts both proximity and malleability.

And now another phone rings faraway, a landline. The doorbell trills. *You can go now,* he hears. *We can handle it from here.* We're used to his funny turns… A second voice… *We've got him.* Hands grope. And from Max, *You're sure,* and the only hand Jack is interested in detaches itself, is replaced by a colder one with wrinkles and three hard mismatched rings.

Adrenaline pumping, he grabs for Max's hand and holds onto it. *I love you.* A tourniquet is fitted, tightens around his arm.

What did he say? Max again.

'*You shall love your crooked neighbor/With your crooked heart.*' A needle slips into his vein. Jack feels himself disappearing.

That's great, old man. That's great.

He's losing consciousness. *No, Max, don't go.* Jack's hand flaps over his pocket. *Take this, Max. This is for you.*

What'd he say?

Max's lips brush Jack's forehead lightly. The contact singes Jack's skin. *Take care old man. Take care.*

Jack smiles. And in the hot garage of his childhood, the

top lifts off a dusty old bottle and murky ginger beer gushes all over his mother's Mini Minor.

He lets his eyes close. When he wakes, he resolves, as he's lifted onto the stretcher, he'll let himself be fussed over. They'll let him sleep, then they'll sit him up in his bed and bring him poached eggs and asparagus as they always do when he suffers one of his turns. God knows why, he's never really liked asparagus, it turns his pee green. Tomorrow he'll be as good as new.

SUBURBAN INCUBUS

RITA TOGNINI

what if my stray of a boyfriend whom I thought of as 'just a friend' my large bellied boy scarred as a child by parents who treated him like a parcel and handed him around to whoever would have him   what if I went travelling the world with him and we found ourselves in a horse-drawn carriage in Central Park New York with snow falling and what if he held my hand and crooned in a heart-melting voice *Around the world I searched for you* and he asked me to marry him   then what if I was suddenly passionately in love with him and wanted to be with him every minute for the rest of my life and I said oh yes yes yes yes and we rang my mother and squealed our news over the phone and we all cried together and we announced that we were coming home to get married   what   if after   we flew home and went back to our jobs and I sold the yacht my dear dead father had left me bought a car put a deposit on a house spent the next seven months planning the wedding of my dreams and on my wedding day I wore a satin ivory-coloured dress with off-the-shoulder straps a bodice encrusted with hundreds of seed pearls a long heavy train that had to be carried by six flower girls   and I had four bridesmaids dressed in graduated shades of mauve and we all walked down the aisle of a cosy suburban church where each of the pews had been decorated with bouquets of pale pink and white rosebuds tied with pale pink and white ribbons

and my face was covered by a veil so that I looked as mysterious as a traditional eastern bride who on her wedding day is carried in a curtained palanquin to the house of a man she barely knows and must serve for the rest of her life

and no-one in the church was dry-eyed my mother smiled so hard in our photos that afterwards I wondered if she was faking it and our reception was in a spacious white marquee on the lawns of Kings Park overlooking the river dotted with yachts like the one my father had left me and I sold   and this time I serenaded my boyfriend now my husband I sang *The first time ever I saw your face* to him in front of all the guests then we sang it together and all the eyes in the marquee were even more moist than they had been before in the church   what if we went on a honeymoon cruise to the tropics and were invited to the captain's table fêted as newlyweds and spent a week in Phuket making love lazing on the beach dressing up at night for fine dining in choice restaurants   and what if when we arrived back home my husband's brother had invited his friends to stay with him in our house and they'd trashed it and there was the house to clean all the gifts to view the wedding photos to choose for our albums the garden to weed the last of my furniture to get from my mother's house

what if that boy who'd crooned to me in Central Park now
farts in bed and snores and I wake in the night and lie there
next to him not able to sleep thinking what if   what if
what if he had asked me to marry him in the car park of
the Coolbellup Shopping Centre or Hamilton Hill or Garden
City even   would I still have said   yes?

OF BOOKS & BAKED GOODS

J. R. KOOP

Half-buried in the snow stands a box. Full to the brim with books, it's protected from the weather by towering trees. Across its roof, *Free Little Library* stands proud in rustic carved letters. Over the years, I've visited this little box, delving through the volumes and pages left there by others. Take a book, leave a book. That's how it's always worked since it first appeared.

No one truly knows how it came to be. One day, it simply…was. Whether it was someone in the neighbourhood wanting to share, or some odd government scheme, I'm not sure. I first noticed it during summer, six years ago. Since then it's become a ritual: because Saturday morning is bakery day. With fresh éclairs on my mind, I grab whatever book someone's left behind for me.

Of course, the library isn't just for me, but it's like Christmas each time I open that little glass door. Or it was, until the books started going missing.

It was slow at first—one or two, here and there. Obviously

someone didn't understand the whole *take a book, leave a book* deal printed just inside the door.

If I peer out the attic window at the right angle, the Little Library can be seen from my house. In the wind, the trees obscure it completely, as does the snow. But on a nice sunny day, when the snow's all melted and you can smell the crisp warmth in the breeze, the Little Library is clear as day.

Like today. The snow's deep from the downfall overnight. Yesterday there were eleven books remaining—a number that's stayed steady, though the books have changed, over the past month. Trudging through the snow with a dog-eared copy of *Great Expectations* in my hand feels like approaching a cliff's edge with nothing but a bungee-cord around my legs. Another step, another shallow breath, anticipation for what I might find. Recently, classics have been showing up—the kind that are loved. The pages half-chewed by pets or frayed from someone gripping them tightly in anticipation. The spine so crinkled it can only be from bending the book right back, grasping it in one hand while multitasking.

The handle cool in my hand, I ease the door open, eyes squeezed shut against the icy breeze. The book feels ever-heavier in my hand as slowly I take a peek and place it within.

There's a book missing.

Another damned book *missing*.

Right.

Snatching a copy of some Rick Riordan novel and sliding it into my pocket, I resist the urge to slam the Little Library's door shut. Next time, I'll bring a pen.

I have to admit I may have started stalking the Little Library.

Sitting up at the windowsill in the attic isn't my usual behaviour. Thank goodness my brother's already moved out, otherwise I'd never hear the end of it. I can almost feel his voice in the back of my head in that nagging tone of his: *Meg, get away from the window, you look like some kind of psycho.*

Munching on the éclairs from the bakery in town, I have to fight myself not to become too engrossed in the quest of a young boy clearing his name with the Greek gods, so I can catch the book thief in the act. Almost a whole day passes; six éclairs eaten, and I can't stop my mind from wandering onto the subject of the baker. I go every Saturday morning, blushing and fumbling as I make my usual order. Her éclairs are like nothing I've ever tasted. And each time, she gives me an extra treat without charge. This week, she'd snuck a cinnamon swirl topped with sugared almonds into the bag. I hadn't realised they'd become my favourite.

The snow's started again, cascading lightly down the windowpane. It's like magic.

My toes curl in the blankets and I shimmy back, almost crushing the pastry box as I bury myself in pillows. I wonder what the baker's name is.

Shoving the thought away, I focus on the matter at hand: Percy Jackson—No. The woman in the plum coat outside.

The colour's a bright spark against the white and birch. Unforgettable. Blonde hair peeks out from under a mustard-coloured beanie. Mustard; a hard colour to pull off.

I lean closer to the window, Percy's adventures with Annabeth half-forgotten as the book slips from my hand to the hardwood floor. The *thud* makes me jump, but no, outside the woman approaches the Little Library. She reaches in quickly and pulls out a black book—which is either Bryce Courtney or Erin Morgenstern, if memory serves. A half-glance back in the direction of my house, and the woman closes the Little Library's door.

The book thief!

Riordan is forgotten on the floor as I scramble up from my chair, bolt down the stairs, and throw myself outside, forgetting my winter coat. Socked-feet slopping around in wellies, I trudge on through. 'Excuse me!' I yell, but my voice is snatched away by the wind before it can reach her. The woman is a few metres up ahead. 'Hey!'

She can't hear me. A glance back to my house and a jolt runs through me. The door is closed. Locked. And I've forgotten the damned key.

Yet up ahead, the woman's still there. Until she isn't.

My light sweater isn't doing well at battling the cold. Wrapping my arms tight around my shivering middle, I can't think of anything worse than this. Damned winter. Damned book thief.

Turning my back on wherever she's disappeared to, I think of everything I might have written when I first noticed the thief. Maybe part of me thought the books would return of their own volition.

The Little Library's door creaks as it swings open, my sugary fingers shaking as they grapple about for the notepad kept inside. The pen beside it is smooth, ice-cold.

Scribbling down what I consider to be a polite—okay, maybe a tad scolding—letter and sticking it in the front, I huff. The books should start returning when they see this.

Percy and Annabeth finished the quest, a very-near scrape, and I feel destroyed. This book has become my life. Damned Riordan.

Another reach into the Little Library and I'm praying someone's left behind the next book in the series. I've no idea who it is; I've never seen any younger readers approach the box. And I highly doubt the eighty-year-old down the street is a fan of fantasy written for young adults, where there are chapters like 'A God Buys Us Cheeseburgers'.

Dozens of books stare back at me now; I hadn't realised so many had gone missing. Amongst them stand new romances, added without a trade. Atop them lays a note in a lazily curving hand: *There's more to come. I'm sorry.*

Well then. I crumble up the note and shove it deep into my pocket. The red wool of my gloves catches on the door as I pull out a volume of Sarah Waters' *Fingersmith*. No doubt some of the little old ladies would have had a fright reading this. I tug on my glove, but it's snagged.

'No,' I almost whine, giving another gentle tug. *Riiiiiiiiip.* Buggeration.

I slam the book down hard on the Little Library's roof, scattering snow. The ice meets my exposed wrist and I hiss, sucking down the scream that I almost let slip.

'Need a hand?'

I turn; I'd been too preoccupied to notice anyone approaching. The someone—the woman in the plum coat. It's the baker. My blood runs hot. 'You,' I grit out, but she's smiling at me.

'Looks like you've gotten yourself a little stuck there,' she muses, that smirk curling her lips with feather-touches. Her lips are a dusky rose, open and plump.

I shake the thought away as she approaches. 'No,' I choke out, 'I'm fine. It's just a glove.' *Only my favourite.*

She sweeps in. 'Here,' she says, the word soft like her freshly-baked croissants as she brushes the snow still lingering at my wrist. The touch of her leather gloves is tacky against my skin. Suddenly I find it's a little hard to breathe.

Without a word, she removes a glove of her own to flick the wool of mine from the splinter. The red thread comes away clean, if not a little pulled, and I pull my sleeves down. The baker closes the door for me and smiles as she takes up my newly-selected book.

A look of surprise crosses her face—a fleeting look, but it's there. A slight enlargement of the eyes, a pinch of the nose. *'Fingersmith?'* She almost laughs, before giving me a look up and down. Slow, seductive.

My god.

She holds out the book, but my hand hates to obey. Slowly I reach up and when I take it in my hand, she doesn't let go.

'I'm Alison,' she smiles.

Nervous as hell, I give a sharp nod. 'Meg.'

That smile of hers only grows; her brown eyes shine. 'You buy my éclairs every Saturday.' She mashes her lips together in a sheepish grin. 'I want to make you dessert tonight,' she says suddenly, her features turning unsure. Eyes widen. 'I mean—make dessert *for* you,' she corrects, with a quick glance at the book between us.

Did she just—?

'To make up for inadvertently stealing the books,' she explains. She still doesn't let go of the book between us; her long-fingered grip is tight like a cobra's. Another flash in those eyes, and I can't help it: I start to feel myself blush.

But Alison shakes her head, and finally releases the book. 'Never mind, then. You probably don't want to go on a date with someone who steals books to get your attention.' A shrug, awkward and giggling. 'You don't even know anything about me.'

Why the hell can't I find my words right now? I'm just staring at her.

'How—how was stealing books meant to get my attention?' I stammer at last.

But she's just standing there, hands in her pockets and looking like she'd rather be anywhere else than here, in the snow with me. Her cheeks plume red. I don't think even she knows why she did all this. I want to reach out and touch her but that feels too familiar. This close, she smells like cranberries and gingerbread. The book still hovers in my hand between us, so I slip it into my pocket.

'Don't worry about it,' she says, brows knit. 'I'll see you next Saturday.'

She turns on her heel—and god dammit, why do I only pluck up my nerve now? Reaching out, I grab her by the arm. There's a surprising amount of muscle beneath my hand when she tenses, and turns back to me with a confused frown.

'I—I'd love to,' I force out, knowing my face is as red as my gloves.

Her face lights up, and I feel like melting. 'Great.' The word is breathless and she points up the street. 'I'm that house at the end of the second block with the blue door. Come over at eight; I didn't think you'd say yes, so it'll give me time to bake.'

Her arm tenses beneath my hand and I jerk back, only realising now that I'm still holding onto her. An awkward sound escapes my mouth, and it makes me feel like burying myself in the snow. But Alison only laughs, clapping a hand on my shoulder and giving me that crazy beautiful smile. 'I'll see you then,' I say, somehow managing to sound relatively human when she leans a little closer.

'Can't wait,' she breathes, the words caressing my cheek before she turns with a wink and saunters off. That bright coat hugs her every curve. I swallow hard, feeling the weight of *Fingersmith* in my pocket.

Eight o'clock comes around quicker than I'd imagined. With all the pacing of my house, debating whether to pick up a book—this one, or that one?—I've worn myself out. The nerves are overwhelming. I haven't been on a date in a long time. And Alison had called it a date, hadn't she?

At last the time is here, and so is the snow. Taking a step outside I curse having curled my hair. It looks like a blizzard's approaching.

Swallowing my nerve, I throw myself outside—this time, remembering the key—and dash through the snow. It catches in my hair, some falling down my collar with a forced shiver, and I know I'm soaked when I reach Alison's front door.

I look like a drowned mess.

But she must have been watching for me, because, slowly, the door opens and Alison is even more beautiful than before. Her colourful coat and beanie earlier had been a surprise; I'm used to seeing her in that beige cap and apron at the bakery. Now, wearing a cream cowl-neck sweater that she knows hugs her breasts, she is more than I could have imagined. The mustard beanie is gone, revealing a carefully-mastered curl in her hair. From inside the warmth of her house, those chestnut eyes look me up and down, this time with concern. She forgets herself.

'My god, come in.' Before I can act, she sweeps an arm around me, practically pulling me inside to the warmth of the fire glowing down the hall. Again taking the lead, she strips me of my coat, grinning when she sees the low neckline of my shirt, and I feel exposed.

'This is… this is a really nice house,' I say, trying to shake off some of the nerves that having her eyes on me ignites.

'Oh,' she looks around, hanging my coat at the door, 'it used to be my grandmother's. My mum was a little upset when she left it to me once I took over the bakery.'

Don't make a weird comment, Meg, I growl at myself. And I make myself look at her, truly look at her, and say, 'I'm sorry,' but she just shakes it off with a shrug.

Taking my hand, she leads me down the hall. I'm surprised by how warm her hands are. 'I made lava-brownies and tiramisu and ice cream,' she says, the words slipping out in a mess, letting me know she's as nervous as I am. A glance back at me, and I can see it on her face. 'I didn't know what you liked, other than my éclairs, and… I got a little over-zealous.'

She laughs, and it's a sound I want to keep on hearing.

The closer we move to the kitchen, the more my mouth waters. Gingerbread, berries, gooey chocolate, coffee, and toffee. 'Can I…' As soon as I open my mouth, she whips around. We've reached the living room with the fire, and I feel the heat seeping into me, like that warmth pulsing from her hand still joined with mine. I almost forget what I'm saying, with her looking at me like that.

Then I notice the room, and I can't hold back my smile. If I've been wracked with anticipation in waiting, then she's gone all out. By the fire is a mattress covered in plush cushions. Beside them stand piles and piles of books. Blankets are strewn in layers across one of the nearest couches, ready at hand should we get cold. And all of it is bathed in the firelight.

Opening my mouth again, I look back at her to find her already staring at me. She's staring at my mouth. I falter, feeling my cheeks flush. 'You did all this, for me?'

Alison gives my hand a squeeze. 'I heard there was a risk of a blizzard tonight, so I thought I'd make you comfortable.' Another squeeze. 'Books seem to be your thing.'

I feel like kissing her, just pulling her to me and tangling my hands in her hair. But I smile instead, returning a hand-squeeze. 'How about that dessert?'

THE CLEAR, CLEAN WATER

MELISABETH COOPER FELL

This is Benny's tale. He's not here to tell it. That's down to me. Unlike some of the others here, I don't want to forget what he was like and it's more than just that he was my brother. He did a good thing. Showed them what kind of man he was. I won't forget that even if it means he is gone forever.

It was in the winter. Days were short, cold and still dry like summer. It used to be the wettest part of the year, now there's no difference. The ground was cracked like spider webs, the dust lifted like spray each time the wind roared up the gully. Everything was brittle and desiccated.

The fire gave them away.

Benny saw the smoke on his low range patrol and tracked them coming up the dried riverbed and watched. They were looking for something. Each day they'd scramble over the stones of the dry riverbed, pushing into the forest on either side if they spied some tracks and return. Everything returns to the river—sooner or later. After four days of tracking, he saw who they were after. A girl, similar to my age, fifteen or so and moving like fire lapped her heels.

The way he told it was it's like when we used to go out shooting and out of the dark comes your first rabbit. Everything narrows in that moment, your breath holds and the electricity makes your finger twitch. They saw the girl, scrambled for their rifles, yelled out and raised them. Benny thought she might have shouted something back, trying to scramble out of the riverbed with her pack on. When the bullet hit her, she slid down the rock face, landing with her leg at an odd angle and the rocks darkening beneath her. It didn't seem right, he said when I asked why he didn't just leave her to them. *It could have been you, Cass, that could have been you.* Instead he raised his own rifle and shot the men. They'd come up too far and he had a border to patrol.

We knew what happened down in the lowlands. The Desal plant that everybody had bitched about being the biggest white elephant in government history ended up becoming the only source of water when the rains failed for three years. Then some die-hard nutters poisoned the pipes. Water became gold. Those who had bores suddenly needed the heft to defend them, those that couldn't got a bullet in the head. We heard stories of people trading anything of use, their families, body parts, anything for water. Willingly and unwillingly. In the end the girl was fuck bait if she stayed below. I can understand why she'd come our way.

But he still should have shot her.

She'd resigned herself. Told him, *just do it*. And turned her head away.

He said he knew he should have. The longer he sat

thinking about it, the harder it was for him to pick up that gun, until it was something that had become impossible.

She didn't look at him until Benny said *I'm not going to shoot you*. She turned to face him. He knew why she'd run then.

The first thing she said. *Can I have a drink of water then?*

Benny signalled the higher patrol and hid the girl, Lyla, in a wombat's burrow. Apparently she passed out a few times as he moved her over the rocks. When Bill and Robbo arrived, Benny had the lowlanders' packs empty, their weapons in a pile and their stash of tobacco in his pocket.

Bill kicked over one of the bodies. *Good work, Benny boy.* Looked around, he saw the other body at the base of the rock face, the bullet wound in the gut. Usually Benny's a crack shot, I can only think of a short list for why he'd miss that badly.

Robbo shook out one of the sleeping bags. Rolled up inside was a book. Benny didn't see the cover but he saw the photo that slipped out of its pages and recognised the face. Robbo picked it up and held it out to Bill. *A girlfriend for ya.*

Bill tucked that photo in his shirt. *They're not going to miss you sweetheart.*

Anything of value we keep, the rest we burn. That was Benny's job.

Bill and Robbo loaded the bodies onto the horses and headed down the hill where the river cuts through the narrow gorge. Here every lowlander that has come up has been hung as a warning. Sometimes with the right wind their bones create their own kind of music.

He waited until the sun started to hit the eastern wall of the gorge before he left the riverbed and climbed back to the wombat burrow. He dragged her back to the fire. It'd be two, three days' time before Bill and Robbo would come back this way. Listening to her breathe that night he wondered if she'd make it through to the morning. She did. Mum had trained him well. Taught us both her skills from her vet days. It made us valuable, needed, she said. In case something happened to her. We know how to splint and stitch but there was other stuff too, stuff that we learnt just by watching her work. Lyla's ankle was splinted, the bullet wound cauterised and dressed and he'd bathed and stitched the wounds on her face while she was unconscious. Then he'd stayed awake, watching her in the dark, listening to her back up one breath after another when she could have just given up. I asked what she was like. *Pretty banged up*, he said. *Could see why she'd run.* Then he smiled. *She's tough.*

The hard bit was what to do with her.

As a group we have a zero tolerance for any outsiders. We staked our claim here, dammed the last wild river in the state and set out to defend it. We have lots of guns and we're used to killing things. No one has come up from the lowlands and lived. Nobody. That's what the rangers do. No one would let Lyla stay. The enemy of our enemy is still not our friend. If she went back or she stayed, she was dead meat. Dead meat on the clock.

We didn't hear from Benny for a couple of weeks and then he walked in one night. Same old annoying brother but different. His shoulders were squarer and he looked up into the trees more. We sat as the sun went down and had a smoke. Sitting side by side as the dark settled is the last best memory I have. When he was finished, he bent down and stubbed his smoke into the dirt. *I have to talk to you and Mum later tonight, private like.*

I remember nodding. His eyes were so serious and stripped of any resemblance to my joking brother, I nearly started laughing. I coughed instead as he headed over to report in to the other rangers. Later I grabbed Mum and we learnt about Lyla.

Mum was livid. Her face splotchy. *What were you thinking?* She grabbed his face in her hands and took the measure of his stare. *Are you in love with her?*

He sat there, not moving, just watching Mum and the door, and waiting. I'm not sure if he was expecting her to run out and tell the others. He knew what he should have done, we all did. *I couldn't shoot her.*

Where is she? I'll do it.

No. Please? He stood up, started grabbing his things and moved towards the door.

Mum raised her eyebrow at that. Before all the rains failed, she shot his dog when she found it dragging its back legs around. He'd hidden the dog too.

Lyla is no dog that you can just shoot. She's like us. I know she can't stay, I just need to get her over the range.

There is no getting her through. She's a lowlander and you know the rules. We let one through, more are going to come. You know this Benny, so why? They'll shoot you for this. And her. They'll hunt her down and shoot her like you should have done the first time.

Mum walked out into that night. Don't know where she

went. I like to think she sat out in the dark, maybe on the big rock, so she could see the whole problem. Looked for the answer in the stars. In the early hours of the morning she came back. Tired, grumpy and trailing behind her an inkling of something unprecedented.

Benny and Mum went out the next day to where she'd been hidden. Mum checked his work. Everything looked good but it would be weeks before she could move over the mountains. Weeks to heal then weeks to strengthen. The burrow was too close to the patrol. Mum carried her pack, Benny carried her and they headed west to the old gold mine, stashed her there with supplies and returned home.

Twice a week Benny went out taking up supplies. Sometimes he'd be gone for days, staying away longer and longer. He'd set out in his brown jumper with the red cuffs and the beanie I'd made last year to match. After a few weeks he came back without the jumper. It was getting cold up there, every bit of warmth counted, especially since she couldn't have a fire. *I haven't lost it*, he promised. During that time we heard reports of people moving below the gorge, more than had tried to come up before, but they didn't come up any further. We were never sure if they were looking for Lyla. Perhaps they found who they were looking for on the rock face.

The days started to lengthen and we'd tipped past the equinox when Mum disappeared with Benny one day. Came back when it was dark. They ate before they said anything. Outside while we were smoking, Benny told me she was ready to go. Strong enough and healed enough to push on.

Will you miss her? I couldn't ask if he would go with her.

I wasn't sure if I could bear hearing his answer. I'd been missing him each time he went to Lyla but he always came back. I feared the possibility of him going with her.

I will. I think you would have liked her.

I imagined meeting her, talking with her like Benny and I did, having her live with us, all sorts of impossible things. *What does she talk about?*

She asked about you, wanted to know what you were like.

And you said good things?

Of course.

I wish she could stay.

Yeah. They've told us what the lowlanders are like and she's not, she's different, kinder, smarter and…

Not the sort to slit your throat in your sleep. I finished. Wonder what it is like down there?

Benny threw his butt to his feet and ground it under his foot. *You don't want to know. Some of it is not for little sister's ears.*

Aren't you the gentleman now? I'd shoved his shoulder but that still didn't clear the sadness from his eyes.

Hardly. He stood up and turned around. *She deserves more.*

But not if it kills you? I didn't get such a brotherly look in reply. He stormed back inside and talked to Mum.

I don't really understand how everything got so messed up. Benny and Mum had it all worked out—he'd take Lyla on high patrol and help her over the range before coming back down. Benny woke me up the morning that they left. He had the red beanie I'd made him last year pulled down over his ears, his rifle slung over one shoulder and the old eucalypt branch he used as his walking stick. He poked me with that stick fair in the guts. I jumped up to deck him and saw Mum kitted out as well, standing behind him in the darkness. Today was *the* day. When Benny returned he would be safe. I gave him a hug. Wished him good travels and they headed off. I climbed the big rock and stretched out, watching them climb up through the trees until they were out of sight.

The sun was just starting to warm the rock when the shouting started. Bill and Robbo rode in from patrol carrying a backpack. They emptied the contents on the ground—Benny's jumper bright amongst it. His name cut into the silence and I forgot to breathe. People poured out of houses, workshops and milled around the rangers. Bill pushed through them heading to our house. Before he could get through I was sliding off that rock and climbing the hill to get over the top before I was seen. And shot. I vomited at the top, I'd climbed that hard, struggled to get control of my lungs and ran along the ridge to where it crossed the path. You never know if you have made the right choice until you do. Sometimes a hand guides you. Sometimes it's a discarded mandarin peel. I turned left. Thankfully Mum and Benny weren't too far ahead.

It wasn't about Lyla any more. Surely she was dead, but Benny still wanted to check, see for his own eyes.

Mum was against it. *They'd expect it of you. You need to run.*

Either way if we didn't get him over the range now, Benny was dead. We climbed, Benny leading at a pace that drowned Mum's complaints into harsh breathing.

There was blood but no body. *Trait...*was scratched into the dirt, the last letters rubbed out by drag marks. We found Lyla's body covered in branches down the slope, her face a battery of bruises, a bullet wound to her heart, cold and blue.

Benny sank to her side, his whole body clenched as he pulled her to his chest. The silence scared me. Then he broke, one sob that snarled free of his body and I was crying too. I knew then he really did love her. He stood up. *How? How did they know?*

I was going to say bad luck when I saw Mum's face as she turned away. Saw the answer to his question in her eyes. Saw Benny see the same thing.

You didn't?

Her face went white.

Then Bill and Robbo arrived, their horse's flanks steaming, rifles raised and dragging hell with them. *Come back up or we shoot.*

We did, obedient as they come when you have guns pointed at you. I sat on the ground, my strength evaporating like sunshine behind a cloud. Benny and Mum stood.

Bill stashed his rifle and dismounted. *You're a fucking idiot, Benny boy.* He pulled the picture out of his pocket. *She wasn't fucking worth it.* Threw the picture on the ground, ground his foot on her face.

Benny didn't drop his head. *You're wrong. She was.*

We'll let the others decide that. Let's get a move on, you've wasted enough of my fucking time.

Bill stepped behind Benny, gave him a shove, then reached for my arm and yanked me up.

She had nothing to do with it. Mum stood in front of him, stopping him from moving forward.

Bill slugged her across the face. *She's here, she has something to do with it.*

I thought we were all going to die like Lyla. I thought

a lot of things, but none that I remember too well. Just the prospect of dying. And Lyla's face, pale and cross-hatched with scars, her eyes open and black. I stood there, Bill's hand crushing my arm and pain surging upwards to invoke a cry I'd never made before.

Benny turned and punched Bill, sent him flying and me sprawling back to the ground. Robbo pulled his rifle out, tried for the shot when Mum rushed his horse, growling as if fending off a wild dog. The horse shied and whirled around. By the time he got his horse under control, she'd flicked out Bill's rifle and brought it up steady. Robbo didn't hesitate, firing his rifle while falling off his horse with a bullet wound in his forehead. Mum's a good shot. Robbo's not so bad himself. Mum folded up on herself, her hand pressing against her belly as blood poured out and knelt using the rifle as support. She took a deep breath, stood up and blasted Bill in the chest as he tried to stand too. Fell down again. By the time I got to her she was gone.

We don't know what she told or to whom. I imagine it was to protect my brother—if Lyla went away, the danger went too and somehow she thought to keep him out of it. I do know Benny rode away on Bill's horse with Lyla loaded up on Robbo's. Bill and Robbo we dragged into the mine and dropped them into the drowned shaft. He didn't linger, wanted to get over the range by nightfall. I asked him to take me too.

You're safer here.

They won't trust me. What if they shoot me?

They won't. They'll need you. Mum's gone. I'm gone. You're the only one with her skills. If I find a good place, I'll come back and get you.

Part of me hopes there's a good place out there with some good people and clean water. I hope they're different than us or the lowlanders. That Benny isn't gone forever. That one day he will come back.

HEART AND MIND

SIMONE CORLETTO

The thump of house music is barely audible over the crowd of horny teenagers that fill the house, spilling out in clumps on the lawn. I haven't been to one of Flora's parties in months. I've never liked crowds, especially when there's alcohol involved. The sound is all-consuming and it would be easy to lose myself. But this is my one chance to see her. The one place I can talk to her without interruption. In the middle of the biggest social event of the year. I'm aware of the irony. But I need to do this. I need to find Meg.

It wouldn't usually be so hard for me to track someone down, but my normal methods won't work on her. And as frustrating as it is, that's part of why I love her.

Love is complicated like that.

I zip up my jacket and step through the front door, dodging flailing limbs as I skirt around the edges of the living room-turned-dancefloor. Meg always spends most of these parties in the kitchen, where she has easiest access to the sushi platters, handing out cups of water to anyone who walks past. She's always the one looking out for other people.

I'll always remember the first time I saw her. A busy courtyard. First day of a new school. A new start. After what had happened at the last school, I really needed it. I remember the sound. Hundreds of voices and twice as many thoughts filling the air, consuming the space like a thick fog. I could barely breathe. I closed my eyes and counted, trying to focus on just one sound while shutting out the rest. By the time I reached double digits, the world felt smaller, calmer. I found a pocket of silence. I opened my eyes and tried to find the source. By the trees, at the edge of the courtyard, I spotted a flash of vibrant red hair like a match on the horizon. The more I concentrated, the quieter it got. I stood, stunned by the discovery. Someone without thoughts, or inner monologue, or at least none that *I* could hear. Someone immune to my curse. Everyone else became a dull hum, so long as I kept my focus on her.

She saw me staring.

Instead of running away or flipping a rude gesture, she smiled and walked up to me.

'Hi, I'm Meg.' She held out her hand. I took it carefully, lest my focus break. She shook my hand vigorously while grinning. 'You're new, aren't you? What's your name?'

'Warren,' I mumbled. I was still staring, but she didn't seem put off.

'Nice to meet you, Warren. Come sit with us.' She pulled me to her group, a blonde-haired girl and an olive-skinned boy, who she introduced as Flora and Jase.

From that day, whenever the fog sunk in, she would

always be there to help clear it away. She made school bearable. She made life bearable. I know it's a cliché. I know many people would view this co-dependency as love. But relying on someone to be a human filter isn't love. I knew enough to realise that. It was because of her immunity that I could actually tolerate getting to know her—the way regular people do. Through talking and time spent together, rather than having her every thought and desire invade my mind like a forceful breeze, impossible to stop. Love came later.

A door opens in the hallway and I step into the shadows, stepping behind a large fern to blur my image. It's not quite cloaking or being invisible, but it should be enough for anyone who's had a few too many beers to overlook me.

Jase stumbles out, mid-conversation on his phone. *'Ti ho detto che non ho intenzione di studiare legge come Michael!'*

Even his thoughts at this moment are in Italian, so I have no idea what he's talking about. He swears, something I do understand, and hangs up abruptly. Slipping the phone into his jeans pocket, he stumbles straight past me down the hall, snippets of Italian and English cursing interchangeably echoing in my mind. That was close.

It's dangerous for me to be back here, after the way I left. I can't trust any of the people I once called friends not to make a scene. Except for her. She's the only one who might understand. Even if she doesn't, I only need a moment.

I can't pinpoint the exact moment I started loving her.

It just sort of happened. Like a seedling shooting out of the ground. Perhaps the seed was always there, just lying dormant.

But people are more complex than plants. Just a tad.

The reasons I love her are obvious. We've been friends for years, best friends. Faced countless enemies and obstacles together, for each other.

I don't know all her secrets.

It's not often I actually care about other people. When you're in their heads so often, you start to see the patterns. The predictability. The anxieties. The fears. They're all basically the same. When it's all laid out there for you, there's no mystery, no sense of discovery. Nothing to pursue. When you can see someone's utmost desires you can manipulate them too easily. There's no challenge when you have the answer key.

This is where Meg's different. I can't read her—not all the time. Sure, sometimes she lets her guard slip and her voice fills my mind like a songbird in an echo chamber. Sometimes I wait a few minutes before reminding her, but I always tell her eventually. I want the mystery. I think that's what love is: slowly uncovering the pieces of a person and, before you're even halfway through putting them together, you already can't imagine life without them.

Over the years, we became close. I learned her secrets, not through force, but because she shared them. After a while, I told her mine. I'd spent a lot of time estimating how outsiders would react if they knew my burdens. I couldn't decide if fear, disgust, or pity would be worse. I'd experienced all of those before. That's when I stopped sharing. People are so caught up in their perception of reality that any dissenting evidence inspires violence.

But not with Meg. She revelled in my abilities. We'd play games, tricks, on people around us, people we didn't like. Entirely harmless, of course. I didn't have to read her to know she wouldn't be too keen on the shit I used to do to people. Mostly out of self-defence, but also sometimes not. It was just too easy to project a person's worst fears back at them and watch them squirm. Or even just the subtle stuff, like small hallucinations over time, so they think they're losing their minds. I'll admit that one was bad, but they deserved it. Everyone has their bullies, but it's always been a more literal interpretation of 'brains vs brawn' when people try to harass me. And who needs to bulk up when you can make someone literally piss themselves without lifting a finger?

After spending so many years trying to hide who I was, pretending I was normal, Meg was a revelation. Even her other friends came around, once they learned. Except Derrick. I could sense his distrust from the beginning. He never liked me, or the fact that Meg and I were so close. It just got worse over the years. I know exactly what he'd do if he saw me here now.

I stop just before I reach the kitchen, taking a moment to scan its occupants. I can hear Flora's drunken anxiety, fixated on whether there's enough chips for the dip, not that anyone really seems to be eating. The only other people in there are the usual frantic drones from our school. No Meg. I know she's here somewhere. Outside maybe? It's a warm summer night and I can hear a bunch of people thinking about either jumping in the pool or pushing someone else. I slide into the kitchen and pass through unnoticed while Flora has her head in the fridge.

I know it's a cliché to fall for your best friend. But clichés exist for a reason. It wasn't weird. It just made sense. More like fitting a puzzle piece into place.

We'd gone on a hike to the top of the hill that overlooks the city to watch the sunset. I recall thinking how clichéd and romantic it was to go up to Hickey Hill right before twilight. I said just as much to her and she laughed. But as soon as I said it, I realised it felt right to be there with her at that moment.

This became my new secret.

We grew distant because of it. I was worried, scared even. She was the only person I could really connect with and I didn't want to ruin the friendship by making things weird. I couldn't read her; I had no idea if she felt the same way. It was just as bad as being *normal* and blindly guessing everyone else's emotions. Her immunity, which I was so attracted to in the first place, had become my nightmare. The irony was not lost on me.

I tried to pretend there wasn't a problem, act like I was normal—I was pretty good at that by this stage. But she realised something was wrong. Even without actual mind-reading, Meg was uncannily perceptive. She confronted me a few weeks later. I was so unused to others seeing through my façade that I confessed how I felt.

I didn't see her again until the big New Year's Eve party. She was especially beautiful then, in a flowing silver dress that shimmered like lightening on the horizon. I saw her smile and laugh with her other friends: Flora, Jase, and, of course, Derrick. He was always skulking around her, had been since he arrived at the school. I could read that he liked her. I hated him, for being around her when I couldn't. Following at her heels like a puppy. It was pathetic.

I avoided them all night. I couldn't be near them, and not just because the large crowd at the party was threatening to overwhelm me. She found me right before midnight. She'd had a few drinks, but only enough to make her slightly unsteady. She grasped my arm as she said those words back to me. We kissed mid-countdown. Her soft lips pressed to mine and a charge ran through me. The room melted away around us. It was unlike anything else, yet it was also all too familiar, like I'd felt it before.

Not personally, but through a thousand other memories that passed through my mind in the fog. Thousands of other experiences, good and bad, drifting in and imprinting upon me. That's how I knew this was love. Throughout everyone's memories this feeling, this warmth, was consistent.

But this kiss, our kiss, felt more real, more special than any of that. I can still feel the way she pressed her chest against mine and bit my lip. I remember cupping her face, a dull pain shooting down my wrist as I moved my bandaged thumb to cup her chin—

Wait.

I didn't have an injured thumb at New Year's.

I remember every injury I've ever had and I've never even injured my hand that way.

So why do I so clearly remember having that injury in that moment?

The realisation hits me cold. *This isn't my memory.*

I lean against the hallway wall, suddenly nauseous. I've

had that kiss, that memory, on replay in my mind almost every night. How did I not see this detail before? If it wasn't me, who was it?

Derrick.

The guy she works so closely with, the friend that fits so easily in with the others. The athlete who had sprained his thumb playing football the day before the party.

Of course it's fucking Derrick.

It comes back to me now, their kiss by the ice statue. Except now I see it in third person. My perspective. Several metres away in the corner of the room. Watching other people live their lives while I experience the memories.

I rub my brow. This can't be it, though it wouldn't be the first time. Memories aren't static. They change in hundreds of big and small ways before they even get to me. But I've never fucked up this badly before. That kiss felt so real. I can feel it so clearly—down to the smell of her perfume. Even when the visual stuff gets mixed up, it's the other senses that are usually the most stable. Especially for my own memories. That's usually how I can tell—it's much harder to smell someone else's memory.

I think back to our other moments. The hike makes no sense. I can't remember the climb itself, nor the smell all those flowers would've had at the summit. So the cliff-top realisation couldn't have been me either. I look over the images again. I—or whoever it is—is wearing a ring with the school crest. The ring the headmaster gives out to the school captain, in an archaic display of traditional bullshit. That's Derrick's ring. So now I'm feeling his emotions now as well as remembering his experiences? Did those two events even happen in that order? What else have I unconsciously appropriated from that asshole?

My head is spinning at this headfuckery. I need to ground myself before I get all existential. I need certainties. Verifiable events, to prove I didn't suddenly invent my whole life.

I find the bathroom and push open the door, closing it a little too loudly behind me. I stand in front of my reflection in the mirror, memorising my identity. My eyes. My nose. That lone freckle on my neck. Any time I see this face, my face, in a memory, I know that memory is not mine. I close my eyes and think back, images appearing and disappearing like I'm channel surfing. I see picnics, funerals, school classrooms. It's all random. I need to focus.

Meg. Megan. Red hair, bright eyes, a smattering of brown freckles across her nose—there she is. We're standing at a bus stop. She laughs. I've said something about ducks. She shoves me playfully. But is this my memory? What can I smell? It's hard, because it's outside. A car drives past, and suddenly I detect the stench of diesel. Thank fuck for these anti-hybrid holdouts. This is my memory. I know this day. It was my birthday, two years ago, before she got her license. We took the bus to the aquarium in the city. Being surrounded by giant tanks of water has the effect of blocking out psychic noise. It was her idea. Derrick wouldn't do this. He doesn't like fish. He's secretly afraid of stingrays. He doesn't trust how they glide through the water without what he would call 'proper fins'. I grin. This is mine.

But did we kiss?

I jump into a new memory. High school. Busy hallway, but I can barely hear anything over the Origin's 'Finite'. Still,

I can sense the mood is…joyous. This was the end of term, our final year. I catch snippets of holiday plans and parties. Meg is emptying her locker beside me. She looks up at me. I lip-read 'kiss me'. I lean in and press my lips to hers. She puts a hand on my chest and pushes me back. She looks confused. I've misjudged this. The cold shame and embarrassment wash over me all over again and I realise why I might have buried this memory. She had said something else. I remember making a quick getaway before the situation became more awkward. Was that really the last time I saw her? It's not the only reason I left, but is that what she thinks?

What *does* she think?

It's the most maddening question I'll never have the answer to, not until she lets me.

There's a shout from outside and I'm reminded of the present. I came to this party for a reason.

I try a new tactic. Closing my eyes, I listen out for thought patterns so familiar they could almost be my own. It's not at all surprising when I find him upstairs. I walk in on Meg and Derrick in Flora's parents' study. Together. She's wearing his ring. They pull apart at my intrusion, and Derrick quickly goes from lust to shock to irritation. The last time he cycled through emotions so quickly he swung a punch at me. Fair, considering I had been sending him unpleasant images all day, but this time there's no fight in him.

'I'll go get us more drinks,' he says to her, dismissing himself from the room. The look he gives me is backed with smug acceptance, without even a twinge of jealousy. I'm no threat to him, to his relationship. I was apparently never even in the fucking running. I want to punish him, but her voice fills my head like a dream. 'Did you really come back from the dead to fight him?'

I turn to her, ashamed. 'No,' I say out loud. 'I came here for you.'

She hops off the desk and wraps her arms around my waist, her face resting on my shoulder. Four months of self-inflicted isolation have at least managed to ease the awkward mess I left behind. 'It's really great to see you, War.'

'You too.' I hold her close, the resentment fading. Her defences lowered, I try to read her, but all I find is a warm platonic sense of affection. She's missed me. I've missed her. But it's not the same longing I thought I felt before. Maybe all this time I've simply missed her friendship. Maybe I was just mistaking Derrick's lust for my own. That's weird. Better not think about it too hard.

When she pulls away, she slaps me. 'I can't believe you just ran off like that for four months. Asshole. Do you even know how worried I was?'

I can't help but laugh. She flushes red and I want to kiss her again. But no. Let's not screw up the reunion as well. 'Sorry. I'm not good at emotions.'

'Yeah, evidently.' She shakes her head and puts her walls back up.

The silence returns but shadows of her remain. It feels more intimate than any kiss I've remembered. Derrick might be *with* her, but he'll never know her like this. Only I could have this experience. 'I promise not to do it again.'

'You better not.' She doesn't ask me to explain. She doesn't need me to. I hold her again and I memorise every detail of this moment so it won't become muddled later.

SPLENDID BUTTERFLIES

LAUREN BUTTERWORTH

I found your book, Auntie Net. Remember the one? It's old now, the pages are yellowed and curl at the edges, but that image of the woman with hair down the left side of the page is vibrant. The reds and yellows you painted of her garland, the bright orange of her drooping earrings. Peak-nosed, elegant and ethereal, 'The Fair Princess Who Would Always Remember'. Mum found it at the bottom of the drawer under the folded linen, pages clasped loosely by a paper clip. A fairy tale dedicated to your niece, my mother.

I'm glad she found it as I've been thinking of you lately. We're very much alike, you see. Travellers. Adventurers. Independent and intrepid women. To be fair, we're both so cloaked in suburban conservatism and easy privilege that our little acts of revolt, to choose travel over marriage, probably seem far more radical to us than they really are. But still, we share the same branch of the family tree, I think. Only I didn't know that until after you'd passed.

To me you were Auntie Net. A poised woman with short

blonde curls and, later, that turban so regally worn. A maiden aunt. Though now I hate it, growing up it was the hushed term used for women like you. Women who lived alone with cottage gardens, who knitted intricate dolls' clothes and crafted ceramic fairies for their great-nieces. Limitlessly talented, these women with time. But always still, a hint of pity. So you can imagine my delight when I read your fairy tale, and no doubt forgive my need to fill in the gaps. To picture you as the woman you were when, at eighteen, you left on an ocean liner to New Zealand, China, then the Continent, and—if the fairy tale is anything to go by—met your Handsome Prince.

I imagine you in your cabin. The walls are white and crisp, with light blue curtains over a porthole that looks beyond foam to the sparkle of sun on the sea. You are neat in your tan dress, one leg crossed over the other, gazing with a half-smile at the wonder of movement. Of the slow tug and pull of the ship carving the water into a wake that jets behind you. The knowledge that you steal further and further from schoolbooks and calisthenics, brown gums and water sprinklers, towards the glamorous unknown.

You rise and emerge from your small cabin, pass a pair of newlyweds in panama hats who nod politely. You smile and continue up the corridor to the staircase that takes you to the deck. The air is chilled, but the breeze is soft. It lifts the short tufts of your golden hair and you wrap your arms about you, wander to the railing and look out over the side. Seagulls dive, riding the wind. You feel a bit like them, free and fearless, letting the breeze take you where it will. I know that feeling. I was the same, standing at the top of Parliament

Hill gazing down over London, with long grass tickling my ankles, alone and freshly arrived. I was escaping then too. That's how I know you felt it. You must have. Because it's all so big, so expansive and overwhelming. You'd never seen anything like it.

I was older on my trip, and though it wasn't my first time in Europe, it may as well have been. It was my first time alone, not just as a solo backpacker, but single. I'd run away after the inevitable end of my engagement, a thing not lost in a single, momentous battle, but through slow collapse and ruin, like Rome. Although it had only been a few weeks I had already grieved and, fully aware of my own cliché, was ready to find myself again. I didn't expect to meet anybody, certainly not so soon, but thinking back now it doesn't surprise me. I was so full of the person that I was becoming, an identity slipped into easily, for she'd existed for years in the imagined space behind my eyes, that perhaps it seemed like we'd always been one. I remember catching my reflection one afternoon soon after my arrival, my dress spilling long in the light of a pond in Kensington Gardens, my hair dark, tumbling energetically. I'd gasped. Did I really know her? Perhaps you felt the same that night of the ball. To discover yourself as the woman you hope to be is quite a remarkable thing, don't you agree?

You are nervous as you stand at the mirror. Your dress is new, sewn from discounted silk from John Martins and although the shoes you have don't quite match the particular shade of red, you decide that in the dark no one will notice. Your heart pounds when you see yourself in it, with your hair done up and your lipstick on, purchased on the same trip, and you twirl, just enough for the hem to reveal your ankle, your knee.

Then you're in that room of dancing figures. A swirling meringue of pinks and blues, black jackets and clipping shoes. It must have been exhilarating: the music, the hum of chatter and the silken mass, waltzing across the polished floors. It is a dream, you think, a fairy tale, but you stand outside of it all. Cross your arms awkwardly across your chest. You wonder if any man will ask you to dance.

He appears as the music lingers, but perhaps it's just your nerves that make time seem to slow. I imagine his hair to be Brylcreem-flat, his face clean shaven. Or, perhaps, he has a dark complexion. Long lashes, a cropped beard. The Handsome Prince, you wrote, had fought in many battles, and so he must have been older, striking in his uniform. It is hard to tell at first where he is from, but you know right away that he isn't Australian. He is too elegant. He mingles for a while with a group of other uniformed young men. They are approached by women in pale dresses and your heart sinks. He hasn't noticed you. So you turn to a girl from the cabin beside yours, giggle and gossip. Pretend you aren't disappointed. You hurry off together to the ladies' room where you huddle in front of the gilt-framed mirror. *Did you see him?* She asks. *Those eyes, that chin. What a dream.* You reapply your lipstick and say you didn't notice.

I was new to it too, Auntie Net. Not just to flirting, though I'd learned a little of that long ago, but to feeling worthy of somebody's attention. Women can disappear in relationships, shrinking to fit someone else's box. Despite the distance in time between us, we both learned that a woman's value comes from a man. My prince was older too, though he wasn't as handsome as yours. Spencer had faded red hair and soft green eyes and he spoke with a Dorset accent that lilted. Not nearly as exotic, but enough to make my skin prickle when he leaned close and whispered. That first night, sitting at the dirty wooden picnic table in the courtyard of a hostel in Earl's Court—hardly a ballroom—I didn't realise that his close attention, his guitar picking and drunken philosophising, were attempts to impress me. That he knew that I was a writer and this was his way of flirting. He didn't need to try so hard; he was a musician, recently returned from working in Denmark, replete with tales of bohemian adventures. I was so new in my skin that I didn't realise through my world-startled eyes that he was exactly what I'd been waiting for.

And so I know you can't help that nervous flutter when you emerge from the bathroom and his eyes land on yours. When he smiles then drops his gaze, scuffs one shoe behind the other. He approaches, finally, and reaches out a hand. He tells you his name and you smile demurely. Jeanette, you reply. He is French, let's say, or Italian. Or maybe even Moroccan, Algerian. The Handsome Prince, you wrote, is from somewhere with mountains that reach to the clouds, where the water is so blue and still that hardly a ripple breaks the crystal surface.

When he takes your hand and leads you to the dance floor your belly cartwheels and your cheeks flush pink. You feel petite in his arms, which is a novelty as you're tall, and, if anything like me, self-conscious about it. But he is taller, with white teeth and peppermint breath that disguises the faintest whiff of cigarette. Of course, this probably doesn't bother you—it is the late 50s, after all, and you are young and fashionable. On your way to work in the theatres in London. Why wouldn't you smoke too?

Spencer smoked. I hated it at first, a stale bitterness that lingered, always, no matter how much gum or coffee or beer he'd had in the meantime. But it has since taken on quite a different association in my memory, tied forever now to easy nights in Camden, and the sticky intimacy of that hot London July. It was at a pub off the High Street with low ceilings, an oaky musk and a bulldog above the door—or a horse, or perhaps a troubadour—that Spencer first kissed me. It may have been the beer, or it may have been that I'd only ever kissed one other person, and had for eight years, but I was both giddy and confused, confronted suddenly with the knowledge that there would be other men in my life. That I was young and, as was becoming quickly apparent to me, perhaps even beautiful. I'd lost the twenty-five extra kilograms that had kept my self-esteem attached to one person for so long, and so it was almost like I was eighteen again, as you were, Auntie Net, when you experienced what must have been your first exhilarating leap into desire.

The Fair Princess and the Handsome Prince danced on until dawn, but you left out the best part. The moment every fairy tale leads inevitably towards: the kiss. Is it under starlight as you arise to the deck for air, cocktail in hand, and stare out across the still and silent sea? Or, when the last of the horns and piano die away as grey turns rosy through the windows and he leans in, fingers tilting your chin, and you close your eyes? There's nothing like a first kiss on the dance floor. The steady pull of music, head dizzy, just a little, with drink. And then waiting, the quiver of an unexpected touch, goose-bumps prickling your arms. The thrill of it. He twirls you and you laugh, trying not to lose your balance. And finally, as he walks you to your cabin door and you say a polite good-night and the rough bristle of his five-am-shadow grazes your cheek, you begin to realise that it has all been real. When you close the door behind you, your cheeks hurt with smiling.

My trip home was less romantic: an early morning bus ride with tracksuited chavs, bleary yellow on brick walls and roller shutters. I don't remember much except the way his eyes smiled when I caught him looking at me. That his infatuation, distinct somehow to both lust or love, glowed, watery and oblique, like moonlight. I wasn't used to that kind of gaze. And it didn't stop. He followed me, puppy-like, along Cromwell Road in a heatwave that melted asphalt, to the Victoria and Albert where we picnicked on Tesco sandwiches in the courtyard. He asked me about art and history and let me blabber about the beautiful extravagance of French aristocracy with eyes that seemed, incredulously, not only interested but fascinated. I didn't realise my heart could skip a beat to watch a man slow and gasp at Japanese prints. Even if he pretended interest for my sake he did it eagerly, though I believe he was as enchanted as I was. And even still, surrounded as we were by the most beautiful objects in the world, I would turn sometimes to find him watching me and my hairs would stand on end. I'd never felt so desired.

It's obvious, reading between the lines, how much the Fair Princess and the Handsome Prince desired one another.

It pulses from the page, that eagerness, the anticipation. It hardly needs imagining. You wait all day for the shade of night and then you emerge. Your lips are contoured and bright, your cheeks pinched. You are shy at first, but he introduces you to his friends and soon they become your own. Nights pass in booths before glass tumblers and ashtrays and all the rest of them squeeze in around you, laughing, while his arm drapes across your back. His fingers play at the silk sash at your waist so your legs tremble. You don't let them see, the others, how your foot glides up his shin. That you know when he turns, the moonlight in his eyes, and places a toothpick just between his teeth, that he's thinking of the velvet of your skin. So you cast your eyes down to hide the blush, giggle as your arms rub against one another. But they all know, and honestly, Auntie Net, they don't care about the young Australian girl and her French/Algerian lover, laughing quietly at the freshness of their love.

I felt self-conscious too, lying in the long grass of a Cambridge common, an ancient brownstone looming across the river. I'd left London to spend a week researching in the reading room, and though he could barely afford it, he caught the bus up every few days to visit. We'd walked the bridges and through the greens and he'd pulled me onto the soft grass, tickled me with stalks. He nuzzled my neck and I remember watching people pass in the distance, hoping they couldn't see our hands, our lips. I'd never wanted to touch somebody as much as I did then. Later, in a market erected in a cobblestone square, he told me lovingly of his father, how he would paint their coastal hometown. For a moment I could almost see it, imagine a life by that southern sea with its limestone ridges, green hills and dinosaur littered cliffs. But I remembered too, as you must have, that this was only temporary.

One night he brings you a necklace, a string of emerald stones more exotic than anything you've ever owned and you think your chest will burst with excitement. He tells you that each stone holds a memory. One for the day the ship docked in Tauranga and you watched the sea pound the sand, the spray a white rush. One for the hike in mountains so tall you could see the clouds meet the rocks and he held your hand fast because you grew dizzy from the height. One for each dance and one for each kiss, and finally, one for the evening you spent in the stateroom as the ship rocked you gently. The evening you'll never forget.

The Fair Princess and Handsome Prince knew that all beautiful things must come to an end. I'd never let myself forget it either. In a carriage on the underground, Spencer told me there was a song he couldn't shake. That it haunted him. 'All My Little Words', he said, and then he sang: *You are a splendid butterfly, it is your wings that make you beautiful. And I could make you fly away, but I could never make you stay.* No one had ever sung to me before. Certainly not in a place so full, and his voice carried such cadence, such confidence. He was serenading me. The marvel of it made me limp. But it is a song of endings, and its significance wasn't lost on me. I believe now that not all loves are meant to last. Some come to us just for a time and pass as they will. When we said goodbye at Earl's Court Station he held me as his voice grew thick. I stepped onto the train with something not quite like sadness in my chest. There was a curious bliss there too. I smiled and watched Victorian row houses pass beyond the tracks. What we had didn't need to be anything more than what it was. What it was had been perfect.

The Fair Princess knew that in time the memories would fade, as memories should. But many princesses have grown old and not known the happiness that the Fair Princess had. And so I don't picture you with longing, or with a sadness so deep it racks you. Instead, I imagine you in your red dress on the dock. He holds you and his voice grows thick. You kiss again and it feels like the first time. Your head grows dizzy, goose bumps prickle your skin. And as you step away, a smear beneath your eyes, you hold the emerald necklace and are overcome with a feeling of bliss. Because you know that the brightest sparks burn fastest, and while all lights fade, they are no less significant. I think this is something we both understand, Auntie Net. The blue ship pulls from the dock and you turn instead to gaze across the murky Thames to the choked chimney stacks of London. It's exactly as you imagined. The porter takes your trunk and you feel so light on your feet you could fly. Perhaps echoes of memories returned to you in later years, as you sipped tea in your cottage garden, or walked the silo-studded beach of your own coastal home. Or, perhaps, as you lay on white sheets beneath radiation beams. I hope it did. And I hope it made you smile.

AFTERIMAGE

CHRISTINE HANOLSY

'Come to the Kimball tonight,' Melanie said. 'They're showing that French movie I told you about, with the dog.'

She knew I didn't speak French, didn't much like foreign films or her friends. But I went anyway because she was tall and blonde and her voice hit me right in the solar plexus every time, y'know?

The Kimball was one of those run-down theatres, worn-out red velvet seats, old-timey 35-millimeter film. Used to be a big deal, before the hipsters moved in. When I pulled up on my Harley, Mel was already there with her art school friends. You know the type: fake-ripped jeans and rectangular glasses. Wouldn't see anything that came out of Hollywood. Therese with her stupid skateboard strapped to her backpack and her white-girl dreads like everybody didn't know she graduated from Payton. And then there was me, in the only pair of jeans that I *hadn't* ripped yet and barely twelve credits at the community college.

My best shot with Mel, I figured, was to make nice with

her crowd, learn their language. Only I couldn't follow half of it: symbolism and camera angles and *people just don't understand Art.* I stood in the lobby trying not to look stupid until I couldn't stand it anymore and ducked out for a smoke. The only other person out there was this tiny little thing in bell-bottom overalls with rainbow suspenders. I barely gave her a second look.

'Need a light?' she asked, pulling out a Bic. 'I quit last month.'

I said, 'Sure, thanks,' even though I had a lighter in my pocket.

I figured I oughtta make small talk, as long as we were both there. Asked if she was here to see the movie. Like a pro.

'Seen it,' she said. 'About thirty times.'

'God, I'm sorry,' I said. It just kinda slipped out.

Her laugh was light, throaty. Turned out her name was Kaya and she ran the projector. 'It's not about the movies,' she told me. She liked being in the booth. Liked the sound of it, the gentle heat of the bulb and the hypnotic motion of the platters.

'Mostly,' she said, 'I like being in control.'

Well. Me being me, I gave her a wicked grin. 'Really?' I said, thinking I was gonna make her blush. Only she didn't.

'Yeah, really,' she said, and shot me that same look right back.

That's probably what started it, that look.

They couldn't run the film without the projectionist, of course, so she had to get back to the booth. And I had to get back to Mel. I sat through that whole fucking movie trying to forget that look while Mel played hard-to-get. By the end of the movie Mel let me hold her hand. She was so goddamn smug about it, like it was this big deal, holding another girl's hand. Maybe it was for her, I dunno.

I started hanging around the theatre, buying tickets with money I didn't have to watch films I didn't like. I learned her schedule, showed up even without Mel. Those nights I'd catch Kaya outside before the show, borrow her lighter. It was kind of a running joke. I'd wait with her, after, until her bus came, smoking cigarettes I didn't even want.

I stopped watching the movies; started watching the blue-white brilliance of the projector's bulb instead. It flickered and pulsed like a heartbeat, and I imagined I could hear her whispers in the steady whirring of the projector, like she was showing these movies just for me, only it wasn't about the movies, it was about the beam of light running through my veins. I started seeing her in the glow of the marquee, the reflection of headlights in the rain. Whenever I closed my eyes, I saw her face in the afterimage.

One night she invited me up to the booth. It wasn't allowed, but what the hell, right? The projector was this ancient mechanical thing, and she had to thread the film on there just right. She wouldn't let me help, just made me sit in the back of the booth and watch.

There's something about a girl who knows how to use her hands.

I don't even remember what the movie was, because next thing I knew she was in my lap and I was thinking, why the fuck was I working so hard for Mel? Kaya didn't care if I thought art films were stupid. Didn't care about making an impression. She cared about the moment, the connections we make, the blue-white arc of electricity when two people touch.

Twenty, thirty minutes went by—we weren't exactly paying attention—and this guy walked in and stopped dead. I don't blame him, really.

Don't get me wrong, we weren't tossing clothes around. We were decent. Only, it was Kaya's boss, who never came by during a show. He kicked me out so fast I didn't even have time to get her number. I waited around outside until the movie was over, and who walked out? Mel. She thought I was there to surprise her, and *wasn't this romantic*, and *hey girls, look who's here.* By the time I peeled her off me, Kaya was gone. Hopped on the bus when I wasn't looking.

She wasn't there the next night, not before the show, not after. I sat through an entire movie with no dialogue, staring at the booth until I thought I'd go blind. And she wasn't there. I don't know who was running the projector, but it wasn't her. Same thing the next night, and the next. Finally, the ticket guy told me she got fired.

I stood outside the Kimball a long time that night, eyes closed, trying to fix her face in my mind.

Just as the image faded, her voice cut through the shadows. 'I hoped you'd be here. Need a light?'

'Yeah,' I said, drawn into the blue brilliance of her eyes. 'Yeah, I do.'

crush

verb

2. to crease or crumple by pressure

   'I wanted to crush the letter into a small ball.'

THE HORSES

ROWENA EDWARDS

You break up. He leaves. You cry, a lot. Friends crowd you, and you need them to. They keep you busy, let your thoughts air. But sometimes you're alone, alone in the bed you shared and the rooms where you laughed together and—worse still—in the room where it ended. You told yourself that these moments would be necessary, that you would use them to feel terrible, because you know that at times you'll need to feel terrible. Company is not conducive to breaking down.

You cry less than you thought you would. It's probably just the shock. You suspected reality would take a while to sink in. You just hope that while isn't too long. You want to feel better already, to be past the heartbreak. But you have to go through the process, you know, you know.

Sometimes you can't bear to be alone, even though you thought you could deal with it, take it as it came. Sometimes you don't want to cry. Sometimes it's just not convenient. You distract yourself. You pull out your phone, get lost in social media. You don't feel safe doing this on a computer because it tells you when he's online. You can't trust yourself to do what you want to do, because what you want and what you need have somehow separated. You want to talk to him, but will it help? Will it enable you to let go or keep you holding on?

You stick to your phone. You promise yourself that being single will allow you to grow. You want to fall in love with the world, to love the world the way you loved him. The world doesn't leave you until you leave it. The world is mother, sister, lover, child, all at once. You're glad you have this spiritual side. It helps.

A page you once liked for the purposes of daydreaming pops up with a new video. You watch. Get on a horse, it says. Come with us and get on a horse. Scrape your savings up and come to Mongolia and get on a horse. Take a train and meet a tribe and learn their wisdom and get on a horse and ride with us. Take a chance and leave your world and get lost in ours on a horse in a herd of a tribe on the plains of wild, soul-driven Mongolia.

Three minutes and twenty-four seconds and your heart has clamped around it. The deal's done. You're going.

You do it. You contact the group and pay a deposit. You take time off work, with an extra week either side for good measure. You find flights—expensive, but oh well. You pick up an extra weekend shift in the meantime. Work is the only commitment you have now, so what's a couple more hours? The weeks slip by. The tide of concerned friends dies down, but the best ones remain. A good sorting process, really.

You feel worse. Your thoughts loop endlessly, doubting his motives, thinking about all that he's given up, all the times it was perfect, the times near the end when your gut wouldn't stop twisting because you knew, you knew there was something bad, and he wouldn't say what it was.

You contact him. You're not sure if it's a good idea, but you feel out of touch with reality and you hope it'll bring you back to earth. It does. It's nothing like talking to him in person, but it never has been, and it's still a better version of him than the one that's been cropping up in your dreams. You smile like you're lovestruck when his replies are the slightest bit funny or reassuring. But you go easy on yourself: you are still in love. Give it time, stay grounded, let the reality sink in but try to find peace with it, peace peace peace, it's ok. You are enough for yourself. It's just hurting. That's fine— it's good. Let it hurt, let it rest, let it be alright.

You need this trip. You know it's foolish to buy into the Eastern Shaman-Black Magic view of Indigenous cultures, but nonetheless you hope for a level of sustained spirituality and guidance that seems to be missing from this life, this city. The horses, too—you've loved those creatures since you were a child. The smells of their wet, sweaty coats, of dust, tar and leather. The spots on their chests that are as soft as rabbits' down in winter; their expressive, dark eyes. The tickle of their breath on the back of your neck when they turn to watch you pick out their hooves. Feeling their power beneath you and their spirit ahead of you when you race together. Yes, you miss that trust.

Time seems to slow down. You don't feel like you're progressing at all, but when you look at the weeks past, you can see the difference between then and now. It's something. Still, it feels like you're waiting, paused until the time comes to pack your canvas bag. Five days out, you begin. Rushing around is fantastic—people to see, appointments to make, things to organise. You think about whether you should see him before you go. You draw blanks. If you don't, seeing him at a later point might undo all the progress you make on the trip, what with the shock of not having seen him since you broke up. If you do, you might not be ready. You might still need to touch him; it might hurt not to. He might not say the things you want him to say. It might set you back. In the end, the decision is made for you: there's no time.

You sit through the flight in a daze. The landing bounces you out of your seat. There's the click of a hundred seatbelts and the thud of baggage, and then you're moving, you're out, you're wobbling down the metal stairs as the chilled Mongolian air hits you like a sharp perfume. You show the taxi driver a napkin with the name of your hotel written on it by a flight attendant. You pay him with crisp notes when you arrive at the run-down, homely building. The woman pours you a small, strong cup of tea; her husband lifts your bag up the stairs. You smile, thank them in a broken English you hope they understand.

Once exhaustion overcomes your buzzing thoughts, you sleep deeply. You dream that your grandfather is here with you and you are worried about how he will cope with the harshness of the trek. Despite this, and despite his visible sickness, you are comforted by his presence. In the morning, the dream fills you with both melancholy and warmth. Your grandfather died three years ago; you were close. It is nice to see him again in your sleep, at least when the dreams are good. When he's happy, not dying.

A van, no seatbelts, picks you up after breakfast (the coffee was awful, the porridge delicious). It is already filled with people, mostly locals visiting relatives, a few tourists squashed conspicuously in their midst. Somehow, room is found for you. The road judders and thumps, progressively more so as the houses, then the bitumen, then the fences, disappear.

The ride is not good for your mental state. Several times, you have to blink away tears, tell yourself to focus on your surroundings, will yourself away from the endlessly looping thoughts and distorted memories that threaten to trap you. There just isn't space for them in this van.

After too long, the drive is over. An interpreter brings you, shell-shocked and overtired, to one of the few solid buildings in sight. You hear the rumble of many voices before he opens the door. Your fellow trekkers are tucking in to dinner, seated on benches either side of long, narrow tables. They cheer when you're introduced, but you can't muster much of a reaction. You notice local people seated amongst the westerners, sun-worn skin, crinkled eyes, baseball caps and traditional silk-adorned coats. Your interpreter gestures to an empty space on a bench and you sink down without consciously deciding to, tired beyond thought. A smiling woman places a steaming bowl of mutton before you. 'Thank you,' you say, hoping she'll understand the meaning, if not the words. The meat is wonderfully unpretentious, the flavour honest, the texture soft but chewy. You wonder if it will taste this good in a fortnight.

Suddenly, you have an overwhelming, mouth-watering craving for Tim Tams. The regret you feel at not having packed any surpasses all limits of reason, but you indulge in the feeling. To mourn for something so inconsequential is an achievement of sorts, a sign of normality.

You are shown to a room filled with bunks, warmed by a fire burning in the middle. Sleep smothers you as soon as your head hits the thin pillow.

Breakfast is served in the hall at dawn, simple fare. The interpreter goes over the day's schedule, words like 'maybe' and 'hopefully' punctuating his statements with a buttery smoothness. You try to listen, but you don't remember much beyond the pre-departure plans. You figure you'll just go along with whatever happens.

Your thoughts trip suddenly, like they lost their footing. The sound he makes when he thinks of something brilliant cuts into your head, clear and shocking. You brace. Feet flat on the ground, fingers pressing into the wooden boards of the table, gaze fixed. Where did that come from? You grab your thermos and gulp down more coffee. You stare at the interpreter, the wide pores of his cheeks, the blackness of his eyelashes, the uneven stubble scattered over his jaw. Be here. Stay here. Just stay here. Slowly, the feeling fades away.

You pack the day's essentials into a small saddlebag and chuck the other bag, the one with your spare clothing and sleeping gear, into the tray of the support vehicle. Then the whole group walks to the edge of town. The horses are tied along a rope suspended from two tree trunks. Brown, bay, roan, grey. No prominent markings—you know from a childhood spent reading horse books that solid colouring is preferred. Some stand with their heads low, dozing, while others prick their ears and watch your approach. One or two nip at their neighbours irritably. There are twice as many horses as riders. The group unconsciously stands in a parallel row, and the horsemen walk in between. They point at a rider, then, slowly and deliberately, turn and point to a horse. When one of them points at you, you feel a shock and hold your breath as he turns. He points to a chestnut and it feels like fate. Not because the horse is special or different, just because you have been put together, for reasons you doubt you'll be told.

You walk to your horse. A mare. You hold your open palm to her muzzle and she softly, lazily puffs into it, acknowledging you. You run your hands over her, cautiously move around her rump, explore the animal who will carry your weight for the next fortnight. It's more than that, you know: this is the animal you will trust, and who will trust you, to make good choices. The biggest choice, the selection of horse and rider, has been predetermined. Everything else is up to the pair of you.

You run your hands down one of her legs, ask her to lift it up. She complies. This is more a test of obedience than an inspection of her hooves, but you see that they widen considerably near the edges, flat and unshod. You move up her neck, twist your fingers into her knotted mane to feel the coarseness of it, lean in to breathe her dusty scent. She makes no objection when you touch her ears, or her forehead. You scratch the whorl of hair between her eyes. She snorts gently, relaxed. But you're not worried that she'll be too calm, too slow: her ears remain pricked, flicking back and forth, listening. You lean towards them. 'Hello,' you say softly, stroking her wide cheek. 'I'm Pippa.' Murmuring the words so that they're just between the two of you, so that the connection stays strong, you close your eyes, press your lips into her mane and tell her, 'I trust you.'

AMOR VINCIT OMNIA

SONALI PATEL

It was dusk and the sun had mellowed on the horizon like a ripened peach. Silvia and Felix watched it dissolve behind a smudge of charcoal. They sat content amongst the fishermen, dangling their bare feet over the jetty.

Soon drowsy and hungry from the heat, they headed off to their favourite haunt. As they veered round the corner they almost collided into a large object.

'What the hell?' Felix cried, steadying Silvia's arm. An enormous metallic shop sign stood precariously on the pavement. Two workmen hurried down a long ladder and hauled up the heavy rectangle. Their old cafe had vanished.

'Patrizio didn't tell us his pizzeria was closing down.' Silvia frowned. 'We just came here last Friday.'

'Yeah, that's strange.' Felix was puzzled by the mysterious smoked glass windows. 'Anyway, it was time for a change. Hopefully it's Thai.'

Many curious onlookers were stickybeaking into the dark interior.

'What does that say?' Silvia asked, squinting hard. Emblazoned in red, the words floated like an apparition— *Amor Vincit Omnia*.

The door flung open and a thin man stepped out. He flicked the neon door sign from 'Closed' to 'Open'.

'Hi!' His voice was smooth as velvet. 'We're officially open for business.' He read the sign with a heavy accent. 'It's Latin—it means love conquers all.'

'So do you serve tapas?' asked Felix.

'I'm afraid I don't serve any food.' The man smiled fleetingly. His green eyes glittered like glass marbles.

'C'mon in,' he said.

To their amazement there were no tables or chairs. The original Tuscan *trompe l'oeil* had been painted over in an obscene glaze of scarlet. Chandeliers hung like suspended drops of rain. The breeze from the open door swirled them gently, scattering fractured diamonds on the walls.

'Geez…you've transformed it!' Silvia said, visibly impressed, breathing in a whiff of French vanilla.

'So what do you sell then?' Felix glanced suspiciously at the mounds of black boxes, each tied with a ribbon of gold.

'This is a place,' he paused for effect, 'where you can find love.'

Silvia and Felix must have appeared astonished, for the man laughed. 'It's not what you're thinking. I'm not a salesman for erotic sex toys.' He continued in a serious tone, '*Amor Vincit Omnia* is the only place in the world where you can find true love.'

Silvia failed to stem a giggle. The man looked offended.

'You think I'm joking?' He was visibly irritated. 'Test

me then—give me some random names. And I'll tell you whether theirs is a true love.'

'Okay…in that case,' Silvia said, scrolling through her mobile screen and selecting a photo. 'This is Pam and Tony… what do you think?'

The man inspected the photo. He closed his eyes for a moment. 'They will part tomorrow.' His eyes narrowed. 'One of them is having an affair.'

'That's bullshit,' Silvia cried. 'These are my parents you're talking about! They've been married for nearly thirty years!'

'Well,' the man shrugged and turned to Felix, 'the truth is hard to bear sometimes.'

'How do you know?' Felix said. 'Are you a clairvoyant?

'I am a Guru,' he said calmly, 'in finding The One.'

'So what's hiding in these fancy boxes? Iron chains? Superglue?'

'You can't control love. Not by chains.' The man pinned Felix with his malachite glare. 'It's true when they say there's one soul mate for every person in this world. The trouble is how to find that person. You could be living together for decades in a false belief. But your heart cannot lie. It feels what your logical brain cannot feel…true love.'

'You're insane…honestly,' Felix said. 'You're not going to try your voodoo on us.'

'I can't believe this.' Silvia was sobbing at the kitchen table. 'My own mother! For God's sake!'

'Hush,' Felix said softly, holding her close. He stroked her hair and lifted her chin.

'Dad has moved out,' Silvia managed in between sniffles,

'and Jim has moved in…our family dentist, would you believe? He's at least ten years older. Has four grown children too.'

'That's incredible.' Felix hesitated. 'I know this is not the best time to mention it but…that weird man was right after all.'

Sylvia remained silent, dabbing at her eyes.

'He was boasting that he had the key to find true love.' Felix paused. 'Maybe your mum could use some of that black magic.'

'How will that change things?'

'You never know. With his help we could get your parents back together.'

They had agreed to meet the next day after work. When they arrived at the store, there was a queue snaking for quite a distance. Silvia and Felix were shocked to see a few familiar married faces.

'I've heard this is terribly true,' whispered a woman in her forties. 'How exciting!'

'My neighbour came yesterday and told me she found her true soul mate,' the lady behind her gushed. 'She'd been looking for ages.'

'This is legit,' a young man agreed. 'Forget all the dating apps.'

Customers rushed out, exuberant with armfuls of boxes. Those still in line looked on with barely concealed envy.

Silvia nudged a man who had just emerged. 'Hey, excuse me…' But the man hurried on, oblivious to the world.

A television news camera was being set up and the presenter

was standing near the doorway filming the commotion.

'If you were ever looking for The One,' her voice was flooded with excitement, 'look no further than *Amor Vincit Omnia*. This brand new business has love for sale.'

Soon a large crowd mushroomed around her. The presenter's voice was drowned out by the drone of the news helicopter hovering above and the frenetic traffic on the street.

There was only one person ahead of them now—a middle-aged, grey-suited man. His eyes darted nervously from under his hat, pulled so low he had to inch it upwards to see ahead.

'I have failed repeatedly at finding love all these years,' he said gruffly. 'Two marriages…three flings and…some casual affairs. Y' know,' he cast a surreptitious glance around, 'some of the ladies I dated might even be in this queue.'

'Not to worry—write your details for me and I'll see what I can do,' said the man behind the counter.

'I'm tired of wasting my time on this emotional rollercoaster,' the man with the low hat said. 'I just want to find someone instantly. The One to who will make my life complete.'

The man with the green eyes scrutinised the screen.

'Are you ready to travel to Fiji? The One is waiting for you over there. But she'll be there just for this week.'

'Fiji? I would travel to Timbuktu if I had to,' the man exclaimed, throwing his hat to the ground and laughing.

'Here are the directions,' the man said, placing three sheets and a tiny gadget inside the black box. 'Wear this on a chain next to your heart. It will send out hundreds of electro-psychic-magnetic signals to your loved one. When you are physically close enough, your hearts will synchronise. Good luck.'

Soon Felix and Silvia stood at the counter, slightly embarrassed.

'Well, you were right about my parents,' Silvia stammered. 'They did separate. But they seemed so happy together.'

'Like I mentioned earlier there is only one soul mate for every person in this world,' he said. 'Lucky if you find them. Or waste the rest of your life searching. You only get one chance in a lifetime…if you blow it you might regret it forever.'

'But what if the other person doesn't feel the same way?' Felix protested. 'Can you make them feel what you feel?'

'If that person is The One for you—your hearts will synchronise. I only supply the transmitter and tell you where in the world that person is waiting.'

'What about us?' Silvia asked. 'Are we destined for each other?'

Felix turned to Silvia, annoyed. 'Do you really want to know? Are you going to trust him?'

'I don't know anything anymore,' Silvia said. 'I'd rather know now than thirty years later like Mum.'

'Maybe,' the man said kindly. 'It's sometimes better not to know.'

The bulging crowd behind them were getting restless. Their shoulders glided en masse from side to side trying to fathom the cause of the hitch.

'Hey mate…it's our turn now,' hooted one.

'Get on with it,' someone yelled.

'Look,' said the man gently, 'have a think about it. No

hurry—come back another day.'

Silvia considered it for a moment. A doubt had smuggled into her mind and try as she might, she could not get rid of it.

'Alright,' she said feigning a smile, 'we'll take a raincheck.'

Felix squeezed her hand and they walked out of the shop—the only ones without a box in their arms.

A few weeks passed and the store's notoriety grew. Along with it came an unusual rise in the city's divorce rates, matched by a spike in marriages. The city seemed to radiate a different fervour.

Amor Vincit Omnia had expanded next door and now employed ten staff to cope with the surging demand. Every Friday Felix and Silvia would amble on the beach then walk past the store front of their new favourite hangout. Each time the columns of customers were so wide they spilled over the entire pavement, forcing them to walk on the other side.

One evening Silvia was cooking penne Bolognese when she heard a familiar voice on the television. It was the man with the green eyes. She immediately switched off the gas and sped to the screen. He was being interviewed alongside the guy who went all the way to Fiji to find love.

'...and there she was,' said the man who still wore the annoying hat. 'Standing in the turquoise water...a frangipani tucked behind her ear.'

'So the transmitter worked? Did you feel the vibrations?' The interviewer was stunned. 'And let's be honest.'

'Honest to god,' said the love-struck man, carving an imaginary cross on his chest. 'Y' know I waded in the water and when I came up to her, the gadget went berserk. I still don't know to this day whether it was my heart or the gadget—or both. Boy was I on fire!' He chuckled. 'Our eyes met and we knew,' he continued in a serious tone. 'It was like I saw myself mirrored in her. She was me and I was her. I don't know how to explain it.'

Silvia sat mesmerised long after the interview ended, wondering how a silly man could suddenly spout poetry. She wondered if love did strange things to people. Was Felix truly The One for her? That seed of doubt had blossomed into a fully-fledged panic—and it was crushing her insides. She would go on the sly this Wednesday, when Felix was working the late shift.

Felix had never given her any reason to doubt his love. She had known him for nearly four years, counting the time they were friends at university. They had not moved in together yet, though they practically lived at each other's places. She had to know for sure before she gave up her freedom. So whenever Felix offered her the keys to his place, she gave excuses.

But lately Felix had been acting strange. He was often lost in thought and she found him daydreaming, which he had never done before. Recently he had marched ahead of her on the jetty for a good twenty minutes, without realising that she had stopped at the shoreline. The other day she was talking to him excitedly for half an hour about their lounge settee and asked whether they should go for blue or red. He had nodded absently saying they didn't need a cat.

The nights got restless for Silvia and she kept dreaming about a gold-skinned boy who shot arrows at everyone. He would aim one arrow at her and another at Felix. She would survive and he would be dead. She woke up with a fright, covered in sweat.

It was Wednesday and Silvia had a throbbing headache. Not knowing was killing her. It was affecting her work, her sleep, her sanity. She made her way to the store after swallowing two Panadol.

As she passed the street corner, she remembered the first time she had collided with Felix. He had a ton of books in his arms which collapsed in a frightful heap. She couldn't believe her luck—this was the cute boy in her class that she had a crush on. She had bent down to help him.

She had offered to buy him a coffee and before the evening was over, they were friends. How easy it was to fall in love, she mused. And yet, how difficult it was to stay in love.

She took a longer route to the store, swinging by the sea. Everything on the beach reminded her of Felix and she felt diminished in the presence of such beauty.

How could she forget that stroll on the beach when he'd steered her towards an abandoned sandcastle. It had turrets and a tiny paper flag. He said how clever kids were these days. She had picked up the flag to read an anonymous scrawl: 'King of the Castle'. But the flag was attached to a scroll. There she read Felix's indelible handwriting. 'Silvia— will you be my queen?'

That moment would remain etched in her mind forever— their first kiss, under a tangerine sky studded with pensive seagulls.

Now she was very close to turning the corner and her

heart was pounding hard against her chest. She made a split-second decision to keep going. When she finally turned the corner, she recoiled in horror—the shop was no more.

'Can't be,' she cried. Her legs felt like seawater and she leaned heavily on the stone wall. It had all gone—the red sign, the mysterious glass windows, the precious boxes—everything. In its place was a barren empty space.

'How could this happen?' Her voice quivered. 'Where is that man? I need to talk to him.'

A passer-by looked at her as if she were a mad woman. She clutched at his sleeve and pleaded, 'where is *Amor Vincit Omnia*? Where is the man with the green eyes?'

'Don't you know? The store closed last week,' said the man, brushing off her hand. 'He disappeared...maybe he realised he was going to be arrested for cheating millions.'

'But he knew everything about love...and where to find it,' Silvia wept in disbelief.

'You're a fool,' he said, shaking his head before walking away.

The man who called her a fool was right, Silvia realised. She had let the fear of not knowing petrify her heart. She left Felix the day after the shop disappeared. All she wanted to do was travel the world looking for The One.

After four futile months of wandering, she decided to meet her mother. Pam was living with her new beau in a city with a name Silvia couldn't spell. Pam had confided some dreadful news. Apparently Felix had planned to propose the very evening Silvia had left. He had been planning it for months and wanted to surprise her. No wonder he was out of sorts, Silvia thought—love does that.

Silvia flew home on the next flight, rushing straight from the airport to the beach. It was Friday evening and she was hoping Felix would be there. She headed to the jetty—the only sanctuary that felt like home.

In the distance she saw Felix's unmistakable silhouette. Her imminent joy turned sour when she noticed he had a gorgeous woman by his side. Silvia's heart shrunk to the size of a seashell and she felt the stabbing wound of the green-eyed man. They seemed so perfect together—so synchronised without having to wear any stupid gadget.

She scrambled over the sand in her heels and stood before them. Felix and his companion looked down at her as if an errant mermaid had sprung from the sand. Silvia noticed that the pair looked uncannily alike—twin bronze gods returning to earth.

'Silvia,' Felix said, 'where have you been?' His face was flushed. He made no effort to hug her. 'And what are you doing in those ridiculous heels?'

'I…I'm so sorry Felix,' Silvia mumbled, 'I lost my way a little. But I'm back for good… If you know what I mean.' She raved on about being the biggest fool. And some odd things like they didn't need a cat but they could have one if he really loved cats. He let her flounder on, listening intently with arms crossed. Silvia grovelled on despite the heavenly creature next to Felix. This time she was not going to give up without a decent fight.

'Silvia,' he said finally, 'meet my half-sister Heidi, over from Holland.'

The sun had distilled into an orange speck burnishing

the sky. Everyone on the beach turned their gaze towards the horizon, but Silvia and Felix hardly noticed.

COLD BLUE TO WARM BROWN

MICHELLE OGILVY

I've been tuning out most of what Sarah says for a while. If I listen to every word, I know I'll find something to disagree with, and Sarah can be unpredictable in an argument. She's equally likely to laugh in my face or become horribly offended.

Pretty soon, I'll be out of this worthless shithole of a town and I might be able to find a girl I can interact with without having it explode in my face. For now, though, I have Sarah.

'You want to go down to the creek?' I ask.

'You mean that you want me to go down on you by the creek,' she says.

Well, duh. That was how every other stroll we've taken down this path has ended.

'Fuck it. Why not? Old times' sake and all,' she says.

We turn off the path to head downwards. It's still early in the evening so I can at least see where I'm placing my feet, which is a plus considering the descent is pretty steep from here.

'Bet you'll be glad to get away from this place,' Sarah says. 'Doesn't really suit you, having to cycle back through the same handful of us girls every year.'

'Is that you being pissed about me hooking up with Kelly last month?'

'Why would I be pissed about that? I don't give a crap what you do.'

And there it is, the thing for me to violently disagree with. There are many examples I could bring up where Sarah had a lot to say about my 'doings', even after we'd broken up. But I have a goal in bringing her out here, and it isn't to get in another argument.

'Where are you headed anyway?' she asks.

'The creek,' I say. 'Didn't we establish that already?'

'No. I mean once the "final bell has rung" and school's out forever and whatever.'

'Are you sure you can't think of any other horrendous clichés?'

'Give me a minute.'

We take a few more steps, then I say: 'Adelaide.'

'Really? Adelaide. That's…boring. Oh.'

'Oh what?' I regret asking as soon as the words are out. I can tell from her tone that it won't lead anywhere good.

'It was Adam's idea, right?' she says. 'Adelaide. You wanted to get out and he didn't want to go too far? You know that this would have been the perfect chance to shake off old Snore Fest.'

'Adelaide was where I wanted to go. Just because I want to get the hell out of this shithole doesn't mean that I have to go to the other side of the world. I'm not that dramatic.'

'Is this where you accuse me of being a drama queen?'

'Actually, I was hoping that we could get past the cumming part of the evening before I make you all offended and huffy.'

'Of course you were. How to get to the cumming—that's, what, 98% of what goes on in that head of yours?'

'Was that supposed to be an insult? Not your best.'

'It was a statement, not an insult.'

I glance over at Sarah. Her gaze is lowered, picking out her way down as I am. Her steps are more confident than mine, though. I can't help feeling like I'm about to trip and face-plant into a rock at any second. It never used to be like this.

'I didn't say that I minded, you know,' Sarah says. 'I'm quite fond of your orgasm face. It's kind of cute.'

'Then let's get *there* as fast as possible.'

'Pfft. You're no fun anymore. Snore Fest's been rubbing off on you.'

'For fuck's sake, Sarah. Are you serious with this shit?' I've reached the bottom of the descent now and I turn to face her. 'It's like you want to start an argument. Why do you have to be like this?'

'Your angry face is almost as cute as your orgasm face.'

Sarah holds out her hand so that I can help her step onto the flat bit of dirt where I am. For a second, I consider ignoring the request. She can get down on her own just fine. She might leave if I don't play along with her, though.

I grab her wrist and almost yank her down the last couple of steps. Not hard, just enough that she stumbles a little and falls into my chest. When she looks up at me, her eyes show a mix of annoyance and arousal. This is normal for us, so I haven't stuffed the night up yet.

'I don't know why you defend the guy so much,' she says, pushing off me and striding away toward the creek. I follow.

'I don't know why you're on his case so much. He never did anything to you.'

'Just sat there in the corner staring at us like a creep.'

'You're paranoid. He never stared at you.'

'Okay. Fine. He stared at you like a creep.'

'Why are we talking about Adam?'

This is not what I had come out for tonight.

'Don't I have the right to be bitter towards the person who broke us up?' Sarah asks.

Geez. I'd forgotten how much Adam hanging around as a third wheel had bothered Sarah. The dude has been so busy with his own girlfriend these last months that I haven't thought of Adam as a third wheel in a long time.

'Adam was not the reason we broke up,' I say.

'Please,' Sarah says. 'Always sitting there, judging me. He never wanted you to be with me.'

'He never gave an opinion either way.'

'Then why did we break up?'

'What do you care? We're both leaving in a couple weeks anyway.'

'True. I must be feeling nostalgic.'

'For what? The "good old days" weren't that good. We were arguing more than we were...'

'Fucking? That's all you can remember. Fighting and fucking.'

'There was more?'

Sarah takes a breath, as if readying to argue with me, but then lets it out again without a word.

'See? That's all we were,' I say.

'Fine. Yes. That was all we were. If you hated it so much, why did you call me tonight?'

I'm not sure how to answer this. It has the aura of a landmine waiting for an idiot like me to wander into it.

'You're the one who turned this into an argument,' she continues. 'I was... Forget it. Let's just get on with the fucking part.'

She starts walking ahead and I let her.

I know what's expected of me when we get to the creek. In fact, I lapse into our old routine like it hasn't been almost a year since we've done this. I squat and brush off anything that might be sharp or uncomfortable, then take off my jacket and spread it on the ground for Sarah. Can't say that I'm not a gentleman.

Sarah settles down onto the jacket-cushion and I sprawl into the dirt next to her. From here, we should be able to see the sunset, if I have to get romantic about it.

'Didn't anyone ever ask why you used to come home covered in filth?' she asks.

I shrug. 'Boys get dirty.'

'Well, this boy sure does.' Sarah leans over, her voice turning low and suggestive.

'In the right circumstances.'

'Get dirty for me, Jason.'

That may be the lamest come on I've heard in my life. All seventeen years. And including all the movies I've watched.

I'm struggling not to laugh.

Then she's kissing me. She's always been good at kissing and I forgive her the lame come on. She presses closer to me, lying against my chest with a leg thrown over mine, the jacket forgotten on the ground next to us. Her rubbing up on me like that is starting to arouse the interest of my less logical head. I slip my hands underneath her shirt, running them up her back.

My fingertips are brushing at her bra when she pulls away and sits up. She doesn't say anything, just stares at me, perhaps waiting for me to bitch about her stopping. I won't take the bait, not when I'm so close to getting what I came out here for.

Her eyes are a clear, bright blue. They always broadcast her emotions with no filter or barrier. When set on me, this usually means pissed off and spitting flaming condemnation. Or soft and unfocused, in the right moment. We'd had some right moments.

All I can see now is a cold pool of blue. No warmth. No affection. I can't see any anger or arousal either. That weird mix of annoyance and attraction we've always had, even ten minutes ago, is gone.

Indifference. That's what I'm seeing. We could do this, or we could get up and walk away. It would make no difference to her. Truth is, it wouldn't make any difference to me either, not really. This was meant to be a distraction, something to occupy my mind so it wouldn't turn to things that I want to go away.

It doesn't seem to be working, though, because here I am with a girl on my lap and all I can think is that if I squint the right way, those cold blue eyes could easily be imagined into warm brown ones. I scrunch my own eyes closed, willing the image to go away. This was supposed to push those thoughts out, temporarily at least.

'Jason? Do you want to—'

'I could have sworn we agreed on a blow job earlier.'

I feel Sarah's weight shift off me and I open my eyes. I can see the top of her head as she gets into position. Really? No more insults as foreplay? I close my eyes again and try to give myself up to the sensations. And it does feel good. I will myself to get lost in it, to not think. It shouldn't be this difficult. What the fuck is wrong with me?

Then my imagination supplies an image of that other someone servicing me instead of Sarah and my mind catches fire.

A familiar car is parked out front when I get home and I wonder for a second if I should go and waste some time elsewhere until Adam leaves. Everyone inside has probably just heard me pull up, though. Besides, Adam is persistent and he seems to like my family more than his own. I doubt that I could avoid the place for longer than Adam would wait me out.

I brace myself for the onslaught I know is about to come as I walk through the front door. Adam's girlfriend broke up with him a few days ago and it's all the guy talks about. If I don't think of some way to get Adam to shut the hell up about it soon, it's going to drive me insane.

'Hey, Jase. Adam's here,' my sister says, stating the obvious, as Adam is sitting right next to her on the couch.

'Uh huh,' I reply, and keep walking through the lounge room and down the hall to my bedroom. I sense Adam get up and follow me so I wait for him to get into the room before closing the door behind us.

'What have you been doing?' Adam asks.

'Sarah. How long have you been here?'

Adam shrugs.

'She wouldn't see me,' he says. 'Can you believe that? I went over there and she refused to come to the door.'

There's no need to ask who Adam is talking about. He means Gabby, the source of all his moaning over the last few days. The last six months really, because it wasn't like she was a peach to begin with.

In all honesty, I think he's better off away from her. But Adam doesn't agree. He spent an irritating amount of time doting on her when they were together so he must have thought there was something good about her. Whatever it was, I never saw it.

I lie back on my bed, cradling my head with my hands and facing the ceiling. If I close myself off, maybe Adam will get the hint and take his stupid ex dramas and go home. Remaining silent, I wait for Adam to either change the subject or go away.

Of course, he does neither. His face appears above me, blocking the view of the ceiling I had been focusing on. He is still babbling about Gabby. I try to muster some empathy, but it's not the night for it. And Adam's face is right there. Looking at me with those warm, deep brown eyes.

I turn my attention to what Adam is saying. Except all that does is focus my gaze on Adam's lips. Red, soft, kissable... Fuck.

I push myself up off the bed so fast that I almost knock Adam over.

'Jay, what are you—'

'Hey. You're into Good Charlotte, right?' I say, hoping he will assume this thought had popped into my head that second and was the reason I'd jumped up.

'Sure. I guess...'

'There's a concert next weekend. In Adelaide. Troy has some tickets but now he can't go. He asked if I wanted them.'

'Oh, well... It's not—'

'You need this. You need something to take your mind off the she-beast.'

'Jay, don't say it—'

'Whatever. You know it's true. She's not going to change her mind, Adam. And you need to stop tormenting yourself over it. It wasn't anything you did. Or it was something you did. Either way, it doesn't matter now. You need to let it go. You need to move on. And a night out with me will do you good.'

'I don't know—'

'Trust me.'

I look into the stupid, haunting brown eyes in front of me and silently plead with Adam to agree. This feels very important. Even though when Troy had mentioned the tickets, I had barely been listening.

'If you think it's a good idea...' Adam trails off.

It's an agreement. Of course it is. That's Adam for you. Always agreeable. Unless there's a she-beast suctioned to his bicep.

'Great. I'll head over to Troy's now and get the tickets.'

'Now?'

'Don't want him to give them to anyone else.'

'You could call him.'

I would come up with some bullshit reason why that isn't an option, but I've already fled out the door. Better that way. The excuses for my increasingly jumpy behaviour around Adam are starting to border on lying. And Adam can never know what has been going through my mind.

I get behind the wheel of the car and take a few seconds to breathe, trying to get my shit together. Then I do the only thing I can think to do. I reverse out the driveway and drive to Troy's house.

UTAKI

KATHERINE ARGUILE

Love, honour and obey. Elizabeth mouths the words as she walks, head bowed by the sun. The first two commands weigh dark and heavy in her heart.

Her disquiet follows her like a shadow. She steps over rocks and roots, lifting her crinoline so her skirts will not snag on thorns. She reaches the clearing: here is the cliff. She stands at its edge with eyes closed, as if the sight of white sand and turquoise sea blinds her. She breathes in as much as her corset allows. Sweat trickles between her breasts, soaking the letter hidden between the whalebone and her chemise. She sweeps the hillside below with her gaze, seeking out movement, and feels a stab of guilt.

She is fulfilling the third command, is she not? Has her husband not instructed her to walk the periphery of this small island, daily—save the Sabbath? It is not easy to navigate the wild overgrown hills that lie beyond the village in this heat, yet she obeys. She is tasked to observe the natives and relate to him their activities, the better to assist him with his mission. *Here* lies the heart of their marriage. Oh, indeed, she obeys him. She obeys him in this, as she does in all other matters.

She must keep faith in her father's choice. He, too, a man of the cloth, knew the best match for her. Her life on these Okinawan islands as the wife of a missionary satisfies her unseemly yearning for adventure while keeping her respectable. If her husband does not yet possess her heart, he is none the wiser. And yet she feels culpable, even as she knows he could no more govern her heart than he could the eagles soaring above these cliffs.

But nor can she govern her own heart.

She has left the house without her bonnet, and the sun beats down upon her head. Sweat beads her upper lip and trickles down her neck into her starched collar. The air is damp and turgid in the undergrowth. There is not even the promise of a sea breeze. Elizabeth wants to loosen her corset, but prefers to avoid another disagreement with her husband like the one she had with him the last time she returned home with loose stays. Perhaps she would faint again from the heat, down there on the fine white sand between the palm groves and the sea. Elizabeth glances once more into the dark wild undergrowth below. Is anybody there? What if she sees *her* there?

It was several weeks ago that she first came upon the women. They wore white robes folded across the chest and secured at the waist, like a kimono. Some wore their thick black hair long and loose, others in a topknot; all had long white bands of cloth wrapped about their foreheads and tied at the back of the head, with the loose ends falling down their backs. They wore glossy green crowns of leaves and their feet were bare. She heard them before she saw them; their voices a soothing rhythmic murmur, hypnotic and strange. She walked the narrow, winding path beneath its tunnel of foliage, so entranced by the dappled light and the sound of the voices that when she came upon them, pacing in a circle, eyes closed, swaying from side to side, she flushed cold with shock.

Elizabeth made no sound, but as soon as she stepped into the clearing, they froze mid-motion and stared. Silence.

Improbably long moments stretched out. The women's gazes penetrated her. Elizabeth felt like a lone swordswoman surrounded by a multitude of swordswomen. Not knowing where to look, her gaze passed from face to face, defensive; they, with sharp eyes trained upon her, their singular object: her tight-waisted corset, her crinolines, her high collar, her buttoned boot-tips peeking out from beneath her petticoats, her sweating, alien body beneath. She did not know whether to walk on, or turn and run, and in that moment, her eyes caught those of a woman near her. Unflinching in their scrutiny, the woman's eyes were dark, bottomless pools into which Elizabeth felt herself fall. Something powerful passed between them. A wild hare leaped within her belly, clamouring to be released. Elizabeth did not know what to do with this feeling. She turned on her heels and ran for home.

That evening, after the girl had cleared their supper dishes, Elizabeth stitched her sampler and spoke of the day while he sat with his bible, nodding, distracted. She described to her husband the sun-darkened men hoeing purple plantains from village fields; the wrinkled grandmothers offering salt and incense at one of the many stone edifices used as *utaki*, the spirit-places; the children playing in sandy alleys between village dwellings; the youths perched on wooden verandas plucking at the *sanshin*—the string instrument peculiar to Okinawa. But she did not tell her husband of her encounter with the women. Her guilt at keeping this from him was appeased by her certainty that he listened to little of what she said. She suddenly wanted to tell him about the way the woman's eyes had made her feel, if only to see if he heard her, but she kept her counsel. She knew that any attempt to turn these feelings into words—feelings she herself did not understand—might destroy the beautiful and delicate thing that had grown from that moment. She pricked her finger with her needle, drawing a perfect ruby sphere of blood. She gasped, sucking on it, and took strange pleasure in the pain.

For some time afterward she sought a different route through the hillside, yet still often ended up at the clearing. There was no sign of the women. She quietened her steps from time to time, telling herself this was so she might hear the cries of sea eagles. Whenever she found the clearing empty, a discomfiting blur of shame and exhilaration boiled within her, and she realised with shock that this was because she was disappointed.

She wondered whether the women lived in the village and whether she would recognise the woman with the compelling eyes should she encounter her again. Her desire to see the woman overpowered her and she was driven to the clearing each day. Summer wound its grip tighter on the islands. Sweating, breathless, undaunted, she searched.

One afternoon—perhaps a month after the first encounter—she heard them again. Her heart hammered violently at her chest as if it longed to flee. The sounds came from a place further down the cliff, from the palm groves at the edge of the beach. She would make her way there quietly. She did not want to be noticed this time. She wanted to watch the women for as long as she could, unobserved.

The sun blazed down with no shade to impede its power. Large boulders marked the transition from cliff path to beach. Making sure she remained hidden, Elizabeth sat atop one of them to remove her boots. It required great effort since they usually required a hook to undo and in her frustration she pulled off a button, which bounced off the stone into the sand. She did not know she had such strength. She searched the sand, but with its disguise of mother-of-pearl it remained camouflaged amongst the shell and coral fragments. Realising her search was futile, Elizabeth righted herself. Her vision began to press in, blurring and blotting out the sun. Alarmed, she steadied herself until her head cleared before stumbling on.

The soft sand made the walk to the grove arduous, though less than it might have been had she still been wearing her boots. She stepped lightly so as not to burn the soles of her feet. She wanted to reach the grove quickly; she feared the women would stop chanting and she would lose them. Her blood pulsed hot and fast in her temples, its rhythm cycling and looping with that of the women's voices; for brief moments the rhythms synchronised, beating time together before breaking apart, then meeting again seconds later. Sweat streamed down her face and trickled down her legs beneath her crinoline hoops. She wished she could wear the white robes of the women, wished she could be rid of her corset, her chemise. She wished she could remove every constricting layer of clothing, down to her petticoats, no, perhaps remove even her petticoats and run naked across the sand and into the sea, like a wild creature. She blushed. What would her husband think of such a thing?

She now saw the women moving in the groves, their white robes glimmering in the shadows. She kept to the base of the cliff, flitting from boulder to boulder, holding her skirts close, taking care not to drop her boots. She drew nearer, could see the faces of the women, saw them swaying side to side as they chanted, making clasping, soundless clapping motions with their hands. She crouched beside the boulder, searching for the woman with the dark liquid eyes, but the dappled light and shadow made it difficult to discern the women's features. The sun glared off the sand surrounding her, blinding her. From time to time she hid her face in her hands, so as to give her eyes relief.

She saw the women had changed their formation; standing in straight lines, they grasped palm fronds with both hands, raising them rhythmically up to the sky. Their voices took on a higher, more urgent pitch. The slow chants became rapid chatter, patterns of strange words repeating again and again, the sound breaking over her like waves. Elizabeth fought the urge to fly to the grove and prostrate herself at the heart of their circle, to surrender herself. The heat made her dizzy; she knew she could not remain there much longer, but must witness their ceremony to the end. She crawled from behind the boulder on her knees, her skirts dragging behind her. She clasped a boot in each hand, leaving a wake in the sand. If she could just reach the edge of the grove undetected, she would hide there to examine each of the women's faces. She needed to know if the woman was there.

Her skirt snagged on a large branch of half-buried driftwood. Tugging at it to free herself, Elizabeth dropped a boot. The hollow sound it made as it bounced off a rock echoed into the grove. The chatter of voices ceased so abruptly that the sound of the waves rumbled into her consciousness like thunder. The women turned as one and saw Elizabeth crouched there. She did not wait to see what they would do; she lifted her skirts and ran, leaving her boots behind. With each step she sank deeper into soft sand until she felt she was hardly moving at all. The far side of the beach, where her path of escape lay, seemed to be receding into the distance. The blood had flooded from her head as she stood, and now her face grew tight, a fizz in her teeth, a roar in her ears, the periphery of her vision darkening. She felt a slap of cold nausea, a strange empty sensation, and then, there was nothing.

She felt heat on her back. A soothing, feathery touch on her neck. Through the pink of her eyelids she sensed moving shadows. She felt herself being turned and her lips kissed the sand. There was a fumbling and tugging at her back, a loosening; a breath—a deep, releasing breath, oh, her ribs ached with the relief of it. She heard a murmur, a whisper. A trace of fingers on her face, rough hands on her cheeks, a cool darkening. Her body rolled back, felt held in a gentle, supporting hollow. The voice again...the hush of waves...

soft heat upon which she lay: the sand. She was on the sand.

She opened her eyes and looked directly into those of the woman. *That* woman. She gasped and tried to sit up. The others stood some distance away, watching. The woman pushed her back down with a gentle hand. Elizabeth felt her corsets had been loosened, her collar and chemise unbuttoned. Palm branches were propped in the sand around her, providing shade. The woman soothed Elizabeth's brow; kneaded her temples; cupped her cheeks. The skin of her hands was rough, but the tenderness in her touch was almost too much to bear. The woman's fingers traced a line to Elizabeth's throat and lingered in the scoop of her sternum. The palm moved down across her chest, and rested, flat, between her breasts. Elizabeth's heart leaped under it; the trapped wild hare. The hand remained there, steadying, hot.

Utaki, said the woman, and smiled.

The smile softened the woman's face, curved the sternness out of her thick black brows. Her lips swelled full, revealing perfect white teeth. Her dark eyes seemed liquid. Elizabeth allowed herself to be swallowed by the woman's gaze. She felt she had known this woman for all of time. She felt an insatiable yearning.

Framed by the impossible blue of the sky, the woman's face with its halo of green leaves seemed to Elizabeth like that of a fantastical being. She reached out to touch it, tracing with her fingers the woman's brows, nose, lips. The wild hare beneath her breast and belly leaped and leaped again, clamouring to be released. *I want to stay here*, said Elizabeth, and clasped the woman's hands. They were warm and dry in her palms; her own were damp and swollen from the heat.

Her wedding band was so tight the trapped blood in her finger pulsed thick and angry.

The women found her boots, helped her into them and back onto her feet. They accompanied her back to the cliff top and stood in the setting sun, watching her go. Elizabeth saw the woman's eyes on her each time she turned back to look. When she reached the final bend in the path towards the village, Elizabeth turned back one last time, but they had gone.

It took her some time to walk back to the house; she was weak with thirst and fatigue. When she reached the veranda she heard the scraping of knife and fork on crockery that meant her husband had commenced eating his supper. She removed her boots to tiptoe to her room so he would not see her dishevelled. But he heard her and drew back the sliding door with a dry clatter. He stood before her, frowning.

You are late. Your supper will be cold. He squinted at her in the deepening shade under the eaves. *Your corset*, he said. *It is undone.*

Yes. I fainted in the heat and so I loosened my stays.

I hope no one saw you in such a state. It is most unbecoming. He seemed impatient to return to his dinner.

Yes. I am sorry. She straightened her blouse. *My dear, I am very tired. If I may, I shall go to bed.*

She made her way back along the veranda towards the sleeping quarters. Passing the kitchen, she saw that the girl had returned with her husband's dirty plates and stepped in. *Gwen?*

Yes ma'am?

If Nabe is still here, could you ask her the meaning of the word 'utaki'?

Elizabeth writes words onto paper, the better to purge them from her mind. The letter will not—must not—be read. Once it is finished, she must take it far from the house. If her husband were to discover it, all that had happened would become impossible to undo. She must undo all this, undo her thoughts. She must conquer her own heart. Love, honour and obey.

The wild hare kicks against her bound corset. As she descends the path to the beach, she wonders what she would do if she were to see the woman again. She must not see her again. In her tight boots she trudges through the sand to the far side of the beach, to the grove of banana palms. Once she reaches it, she pushes between the creepers and into the cool dappled shade of the clearing. Her eyes take some time to adjust out of the glare of the sun.

The women's feet have left a circle in the sand. She steps into its centre. What could she do? Undo her corset. Remove her boots. Let down her hair and weave flowers through it. She could wait here until the women return. She could leave with them; she could leave her husband. The impossibility of this strikes her with such force that she sinks to her knees. For as long as she sits there, she remains safe in this *utaki*: her sacred place. Under a fig tree on the far side of the clearing, there is a stone altar scattered with incense ash and offerings of rice and flowers. Light glints off something lying there. Elizabeth stands up, dusts sand off her skirts and goes to examine it. Next to the waxy red petals of a fragrant flower is placed a tiny piece of mother-of-pearl. Her boot button.

She will not walk this way again. Once she reaches the place at the edge of the grove where she had hidden the week before, she takes the letter from her bodice, the damp paper limp between her fingers. The words have blurred with sweat and ink smears her fingers. She kneels, digging deep into the sand with her hands, and buries the letter there.

If her eyes were red from weeping once she returned home, if her expression were one of sorrow, her husband did not notice. He did not look upon her once that evening. He did not hear her silence.

BLOOM

RIANA KINLOUGH

Red Rose (Rosaceae): Respect, love, and courage

For weeks after the funeral, the man's house is filled with bouquets of dark red roses and lilies. He fills vases and glasses and even empty soft drink bottles, but it doesn't seem to help—he drowns in floral sympathies. The house develops a heady, sweet musk that makes him think of the cinema of their first date, shyly slipping his hand into hers in the back row and later, outside her doorway, leaning in, breathing in her perfume as he kissed her for the first time.

Asphodel (Asphodelus): Regret

His wife has been gone for nearly a month when her phone rings. The seeds she ordered have come in. He picks them up and a friendly-faced assistant with a crescent of filth under every nail serves him.

'Are you planning a garden?' she asks, smiling, while she packs the packets into a carry bag.

'Kind of.' But when he gets home, the bag and its contents

sit in the garden shed for months.

Orchid (Orchidaceae): Grief

The phone rings in the middle of the night, pulling him roughly from sleep. He'd been dreaming—ivy, thick and cloying, wrapping his limbs tight from the lungs outward. At first, he listens to it ring and ring and ring. He's waiting, he realises, for her to pick it up. He almost doesn't answer— he recognises the number.

Dogwood (Cornus): Constancy

A machine breathes for her in noisy gulps: suck, *whoosh*, suck, *whoosh*. Any trace smell of humanity has been eradicated by something chemical. A single chair is placed near the bed, waiting. Every surface is covered in flowers, suspended in vases of scummy water. The room is full of half-life.

Iris (Iridaceae): Hope

The wheelchair is on loan from the hospital and not equipped for the paths in the botanical garden. She pushes it herself, a picnic basket in the seat. It's slow and he hovers anxiously, ready to take over if she needs. She waves him away and points to the huge banksia tree. 'We have room for that in the garden!'

He eyes the towering trunk doubtfully. 'There's no room for *us* in the garden.'

She abruptly abandons the wheelchair and walks along the flowerbeds, feeling the leaves, smelling the flowers. 'Get the notebook.'

He pulls a dirt-encrusted, pocket-sized book and a pen from the inside of the wicker basket. As she meanders, she reels off the common names of the ones she likes and he makes a list. He sketches the blooms she can't name. When she's excited about a plant she lists not only the common name, but the botanical name, which makes him giggle.

'It makes them sound like Roman emperors,' he says.

She makes her eyes wide and tilts her head towards a wild soursob. '*Oxalis Pes-Caprae*. He's the worst one.'

They wander so far, absorbed in their task, that the wheelchair is forgotten completely.

Heather (Calluna vulgaris): Loneliness

He lies in their bed, thinking about his wife in her narrow hospital bed with its clinically green blanket and starchy sheets. She was sleeping when they kicked him out, breathing gently through the tube tucked into her nostrils. He worries that she'll be cold—she always felt the chill at night. Restless, he starts opening drawers, making a small pile for the next day. He would bring her the quilt off their bed. It was a wedding gift from his mother and is embroidered with tiny garden creatures. Bed socks too—she used to press her frozen toes into the backs of his knees during the night.

His fingers find a dried sprig—heather. This cutting, according to his wife, would stave off loneliness, and therefore the kind of separation that results in odd socks.

When he finally goes back to bed, he finds another spray tucked into his pillowcase.

Rue (Ruta graveolons): Remembrance

A wedding anniversary, their last. In an uncharacteristic show of domesticity, she announces she will cook for him.

She won't tell him what and she hums with the excitement of her secret. The fridge is full—carrots, corn, broccoli, a huge cut of meat. There's so much food, he begins to question how many people he'd married, exactly. He's banned from the kitchen, so he sits in the lounge room under the pretence of watching television. Really, he's listening to the endless string of curse words and banging coming from where his wife is cooking.

Eventually, he wanders into in the adjoining dining room. She appears a moment later, flustered, holding two plates. He still isn't entirely sure what he's supposed to be eating. There's something round he thinks may be a potato. He taps it with his knife and it sounds like knocking on wood.

She saws off a piece of something charred and nibbles at it. After a moment, she puts a napkin to her mouth. He bites his lip, trying not to smile. They throw the meal into the bin, plates and all, and he cooks frozen fish and chips in the oven.

Snapdragon (Antirrinum): Falsehood

'What did the doctor say?'

'Nothing life threatening.'

Peony (Paeonia): Happiness, a happy marriage

He carries the ring—a twist of gold made to look like intertwining vines—in the coin section of his wallet for weeks. They have been to so many fancy restaurants in the period that she suspects something terrible to come. None of it is right: the restaurant is too noisy; the food is bad; he feels stupid in his nice clothes and she looks strange out of her dirty jeans. So the ring remains in his wallet.

She takes him to the garden centre. They wander through the plants. She points to flowers and tells whether she likes them or not based on the colour of their pots. They hold hands, loosely, just the fingers interlocked. Then, in front of a huge pot of pink peonies, she goes down on one knee. He says yes.

Purple Hyacinth (Scillodae): Apology, forgiveness

She's shouting and crying and curling and uncurling her fists. He doesn't remember what started the fight—argument over the rules of a card game, maybe; it's all slipping away now. He does remember leaving, letting the door *thwack* shut behind him.

By the time he pulls into his driveway, the fight has steamed right out of him. The neighbour's yard is overflowing with vibrant purple hyacinths. Leaning over the short fence between properties, he yanks out a fistful and binds them with a rubber band he's found in his pocket.

On the way back to her house, he notices her sitting at the bus stop and pulls over. She has a bundle of hyacinths for him.

Rosemary (Rosmarinus officinalis): Grows strongest in the garden of powerful women

It's a beautiful day—sunny without being overly warm, cloudless. It's the first reasonable day after weeks and weeks of rain, so they're taking advantage. He tucks a blanket and a book under his arm and she her gardening things and a hat. He lies on his stomach, pretending to read his book—some crime thriller—but really he's watching her prune the rosemary bush.

REVOLUTIONS

BERNADETTE SMITH

(i)

The birds' announcement of morning is meek at first, their songs isolated. The light disperses slowly. Like a yabby in boiling water, Ted has to blink twice before he realises that the night has gone. At the man-made morning of the alarm, Joan wakes and moves off. Muffled sounds carry from the kitchen, the bathroom. Back in the bedroom, her face and hair have been sculptured, made plastic.

'Coffee's brewed.'

Her scripted routine. She goes out to her day.

Ted might get up just after her car leaves, or it might be much later. He's wondered how he comes to make this decision each day; there seemed no link to the time of sleeping the night before. He's thought about this for hours, lying prostrate with the covers thrown back.

They have a dinner on tonight, Joan's sister's birthday, her half-century. Ted will cook the required vegetarian meal. People like coming to their place: in the day, wrens and magpies; at night on the porch, shadows leading to total darkness, which makes a bowl around them.

There's mail to collect, emails to check, recycling to take down the drive. Some days these could take up the good part of the day, all the fiercest hours of the sun. Watering the garden and pausing expertly over the new bulbs. No neighbours are in sight, he could go naked if he chose. His work has slowed down, that tired end-of-year time. It feels like summer holidays as a child: breaking the day up into small units, mental lists of small things which once ticked off are achievements nonetheless, and the trick is not to do them all at once or a chasm could open up. He's an experimental one-man one-act play.

The domestic obligation of dinner feels like an intrusion but just for a minute until he corrects himself, thinking about days past and loitering near the phone or pressing *inbox* over and over even though it checks automatically.

There is an email from an author he is working with. Catherine is local, softly spoken, and the publishing house will probably take on her novel. He wonders if she thinks it is ultimately up to him that they sign her. After twenty years as an editor he is sure he isn't biased by the ease of working with her. He reads one of her new lines: *It is summer now and the flies are welcome because of the energy needed to deal with them.* A bad line. A *great* line? It's a novel with the big themes of regret and apathy—of course, she is still young. Regret *of* apathy perhaps. No, she probably hasn't found that god yet.

One more cigarette and coffee, a sweep of the porch for murdered bugs. He symmetrically lines up ingredients on the kitchen bench. Everything that can be done is done, just a re-heat to come, some cheese to be put out to induce bonhomie. He pours a glass of wine.

A phone call from Joan.

'Everything fine?' she asks.

'Yes, all good.'

'So they'll be around at 7?' She knows, she is just reminding him. 'I'll try to be home early. Oh—the present?'

'Wrapped. Ready. You just need to write in the card.'

All ship-shape.

Catherine jokes about him being her absent and coy god, a *riddle-wielding Sphinx*. She wants to meet up next week for dinner. They've met before, briefly and formally; the bulk is the written word.

He reads: *Don't slay me*, but—*I am struggling with the directness to the end. So, all I've been thinking for long enough to give it merit, is: cut the end, the destination, but leave the pretence of direction. That frees us all up.*

Great, the editor's death toll: a paranoid reshuffle after months of mixing, a youth grasping, irritated at the non-linearity of all things. He is more psychoanalyst some days.

He begins to write, something about the duty of art to climax when we can't, but erases what he starts and agrees to meet next week for dinner.

Six pm. Joan should be home. They only break their routine in times of crisis: dead mothers, the fall of communism, a broken leg, the affair. The cat musters a jump and just like that, severity arrives. It's 6, past 6. She only had one move to do today, to be home on time and laugh at the saccharine card he'd picked out. He calls her phone. No answer. More wine and smoking in the house.

If she had come home just then he would have given her his glass, relaxed her hair. Initiated quick sex to leave them joined through the dinner party, the enviable couple with secret glances like children. But she is ten minutes more and his thoughts cement. Cooking food he doesn't like for her sister's birthday. He thinks of all the offensive and dull things Joan's sister has ever said, the thickness of her—her wrists, her nose. There is a line in a novel about women who refuse to make themselves attractive, inexplicably. Joan makes an effort; she makes a monument of herself each morning, but not on weekends. If he were younger, he would have thrown out the dinner and drunk all the wine.

She comes through the door. He didn't hear the car and he's forgotten to think of an opening line.

'Smells good,' she calls. 'How's the wine?'

'Nearly finished.'

'Sorry, I got tied up. Late meeting. You know what it's like. What else needs to be done?'

He points to the card on the table. She reads the front and inside punchline as though it's for her, signs both their names.

He moves out to the porch and she follows. The light streams through horizontally, moulded by the hills that are purple as an oil painting. Moths and mosquitoes start up on cue. Joan lights his cigarette and places a hand on his neck and they watch headlights come down towards them.

(ii)

The city was alien for the first days. People seemed darker than before. There was more advertising; the billboards featured more skin. It's a country obsessed with museums and galleries, memorialising all. They took a bus to the outskirts of the city to the park that had been built a few years before. Any monument that hadn't been destroyed, pulled crashing down into the street by crowds, statues that had been collecting dust in back-sheds, were gathered together in a field, surrounded by farmland. It was Ted's 40th birthday. They sat under a huge smiling bust of Stalin and drank champagne out of the bottle. A deer appeared on the horizon and stared. They sat quietly as the cold came in.

In the morning, they went to the central market with the sparkling blue and gold tiled roof. Great reams of hanging lace and hand-made wooden games; spices piled up like dappled sawdust. He walked her along the route he used to jog and they jumped out of the way of trams going the wrong way. Tomorrow they would go to Szilvasvarad, with its clear trout streams and postcard shots at every turn of the head.

They didn't plan it. They were in need of sentiment enough to return to this city, but not to the very place where they first met. They are walking along, arms entwined and tangled in coats, when Joan stops with an *Oh my god*.

They've accidentally walked past the Cello Bar. It is closed—the city light-years away from being 24 hours—and has been redone in plastic with all the wood removed or hidden.

Joan says, 'Remember how you scorned me for smoking, and then only months later you were smoking more than me? I mean, who takes up smoking in their late twenties?'

He drags her off again, happy to hear this for the fortieth time and to repeat the answer that he was a true connoisseur, not an addict.

'You were such a health nut then too. Body of a god.'

Ted smiles and listens to the word *body* ring out on the near empty street.

They walk over the suspension bridge to the other side of the city.

'It's still the ugliest bridge I know,' Ted says.

'I don't know. It's just raw. A skeleton.'

'Exactly. It makes me think of torture.'

The name of the bridge translates to Freedom Bridge but it was called something else under the People's Republic.

They choose a restaurant they guess will have something other than slabs of meat on the menu: *the final frontier of globalisation*, Joan called it. An extended family in the corner talk over each other, talking with their mouths and bodies so they look like they are performing, even the children. Joan and Ted listen to the language they can still get by in. They have things to say to each other, which is why they travelled halfway across the world. Ted knows he should wait for the warmth from the thick local wine, exaggerated banter with the waiter, but he can't.

'You look just the same you know.'

She gives him a short smile. 'You should be able to do better than that. You're a writer.'

The oblique reason for the trip: for him to write.

They drink from glasses without stems, which are heavy in their hands. A group of younger men sitting at the next table grin unabashed at them. This is what they loved about this city: a community drawn together by a painful past of missing fathers. Joan wonders how young they are and sits more upright, but this is not conscious, just habit. One leans and asks if they are American, the default nationality. Joan tells him and the group repeat approvingly, with thick sticky vowels: *Melbourne.*

'Is this your honeymoon? This is a very romantic city.'

'We've been married for seven years.'

This is deserving of a toast and vodka is forced on them. When the man talks, he talks to Joan.

'This city isn't ours anymore. It hasn't been for generations. You must go to the countryside to see us.'

Joan thinks of mantras being passed down to children who never rebel. She thinks maybe it's just the men who repeat them as dogma, the first-born. The men turn away to eat.

'So, do you think it was a mistake?' she asks.

He smiles, thinking of all the things he could take this to mean. She could mean the whole thing, getting married in the first place when they didn't like each other's friends. The few short stabs at trying for kids, then being washed over by everything that happens when you aren't paying attention. He knew what she didn't mean: the image comes to him, when he followed her and she sat with a man in the park, hands disappearing under clothes, but the image fades and he answers her.

(iii)

Ted sits upright in the window of the Cello Bar on a stool that is bolted to the floor. He moves his head side to side, his shoulders taut, controlled muscular awareness. The lights from the bar reflect its hard wood and taint everything a similar colour. People walking outside are bent as though from the weight of their coats and in the window he can see his own silhouette, an outline of sharp edges. A second silhouette arrives with a tiny *Hi* and he swivels around with too big a smile. In this light, Joan's skin glows red.

They move to a booth. The leather on the seat is cool against her bare legs and she moves them up and down under the table. They put the menu and tubs of sauces to the side and the phrase *Opening up the battlefield* runs through Ted's head. He talks about people they both know with affectionate put-downs. She keeps looking around which makes him continue with exaggerations, then she jumps up and grabs the discovered ashtray. Lighting her cigarette, she acclimatises, instantly focused. She leans in to speak.

'You know how they pronounce this place? They say *Sch*ello bar. They anglicise it to get the students in but still pronounce it their way. They just can't take the thickness away.'

'We should say it too then. Next time you are at a concert, you have to turn and say: *Isn't that* sch*ello player just magical.*'

She laughs and says, 'You know it's my birthday today?'

'You're kidding?' He will wring the neck of the mutual friend who set them up. He'd been told her favourite colour but not this.

'Fuck. Happy birthday.' He raises his glass of beer and she leans across the table to get kissed on the cheek.

'We need bloody champagne now, don't we?' he says. He doesn't think of his early start in the morning, his dawn jog around the market area, which came alive before anything else, so only a few people saw him slipping on the tram-tracks covered in fish guts.

'I've got the perfect present for you actually. A perfect accidental present. Do you have a courtyard? You need one for the present.'

'Hmmm, I do. Is it a pony?'

She plays the game and begs him to tell her but he refuses.

The ease of dumb jokes falling out of their mouths, feeling special in a foreign place, talking about news from their friends in Melbourne, talking about what this city reminds them of: *It's like Istanbul—What? It's closer to bloody Auckland than that.*

'I hear you're a writer,' she says.

'Well, not exactly. Trying to be, I guess. Have you been to Szilvasvarad yet? That's what I'm working on now; it was the last hold when the Ottomans invaded. They conquered everything, smashed everything aside, but this one tiny town kept them at the gates for weeks, so they gave up and left the country altogether. Just one little thing can break everything apart.'

'Or keep everything together, depending whose side you are on.'

He smiles at this open insight, the duality.

'In the town square, there is a giant statue of a man on a horse—its teeth bared, you can smell its breath—and this man is cutting the throat of a falling Turk. And it's odd you know: this is where people sit around happy with sandwiches on their lunch break. Imagine a statue of Diggers getting mowed down at Gallipoli, it just wouldn't wash. We work in discrete timelines. Up to some date, things are sacred and a part of us but beyond one arbitrary date, it just becomes history.'

'You should take me to Szilvasvarad.'

He will a month later and they'll watch laughing children climb up over and under the giant horse.

Walking home from the bar, she grabs his hand within

minutes because she knows it's not a long walk. They both live where all the other foreigners live, right in the city, close to the river that is ten times as wide as the Yarra. He asks her up to his apartment. The boxy lift screeches and the thick concrete that makes up all of the old town falls past slowly. Things crank behind the cracked walls.

'We think all this stuff is magical. The locals are ashamed to live here now though. They need dishwashers.'

It's a tiny apartment. He gives her a joking tour, throwing doors open, big-armed. In the corner of the kitchen, dull and bent like it was ashamed: a lemon tree.

'It's yours. Happy birthday, Joan.'

She kneels down beside it.

'It's perfect. But I can't. It's yours.'

'But it won't live. I thought it would get enough sun through the window, but it needs more. It needs some quiet courtyard somewhere to spend the rest of its days. You can always bring me lemons.'

He kneels down and shows her the mottled yellow on the underside of the leaves that is a cry for nutrients. She will end up moving in after two weeks so won't take the tree after all. After one final lurch of four tiny lemons they'll put it out on the street, clasping hands in mock memorial.

He gives her a coat to wrap around her and engulfs his head in a scarf. They sit on wooden chairs in the kitchen. Joan lights a cigarette and ashes in the sink like he's put it there especially for her.

'You smoke a lot,' he says.

'What you gonna do? When in Rome.'

She puts her legs across his and he blows warm air on his

hands and runs them up and down her calves.

'You were turning heads out on the street you know. The locals don't usually bare so much.'

'Well I bet you wear those little jogging shorts.'

'That's different. My legs are awful.'

She smiles and stares with heavy eyelids. Now they will revert to gender roles. His hands are on her thighs and when he speaks his voice is thick.

'You can't smoke around the lemon tree, you know. You'll clog up its pores. It needs space and sun and air. All the good things.'

'And company? Should I whisper to it at night?'

'I might get jealous if you start doing that.'

He takes the cigarette from her hand and examines its glow, takes a puff and drops it into the sink with a hiss.

crush

verb

3. to hug or embrace tightly

    'She held her in a skin-tight crush.'

LOVE OF MINE

AMY T. MATTHEWS

Love of Mine,

Today you are sad. Lost in the dark woods of yourself, you are a small and hurting being in wilds that stretch as far as the eye can see. Today the smallest things not done fill you with despair. You see cracks in the walls, dust on the shelves, dirt on the windows, unpaid bills, unwashed clothes; you see all that is undone and you are undone. You look at your flesh and it revolts you. You wish you had never been. When you get like this, there is nothing to do but to climb into bed beside you. I pass warmth from my skin to yours and wait it out with you, knowing that it is the most I can do. Sometimes, I rub your back. And sometimes I talk, following my thoughts as they swim to the surface. This is something you laugh at, when you are well, my urge to say everything I think. Today I am thinking about you. You lead me to love and fate, and to the flow of all things.

There is an old story about a red thread. In the story, before you were born the gods took care to tie a red thread around your ankle, a thread that leads to another knot, around another ankle, to a person who is your destiny. Connected by the red thread, you are lovers before you even meet, joined by this tenuous fibrous fate. According to the stories, the thread may get tangled, it may stretch, it may snag into unimaginable knots, but it can never be broken. You may be remote, removed, separated by time and distance and impossible circumstance, but nothing can sever that thread. Snug against your ankle (barely noticed, forgotten, or so tight it pinches the circulation) it vibrates, transmitting every twitch from one lover to another, even if they cannot touch. Wherever you are in your dark woods, there is a thread around your ankle, leading you back to me. While you have it, you can never be lost, because here I am, at the end of it.

But the red thread is not the only way home. According to other stories, you can never really be lost, and we can never really be separated. The story of String is a story of our smallest level of being, our micro-selves: at this level we are all immaculately tiny vibrating strings. Instead of a single red thread, we are many. Trembling strings connect us to everyone we have met or will ever meet. I feel the vibrations, all my strings shivering through time. You twitch and I feel it, across time and space. We are entangled.

This is our secret music, a shared sub-audible symphony, sometimes melodic, sometimes cacophonic. The disharmony is unsettling, but far worse is silence. In the silence I get scared. I worry that you are lost to me forever. I look into your eyes and it's like looking through a window into an empty room. There have been times when your 'bad thoughts' have settled in, like an ice age. I know that you might do something to stop them one day. Something permanent. I feel this would break me. But there is no breakage in the universe. That's what I tell myself on the worst of days. There is only change. Nothing ends, all matter transforms. If you left me, you would still exist. I would still feel your vibrations. You would still be part of me. And I can't control the length of time we have.

In the old stories, our threads passed through the fingers of the Fates, our single strands joining to make a pattern more complex, more magnificent, than anything a single thread could manage. If the Universe is a tapestry (and why not?) and our lives are the threads, these are the three who determine the weft and weave, who spin our stuff and clip us when our part of the pattern is at an end: Clotho the Spinner, Lachesis the Allotter, and Atropos the Unturnable. Not even the gods are exempt; we are all woven from the same stuff. Their threads might be brighter, more dominant, shot through a greater portion of the pattern, but they are twisted into the same febrile strands, and eventually even they are clipped, when their role is done and a new pattern emerges. Gods come and gods go, but the tapestry continues, the weavers tireless. God and child, universe and proton; all remain, our pattern permanent in the tapestry. We are there, deeply ingrained, our existence so tightly woven with all the other threads that we cannot be teased apart without unravelling the whole.

In our time, the Age of Science, this ancient story of entanglement is reflected in the Universal Principle of Natural Order; we reach equilibrium by becoming entangled with the world around us; coffee cools as its particles entangle with the air, quantum uncertainty spreads as particles become increasingly entangled. We, my love, are entangled. And when I look at you, I see all the wonders of the universe.

You are quarks and leptons and force carriers; you are top, charm, strange and beauty. Your subatomic self is as vivid and active as the furthest flung, hottest, spiralling galaxy. Gluonic jets are sparking through you like comets; the gravitational pull of your force carriers—gluons, bosons, photons—are forming minute protonic planets; ordering you, structuring you, creating this hand, this face, this momentary flicker of thought that chases through you, causing this crushing black depression. None of it is fixed, none of it is certain; all is vibrating, shifting, in constant motion. You are a universe.

I see you and I rejoice.

And whether joined by a single red thread, or spun from the stuff of life, passing through Clotho's eternal crabbed fingers; whether sub-atomically entangled, or vibrating with our secret sub-audible music: we are. You and I. And it is grand.

One day soon you will crawl out of the dark woods, where you are feeling small and alone and unsoothable, but for now you are out of reach. Except I am with you, tangled into the deepest fabric of your self. Me and all the universe: whales and matchsticks and violets and violins and sandhills and peridots and pomegranates and the smell of salt on the wind.

THINGS AND THE NATURAL WORLD

CHELSEA AVARD

More than one woman has fallen in love with the Berlin Wall. There has been at least one marriage ceremony between a person and the Eiffel Tower. The women communicate with the objects; they love and their love is returned. I don't like to use the word 'it', one woman says, because he is not an inanimate object. He is an archer's bow.

I know a human magpie. He collects objects from what he calls the natural world. Rocks, stones, twigs, branches, knots, bird's nests and eggshells and seedpods, gumnuts and 'haycorns'. When he was three, he brought home a Jacaranda pod, hiding it beneath his bed in a paper bag. When he opened it a month later, it had burst in the bag. Its tiny opaque seeds were released into the air between us and settled in our hair, on the bedspread, the floor, our fingertips. I swept them up and took them outside to let them go in the breeze, holding his hand and my breath as he wept. When he pulls the bath plug, he repeats a ritual from his babyhood: Goodbye Water. I love to play in you and wash in you. See you next time,

Water. When he was two, he spent one Autumn afternoon at the park attempting to convince me to put the fallen leaves back on their branches, where they belonged. All recyclable materials are to be checked for their 'craft' potential before they hit the bin. Broken toys are loved best and jealously guarded.

I am not concerned. Sometimes, as he falls asleep, he lists the names of the people he knows love him. When he wants attention, he asks 'What's more important, the news or your child?' He is moved to tears by the tears of others. He comforts and seeks comfort.

I am terrified. I can't put the leaves back on the tree. Tomorrow's water will be both different and the same as today's. If I could put his ideas of love and safety and home and forever in a paper bag and hide it beneath his bed, I might be tempted to do it. But very soon, instead, I will have to hold his hand and my breath and let all these tiny, opaque pieces of our future selves free in the wind.

The beginning of my story does not fit with this ending. These women who love these objects have nothing to do with me or my magpie. Nothing to do with loss, or with leaving. Only, I needed to start somewhere, and sometimes it is impossible to tell the truth.

We are not objects. We are archers' bows.

THE MAN WHO ROWED AWAY

JENNIFER MACKENZIE DUNBAR

Mhairi liked the word stealth. It was how things happened in her life. Slowly, slyly. She was working on an article for the local paper about the role of ancient folklore in modern Hebridean culture and the word kept coming to her.

'The move away from an open belief in the second sight happened not by stealth but by sword at the time of the Clearances. By the early 20th century stories of the Other People, the fairies and the selkies have become just that, stories for entertainment rather than an esteemed truth.'

Since she'd moved to the island and begun freelance writing she'd become interested in Celtic myths and legends. Seamus thought it was all nonsense but he knew better than to criticise; she had, after all, given up her position at the *Inverness Times* to marry him and join him on the croft. Her idea for this article had come partly from a conversation she'd had in the pub with her great uncle, Old Jock, about her Gran's premonitions—her second sight. He'd made light of it, as if it was nothing or, at least, everyday.

'Och, she just knew things ahead of time,' Old Jock said. 'Not everything, ya ken—just the important stuff.'

But Mhairi's curiosity was personal too. She too had been having experiences she'd come to think of as her *calling*. 'It comes on me by stealth,' she'd tried to explain to Seamus. 'Like a slow hunger. I get a pull to do something for no logical reason.' Once her calling led her to a lamb, stuck in the fence. Another time she'd been drawn to an old cavern once used for kelp drying and found an intricately carved chess piece. Old Jock said it was part of the famous Lewis Chessmen and might be worth something. But Mhairi liked it too much to sell.

Trying to ignore the growing restlessness that always preceded the *calling*, Mhairi pushed away from her computer and picked up the photo of her and Seamus, taken on their wedding day. They were both laughing; their new life together stretched ahead of them, unblemished and full of potential. Now, well, now it was different. Not bad, just different, she told herself.

She put the kettle on but the *calling* was too strong. It would not be denied.

Wrapped up in Seamus's old fishing coat she headed across the dunes. The previous night's storm had made a mess of everything. Bits of bark from the nearby wood yard lay scattered across the sand and tangled seagrass scratched at her legs and wrapped around her ankles as she pushed on to the cove. She felt the salt air deep in her lungs. Above, seabirds screeched, fighting for the debris of shellfish smashed against the granite-lined shore. The *calling*'s pull grew stronger the closer she got to the mounds of sodden kelp. Stepping up onto the highest stack she sank almost to her knees. It was then that she saw him, at the water's edge. At first she thought he was a sea lion but the next wave rolled him over and she saw his human shape. A man.

She knew he must be dead and that she should go for help: retrieving bodies washed ashore was no work for a woman on her own. But the *calling* enticed her into the shallows.

Wrenching the kelp away from his face and torso it was clear he'd been a strong man. She was about to tackle the weight of weed on his legs when a glorious fountain of salt water and mucus erupted from him and his chest heaved. He had risen from his watery grave.

Pulling at the kelp encasing his legs she helped him sit upright. He spoke in a guttural language Mhairi did not recognise. When he tried to stand, his legs collapsed and he groaned with pain. Mhairi looked around for help but their only companions were the circling gulls.

'I'll bring help. You must stay still. You'll be alright, the tide is going out,' she said. He grabbed her wrist, pleading in his own language. His animal smell filled her and emptied her like a crashing wave.

Mhairi removed her wedding band and placing it in the stranger's hand, folding it into his fist.

'See? I'll come back. You understand?'

He nodded and, put the ring to his lips and took her hand in his. His hold had a strength that belied his plight: commanding, exciting, dangerous.

Mhairi brought two of her neighbours to retrieve him. By

the time they arrived at the shoreline he was standing, a little unsteady on his legs, but able to walk with assistance. She instructed that he be taken to the nearest croft.

'Seamus is away in Inverness,' she said by way of explanation. As she watched the three men make their way back across the dunes she felt the weight of the *calling* lift.

The stranger's leathery coat, slashed to pieces, lay nearby. She took it back to her cottage and laid it across the chair nearest the fire. Stroking it, as if to heal it, she realised it was not cowhide but seal skin. She tasted its salt. Catching sight of her bare ring-finger she drew back, resolving to return his coat and retrieve her ring the following day.

The shrill ring of the telephone startled her but she was happy to hear Seamus's voice. It was not the news she wanted however.

'I have to stay a bit longer. The Minister has asked to see us. I think we can secure our fishing rights if we meet him in person. Is that alright?'

He and two other islanders were at the annual crofter's meeting. They'd been fighting to regain the right to extend the boundary of the waters they were allowed to fish. They only asked to have what their great grandfathers had once had, a right taken away during the Clearances. Seamus was their spokesperson; he was the only one who'd been to the mainland to complete his schooling. But this year Mhairi had asked him not to go.

'It's my time Seamus. We need to...' She'd left the rest unsaid; he knew well enough. The doctor determined there was nothing wrong with either of them. IVF was an option but not yet. Mhairi and the local midwife had worked out her cycle and she'd marked her fertile days on the calendar that hung on the wall above the kitchen table. Seamus's scrawled 'Crofters Meeting' left little room for her crosses.

Since the trip to the specialist six months ago Seamus had refused to discuss their troubles and whenever Mhairi drew him to her he'd pull away. They'd come together last month on her days but two weeks later her blood had flowed as fresh and defiant as always.

'I'm the spokesperson Mhairi. I have to go,' he'd insisted. 'I promise to be here next month.'

'Next month might be too late,' she'd snapped back. At thirty-eight her body was running out of time but that was not what she'd meant, and he knew it. And now here he was making excuses again. She could hear the loud voices of the other men in the background. The crofter gathering was held at the castle in Inverness and there was always plenty of whiskey.

'Are you asking me or telling me Seamus?' she asked. 'You know you'll stay as long as you need to, with or without my approval.'

'Aye, lass I will. As long as I *need* to but longer than I want,' Seamus replied. Mhairi could hear the tiredness in his voice but her anger felt good.

He broke the silence. 'So what's happened there?' Mhairi had planned to tell him about the stranger but now she wanted to keep today to herself, to hold on to something of her own.

'Nothing. Nothing at all. I need to go,' she said and hung up.

She arrived late at the pub and squeezed past a couple of the other village women to take up her usual place in the nook. Even with his back to her she knew it was him. His chest and shoulders strained against his borrowed shirt, his head sat heavily on his thickset neck; his tanned seafaring skin reminded her of leathery kelp. She remembered the sea lion she'd found this time last year, next to the well, strayed from the cove. If Seamus had been home he'd have used the scraps from the day's catch to lure him back to the sea but Seamus had been away so she fed him the best of the fish, there in her garden. He'd stayed for one day and one night and Mhairi had felt curiously drawn to lie beside him, to align their bodies to the earth and each other.

He left as he had come—unnoticed. 'With stealth,' Mhairi whispered to herself as she sipped her drink remembering the sadness that had filled her that day, much like the despair which clouded most of her days of late.

'Last drinks,' the barman called. The stranger turned to her, and raised his glass. His grey eyes seemed to hold the wisdom of the ocean. Mhairi hoped no one could see the ripple of desire that ran through her. She stood to leave but a dram of whiskey appeared in front of her.

'Our visitor has bought a round for all his rescuers,' the barman said.

She looked up to say *slainge*, cheers, but he was gone.

The pub emptied quickly. Old Jock walked with her to the corner. 'Tell Seamus to be sure to mend that boat of his before he goes out next. The fasteners have loosened and it was taking in water when we took it out last. He should be buying a new one but he's as stubborn as his father before him. He won't listen to me.'

'I'll try, Jock, but he's not listening to me too much either these days.' She tried to make it a joke but Old Jock was no fool. His next remark fell like a stone.

'He'll need to come down off his high horse when the bairn is born.'

Mhairi turned to him in anger. 'And what gives you the right to talk about a bairn, Jock? For your information we've chosen to not have children.' The words were out and she knew that they could not be taken back. Was this what she would be telling everyone from now on?

Old Jock took her hand. 'You'll have a child alright Mhairi, sure as the tide follows the moon.'

Mhairi's temper cooled as fast as it rose. Stupid old fool, she thought, he's losing his good sense. But his words stayed with her as she walked in the moonlight the two miles to her cottage.

She didn't see him at first, sitting there in the garden next to the well. When he stepped forward she startled but as he followed her into the house no words were needed between them. He pressed the ring into her into her hand and her to the bed. She should have felt guilty but she didn't. She could have blamed the whiskey, but she knew better.

Their bodies moved together as if swimming in a silky sea until the moon sank low in the sky.

She wrapped herself in the quilt, passed him his tattered coat and watched until he disappeared over the cliff to the cove. Minutes later she saw him in a river of moonlight, rowing strong and slow towards the horizon.

They never found Seamus's boat. Old Jock said it was good thing too. Seamus returned home the following day, ahead of the others.

'I've done my work there lass. Now it's you who needs me.'

Their lovemaking was tender and profound. When the child was born everyone said he had the look of a seal pup with his languid eyes and skin already the colour of the winter sea. She called him Roanan, the little seal, and told him the legend of the selkies.

'They leave their home in the sea and come onto land,' she whispered to him as he suckled. 'They shed their skin to take on the form of a man and live happily as land folk, sometimes taking a wife. But when they achieve what they are sent to do in this world, the *calling* comes and they return to live once more below the waves.' He pulled away and she smelled the ocean in his breath.

SIREN LATITUDES

A. MARIE CARTER

She went down to the beach late in the afternoon, carrying her towel and her book, with her bikini on under her shorts and singlet. Back at the beach house, her parents and their friends sat with their glasses of wine and their murmured conversations. Maggie hated the way they spoke in low voices as though everything was a secret she shouldn't be allowed to hear, as though she were six rather than sixteen. And then, to make it worse, they'd all erupt into brash laughter like the joke was on her.

She was away from all that here by the ocean, though she had no actual intention of swimming. The water scared her on some primitive level. She admired it and loved it, but she preferred not to be in it. It felt unnatural, profane, to take her land born body and thrust it in the sea where the creatures that belonged there would swim past curiously, brushing against her legs, demanding to know why she had ventured into their realm. No, it was better to sit on the beach and read.

The first year Maggie had come here with her parents she was only five and her brother hadn't even been born yet. It was only the three of them then, and Maggie had vague memories of being terrified of the seagulls after one stole a sandwich right out of her hands. Her mother had laughed, but Maggie had erupted into inconsolable tears. At least that's the story her mother told, and Maggie wondered if she really remembered it happening at all.

She did remember riding a camel along the beach, her father seated behind holding her tightly. The camel was beautiful, with swollen black eyes and long, dark eyelashes. Maggie had furtively wound strands of its sun-bleached fleece around her fingers, and later, washing the mix of the animal's smell and the grit of sand from her hair, she pretended they had just returned from a journey across the deserts of Arabia. After that first year, her parents had extended the invitation to stay to all kinds of friends and family and every summer, from Christmas to New Year, the beach house was full of people coming and going.

This year her brother had brought his friend, Tom, who Maggie constantly caught gawping at her. He'd already walked in on her in the shower twice under the pretence he hadn't known she was in there. The house, with its rusting charm and its weatherboard walls, had no locks on the internal doors, only latches that could be jimmied free of their hooks by twelve-year old boys. When Tom wasn't pestering Maggie he was with her brother playing video games in the lounge.

Maggie much preferred the company of the adults, and this year Maggie's mother and father had invited their friends Mel and Gus to stay. Mel's younger brother, Seb, had come as well, having flown over from Hong Kong where he lived to spend Christmas with his sister. She noticed the look on Seb's face as soon as they were introduced; that look older men got when they saw a teenage girl in shorts and a crop-top. The look that passed in a second, that they pushed down and away and pretended hadn't happened. Sometimes she caught the male teachers at school doing it, especially her PE teacher. But in Seb that look sparked her attention.

Seb was an engineer, her mother told her, but he didn't look like an engineer to Maggie. He had a blonde mane long enough to tuck behind his ears, and the tight, muscular body of a surfer. Maggie liked the thick, mannish curl of fair hair on his arms, and when his blue eyes caught hers she felt a flutter of anticipation. If he hadn't looked at her like that she might have ignored him, relegated him to the world of her parents' boring conversations. The look, however, made her wonder if she could catch his eye again, and it was a challenge for her to make sure that she did. At lunch she sat opposite him so that he had no choice but to look at her every time she leant over the table to get the butter.

After lunch they all walked down to the foreshore to buy ice creams, and Seb walked slowly, behind the group of other adults, waiting, she knew, for her to catch up and walk next to him. She dutifully complied, and they talked amiably about her schoolwork and the music she liked to listen to. He told her he played the guitar.

Back at the house the afternoon dragged along at its unhurried pace, the boys still playing video games, the adults drinking more wine, and Maggie lazing on her top bunk, reading. But there was too much noise, the house full of the adults' drunken laughter, the insistent hum of their chatter and gossip, the explosions and gunshots from the boys' video game.

Maggie covered her skin in sunscreen, conscious of the damage that too many freckles would do to her looks. She took up her things and headed to the beach, finding there peace in the motion of the waves and the distant clunk of bat hitting ball at a family's beach cricket game a little way off. She opened her book with her greasy fingers but her thoughts drifted, and she let them. She took pleasure in having nothing more pressing to do than think, and she let her mind roam to all the things she would do soon. The places she would go. When she was old enough she would go to Europe, to see the castles and the galleries and the mountains and the snow. She'd never seen snow. She would start in Spain perhaps, and then make her way up to France, then to Germany, Italy, Greece, and to Eastern Europe and across to Russia. Or perhaps she would go to Africa instead. To Morocco and Egypt. Or to New York. Or to South America. Anywhere. Wherever she liked, she would go there. She would go everywhere before it wasn't there anymore, before it was blown sky high, or swallowed by the sea. It was all there before her, on a timeline, stretching out and out, while everything else receded. She thought about these things and dreamed until it became early evening and the beach-goers packed up and went home and the sky faded from pink to red to purple, and then to a dark, navy blue. The waves were calm and the ocean as flat and as dark as the sky.

He came to find her then, just as she knew he would. They'd eaten dinner, he told her. There was pizza left over for her, her mother wanted her to come home now it was dark.

'It's nice out here though, isn't it?' she asked him. 'Now that the sun's disappeared.' And now that he was here with her in the cool night.

'Do you want my jumper?' he asked.

'No, no thank you.' She was shivering a little but she preferred it for now. She wanted him to see her body first, to make sure he had really paid attention to its curves, to her waist, her goose-pimpled arms.

'How old are you?' she asked, so suddenly it made him laugh.

'Twenty-eight,' he said.

'Twenty-eight!' She couldn't imagine being that old. 'You must have done so much. Seen so many places.'

'No,' he replied. 'Not many. I've only travelled overseas once, to America, when I was twenty. And Hong Kong, of course.'

She tutted at him. It would not do. She would see so many places, she told him, and she would travel all her life. She was learning German at school and one day she would learn French and Italian as well, and perhaps Spanish too, even Arabic, if she had the time.

'As soon as I'm old enough I'm going to go Egypt,' she said. 'To see the pyramids. Do you know they're crumbling? Even though they've stood for thousands of years, now they're affected by pollution and they're slowly falling apart? In another hundred years who can say how much of them will even be left?'

Yes, Egypt. She would go as soon as she was old enough. He was laughing at her. Would he kiss her? She was scared he might, hoped he would. She had never been kissed by a man, only boys. Stupid boys of sixteen and seventeen who didn't know what to do next, who fumbled and groped about blindly at her, awkwardly failing to undo her bra until she herself had to unhook it while listening to their terrified breathing, their unsure, cloying words: she was beautiful; they loved her. They didn't need to talk like that. She wasn't an idiot. She knew they didn't mean it and that was okay, she didn't need them to mean it because they were only children, boys she would forget, or despise, in a month or two, their names all lost to her. But if *he* kissed her that would be something. A man of twenty-eight, who had been to America.

She patted a patch of cold sand beside her, motioning for him to sit. It was an innocent enough gesture but she saw him hesitate, a bemused smile creep up for a moment, then vanish. He was conscious of her looking up at him. She knew it now, was sure, that smile meant he would kiss her. That smile meant he wanted to kiss her, he was thinking only of kissing her, but he was terrified. Terrified like the boys she'd known. Just another terrified child.

He folded his legs beneath him and sat cross-legged on the sand. He seemed to sit a little at a distance from her, purposely, as if restraining himself, so she shuffled over. The shock of the unwarmed patch of sand against her rump made her shiver. Their knees hovered a few centimetres from each other, and the tiny space between them was more wonderful than if they had touched.

'Can I have your jumper now, please?'

He pulled it over his head, his t-shirt taken up with it

for a moment, exposing his flat, hairy stomach. All the boys Maggie had known were smooth and hairless, practically pre-pubescent in comparison. She took the jumper from him and pulled it over her head, pushing her cold arms through the warm sleeves, smelling the musty scent left by the mix of his deodorant and the sweat of a day in the sun.

'That's better, thanks,' she said. But she didn't tell him that her thighs were still cold, that, having moved off the patch of sand she'd warmed all evening like a mother hen, the coldness of the earth was almost painful against her skin.

'What are you reading?' he asked, pointing to the book that lay face down on the sand, as if ashamed of itself and hiding.

'*Lolita*,' she replied. He laughed at that. He laughed knowingly, quietly.

He picked it up and began flicking through the pages.

'Careful!' she protested. 'Don't bend the spine!'

He looked at her and frowned.

'It's only a second-hand copy,' he said, teasingly. She felt stupid. Of course he was right. It was only a daggy cancelled library book that she'd picked up for a dollar. He stopped at a page, pressed it out flat—she fought the urge to protest—and read at random.

'"A faint suggestion of turned in toes. A kind of wiggly looseness below the knee prolonged to the end of each footfall. The ghost of a drag. Very infantile, infinitely meretricious."' He paused. 'Meretricious? Do you even know what that word means?' he asked.

'Yes,' she replied, 'I looked it up. It means...' But she'd forgotten. Plausible, perhaps? Or showy? She couldn't remember which. 'Do you know?' she asked.

He laughed again, and handed her back the book. She took that to mean that he had no idea, though he intended it to seem like he knew but wouldn't tell. He was trying to impress her after all. He would kiss her, she was sure.

They sat quietly for a while but the sound of the ocean filled the space between them and neither felt compelled to speak. Maggie dug at the sand beside her feet with a stick, drilling a small hole and then filling it back up with sand and repeating the process. She rested her head on her knees, tilting it to look up at Seb, and letting her loose hair fall over her face for a moment, obscuring her vision. She brushed it away behind her ear and he was looking at her, smiling. She smiled in return and prodded at his ankle with her stick. He gently caught her wrist and held it briefly before leaning in towards her. She raised her head up to meet him, knowing that she was right all along. She was young and beautiful. He kissed her.

They fumbled in the darkness, but it was not hard and brutal like Maggie thought an older man might be. He was just like her boys of sixteen, all nerves and awkward gestures, halting touches on her waist, her thighs, her chest. When he was done he asked if she would come in the ocean with him, to clean up before walking home. But she didn't want to go in the ocean.

'Just a little way in,' he insisted.

He wanted her to wash the scent of him off of her, she knew, to wash herself clean of any incriminating evidence before they returned to her parents. She grudgingly consented and waded out, till the water reached just to her waist, washing the man from her, rinsing herself clean. A measure of him was trickling out of her into the ocean, catching in the tide, sweeping out to sea, out to the endless dark deep where it would be swallowed by dolphins, eaten up by sharks, impregnate unsuspecting mermaids. He called to her to come back to shore, to head home to the beach house.

'I'll come soon,' she called back. Let him go ahead first, it would look less suspicious.

He was heading back to shore, his man's body firm and hard and foreign to her though she'd just been in his arms, she'd just held him fast and close. She watched him go, shaking himself on the beach like a dog before slipping on his shorts and thongs. And then he was gone, back toward the streetlights of the small, quiet coastal town, up over the dunes and out of sight.

She was aware of her feet sinking in the wet sand, the coldness seeping into her, and the quiet waves pushing her off balance. Aware of the orange glow of the little town's lights, all burning on the other side of the rise. Tomorrow she would need to find a chemist, she supposed, need to quell the life that threatened to spark inside her. But that was okay.

She saw the long days reaching forward, ahead of her, outwards and askew. One day soon, when she was a little bit older—eighteen perhaps, or twenty—the world would be whatever she made it. She would go anywhere she wanted and love anyone she wished. And then, one day after that, she would be thirty, then thirty-five, then forty. But no, that was impossible, she would never be forty. She would never not be young. She would always be this way, young and beautiful and admired, always on the cusp of something new, of something wild, of life at its best: wonders and love. And what did it matter if now, here on this beach, in this little town, she should be alone. She would not always be so. One day she would be loved.

Yes, what did it matter now? She had the rest of her life for that.

GLITCH

ELAINE CAIN

Along came Kevin out of the blue. Not a nice sunny day, I can't pretend. It was still early spring, with a tail-end kick of winter some days. A few dates at the end of last summer had made me more than gloomy and I had pulled my profile, squirrelling away inside at home for winter. With the summer coming, I was back online to see who was out there. Things were looking up. I sent out some virtual kisses to likely candidates and had a couple of reasonable dates. One guy even made it to date three—he was disappointed that I wasn't as keen as he was. Kevin was keen though and made first contact. I like a man who can take the lead a little, rather than me chasing all the time.

Kevin was not a name I was instantly attracted to, but his profile picture was okay. He sent me emails and after a couple of funny chats, we decided to meet for a coffee. I picked the location, keeping it close enough for me to bail if needed but far enough away from home that, if it went badly, I wasn't in my own neighbourhood to be followed. You can't be too safe.

On the night, I was ten minutes early and found a good seat with a view of the door. I had just gotten settled when someone approached me and said hello.

Kevin was not Kevin. He explained quite animatedly that he used his brother's photo online so his work mates didn't know he was looking. Lie one. He also admitted he wasn't the age he said he was online, he was a couple of years younger. Lie two. His name *was* Kevin so there was a truth among the bull. He sat down and I gave him the benefit of the doubt as our chats by email had been interesting. Plus I love it when someone makes me laugh without trying.

First date done we talked about another one soon. It wasn't long before we had dinner, then date three was a movie followed by drinks and supper. A hike was date four; daylight was a nice change and I could see how he handled one of my favourite things.

Date five. Kevin booked a café for lunch, a new one for each of us, and the day was looking warm—a blue-sky day that hinted at summer strolling into the city soon. I arrived on time to find him already there with flowers for me. I hadn't brought him anything and he didn't seem to care. Orders out of the way, he started to babble about his family and how excited they were that he'd found someone. He'd told them all about me and our dates, our conversations, about what I was interested in. He confessed he was falling for me already and wanted to give me a key to his place so we could share our lives more. Be open, trust each other. He produced a small gift-wrapped box and pushed it across the table to me. The key was inside.

I don't have a poker face. As far as I was concerned, it

was still early days. I hadn't seen this coming and I wasn't sure whether he was crazy or just prone to loving quickly. I politely refused the key, letting him know that it was too early for me to have that kind of commitment; I suggested we still keep getting to know one another as we had been. Hell, we hadn't even slept together! I laughed at my own comment—he didn't. We ate lunch in silence and he soon left. I drove home wondering whether I *should* see him again.

The next weekend it was Mum's birthday. Even though the years had passed since her divorce from Dad, I wasn't surprised to see his car there too when I arrived. We'd grown up making a special effort for birthdays. There were only four of us after all—my older sister had married and moved overseas two years ago but there were always calls on our birthdays. With a beaming smile Mum greeted me at the door. It was so good to see her happy and I asked why. She giggled and said I should know, it was a better than normal birthday. Walking into the lounge I realised why—Kevin was sitting on the couch, Mum's cat asleep in his lap. He was chatting to Dad who was laying out lunch at the dinner table. Kevin grinned at me, like a kid who's just found the local lolly shop has a sale on. Dad asked where I had been hiding him and why they hadn't met him earlier? If I had been a fish, I would have been a mullet—stunned, gawping for air with my mouth open. What the fuck?

I signalled to Kevin to join me in the hallway. He shook his head and went to the dinner table. Mum and Dad were fussing around him, helicoptering food and drinks, asking questions all the while. If it hadn't been Mum's birthday I would have been out of there, calling the police on the way out the door. But I sat, ate, smiled and said little. After lunch, Mum and I cleaned up while Dad turned on the telly to see if the footy was on, still chatting to Kevin. Mum asked why hadn't I said anything? How long had we been dating? Had I met his parents yet? She was non-stop with the chatter, happy because she thought I'd found someone.

I grabbed her arms to keep her still and asked her to stop.

'I didn't ask him to come and I had never said where you lived. We aren't serious enough to meet each other's parents yet. Something isn't right here.'

Her reaction was denial. Kevin had known things, had told them of romantic dates, of long conversations and chats about our future. Some of it was lies, some of it real. Her words were harsh—why would I push away a great guy like this? Do I want to be single and childless forever?

Sasha was one of the most beautiful girls I had ever seen. She had the look—the gorgeous golden hair that lit up her face with a halo, and eyes with a bit of glint in them. I knew those eyes would understand what I needed. I didn't hesitate to use Brad's photo, Brad my imaginary brother. I wasn't going to put mine up on the site, not after what happened last time.

I looked up some lines from a couple of comedians, watched a few YouTube videos of stand-up and had enough banter ready when we emailed to make her laugh.

Sasha and I met for coffee after a few email chats. She was so amazing in person. Full of life, really understanding about the photo thing, happy to keep getting to know me past date one. A real connection, that's what it was. After our second date, I followed her home. I vaguely knew where she lived, what suburb, as her online profile had mentioned it. So it didn't take much to work it out, driving a distance behind, parking a few buildings down. Then I drove back there early the next morning and waited. I watched her leave for work, walking in to the city. She looked so perky.

Date two, I prepared by reviewing a few sites with restaurant reviews and made a suggestion. It was such a hit I prepped again for the movie. I gave her options of course but mentioned which one I thought would be ideal for us. Meanwhile I started walking hills on the treadmill at the gym—she had said she liked hiking and I wanted to be prepared so I didn't seem too unfit or sweat a lot. When I chose a hike and asked her if she would be interested for our next date, I could tell she was impressed.

Dad had asked me one night, after date three, whether I was a faggot, not into girls. I yelled at him I was sick of that talk and yes, I had found a nice girl who loved me.

It was disappointing when she refused my key. I had just found a great little unit for us, moved out of Dad's and started to sort out the IKEA stuff. It's not easy following those weird diagrams they give you.

By the next weekend, her mum's birthday, I knew her mood about moving in together would have passed. It would be so romantic to surprise Sasha. I had looked up her mum's address—it wasn't hard to find her through the work databases. And to meet both her mum and dad at the same time was so much more than I expected. I took her mum more of the same flowers I had given Sasha last week. I'd bought a few bunches and taken out the grungy ones so Sasha would have a pristine bunch, all hers, no wilting or damage.

There were some good ones left. Her mum liked them, she said. Sasha's parents were nice and asked so many questions. I had a hard time keeping up, but once Sasha arrived, I knew I'd done the right thing.

Later that week, I stopped in to see Sasha at her townhouse. I hadn't heard from her since the birthday lunch. When I buzzed the doorbell, it took her a while to answer. She spoke to me through the security door and wouldn't let me in. How did I know where she lived? Was I following her as well as stalking her mum? She was being such a bitch. I screamed at her. All I had done, I had done for her. Didn't see she I loved her? I wanted her to be happy. When her neighbours came outside, I screamed at them too. Then the police arrived. I screamed some more and left.

I know this is just a glitch, one of those arguments that happen when you are in love.

THE DEATH OF STARS

DANIELLE ANGELI

The night air was hot and dry. Khari breathed it in anyway, relieved to be outdoors again. He'd been swaddled in expensive silks all day, and now his limbs felt loose and free. He wore a cotton shirt that once belonged to his best friend, Ilyas. Khari had always felt an odd sort of comfort wearing his shirt. Like he was safer, somehow.

The market square was deserted, its pale stones shining like illuminated bones in the light of Eea, the brother moon. His sister, Seda, had already sunk behind the rooftops, beyond Khari's sight.

Khari was halfway across the square when a breeze stirred his hair and he froze. Only shadows edged the streets, but the prickling on the back of his neck told him he wasn't alone.

Above him, crouched on the rooftop of the nearest building, a figure paused. Blue eyes caught Khari's over a scarf that covered the bottom half of his face.

Rohak. The *hashash*.

Khari would've known his eyes anywhere.

He leaped off the rooftop and the wind knocked his hood back. Locks of dark hair curled around his eyes.

'It isn't safe to be wandering alone, Khari.'

'Go away,' Khari growled, frustrated by his meddling. Not only had his father hired a *hashash* to protect their family, Khari was certain he'd been instructed to keep an eye on him. As if his father suspected him of doing something reckless— like sneaking out of the house every other night.

Rohak's face was unreadable beneath the scarf. 'Go back to the house.'

Khari pinned him with a glare, then turned on his heel and marched away.

When they were children, Khari and Ilyas considered the bazaar their personal playground. Ilyas taught him how to climb the lower buildings and together they mapped out routes to travel unseen above the shops and stalls. They'd spent hours on the rooftops, spying on vendors or soaking in the sun while the scent of spices and the murmur of conversation drifted up to meet them.

It'd been years since Khari travelled the rooftops, so it took him a few attempts to climb the tea merchant's building. He knew he was unlikely to lose the *hashash*, but he could feel him watching him from above and it made him feel like a mouse with a cat on his tail.

His shoulders strained as he pulled himself over the lip of the roof and onto his stomach. He lay there a moment panting, then forced himself into a squat and scanned the rooftops.

No sign of Rohak.

He sat back and wiped the sweat from his brow.

'Not as graceful as you imagined?'

Khari's head snapped around. The *hashash* was perched on the roof's peak, scarf tugged down to his neck. A dimpled smile curved his lips.

'I told you to go away.'

'And leave you alone in the streets after dark, with such unrest in the city?' Rohak climbed down and settled beside him, hugging long arms around his knees. 'I'd hardly be serving your father if I did that, now would I?'

Khari glared at his side profile, then turned away to face the night. The sister moon, Seda, was a deep gold crescent trimmed in red, so low on the horizon it looked in danger of slipping into the sand.

'If I'm to understand you correctly, Khari,' said Rohak, 'you'd happily risk your safety for a little taste of heartbreak?'

Khari stiffened at the implication, but he kept his voice steady as he said, 'I don't know what you mean.'

The *hashash* must have seen something in his expression, because a slow smile spread across his lips. 'Coincidence, is it, that you sneak out on all the same nights as Ilyas Nejem?'

Khari glared and Rohak chuckled, stars twinkling in his eyes.

'You can hardly scold *me* for stalking,' said Khari.

Rohak shrugged. 'It's my duty to guard your family.'

'Then why haven't you told my father?'

Rohak sat back, drumming his fingers on the roof tiles. 'You deserve your freedom. But you're the son of a powerful lord, and the night is unkind to precious lordlings.' He glanced at Khari sideways. 'Let me train you, and I will keep your secret.'

'The high born don't become *hashashin*,' Khari said with a snort.

'You don't need to be a *hashash* to be strong. You don't need to be anything you don't want to be, Khari.'

Khari met his gaze, but could find no mockery there. A little thrill crawled up his spine at the thought of being trained by a *hashash*, of learning skills—*useful* skills—that had nothing to do with impressing ladies or entertaining guests. But...

'My father would never allow it.'

'I can be very persuasive.' Rohak gave him a low-lidded glance that brought a flush to Khari's cheeks. But something drew the *hashash*'s attention before he could tease him. 'Your friend is near.'

Khari's heart plummeted, along with the foolish hope that tonight Ilyas wouldn't meet Atiya, that something would turn bad between them, that he'd realise he'd loved Khari all along.

Rohak surveyed him, and the pity in his eyes flooded Khari with shame. He turned away and pushed to his feet. 'We should go home.'

Khari took a leap to the next building—but his foot found a loose tile and with a sudden *whoosh* the roof slid out from under him.

For a sickening moment, Khari fell. Something caught his sleeve. He glanced up in time to see Rohak, before his shirt tore through a seam and he hit the cobbles in a crumbled heap.

'Who's there?' a familiar voice called, followed by the sound of quick, booted footsteps.

Khari rose tenderly to his feet, cursing his luck. Rohak was beside him, but there was no time and nowhere for them to hide.

'Are you alright?' asked Rohak, but Khari barely heard him.

Ilyas is going to find me. Going to find me and know I followed him.

He grabbed Rohak by the shirt and pulled him close. 'Kiss me,' he hissed.

The *hashash* looked down at him and blinked. 'Wha—'

'You have to kiss me, *quick.*'

Rohak's brow lifted as understanding dawned in his eyes. Khari's breath hitched as Rohak cupped a hand along his jaw. Rohak leaned down and parted Khari's mouth with his.

'Khari?' The disbelief in Ilyas's voice doused the moment like water over a fire.

Khari pulled away from Rohak, his face blushing pink as the dawn.

Behind Ilyas, Atiya peeked out at the two of them.

'The *hashash*?' Ilyas blinked, dark brows knitting together. 'What are you doing here with him?

'I could ask you the same.' Khari nodded toward Atiya, not quite masking his bitterness.

'She... I...' Ilyas cleared his throat, and Khari was satisfied to find that his cheeks were a little pink. 'I've asked her to marry me.'

Khari's heart dived down, down, down. Through his stomach, through the ground, through the earth and into cold, hard, nothing.

'We haven't told anyone yet,' Ilyas said quickly. 'We

wanted to wait until her father returns from the war.' He looked at Khari, waiting for a reaction.

Khari couldn't move. Couldn't speak.

I've lost him forever.

'Khari, aren't you going to say anything?'

His own voice sounded hollow. Distant. 'I'm glad for you.'

That was what he was supposed to say, wasn't it? Even if it wasn't true. Even if it was tearing him apart.

Ilyas placed his hands on Khari's shoulders. His eyes were wide and dark and full of guilt. 'I'm sorry, Khari.'

Khari looked into those eyes he knew so well, eyes he knew better than any, and he realised that Ilyas knew. That perhaps he'd always known. That he was foolish to think there was anything unsaid between them. They'd never needed words.

It was why he loved him.

'Come on,' Rohak whispered when Ilyas turned away and Khari's heart cracked and caved in on itself. 'Let's go home.'

The *hashash* walked silently beside him through the streets. Khari was so numb that he forgot his shirt was torn until Rohak offered his instead.

Khari thought of refusing, but just then it felt like too much effort. The *hashash* was less broad than Ilyas, but taller, and his shirt felt strange and new when Khari slipped it over the top.

Rohak helped him climb the compound walls and sneak onto the second story balcony. He accompanied Khari to the doors of his quarters. Just as Khari was about to go inside, Rohak caught his hand.

'Even the stars die.'

Khari looked up at him through swollen eyes. 'What?'

'The stars. New ones are born, of course, but every star dies eventually.'

'Are you trying to make me feel better?' asked Khari.

'I'm trying to make you see that all things must end.' He paused, and a tiny smirk curled at the corner of his lips. 'Just as they must begin.'

Before Khari could discern his meaning, he'd already started walking away.

'Rohak.'

The *hashash* turned, lifting a brow.

'I…I do want you to train me. Like you said.'

The blue eyes held his and he smiled, then continued down the corridor. 'By the way,' he called back without turning, 'I enjoyed that kiss.'

Khari leaned against the doorframe, watching Rohak's bare retreating back. He almost called to him again, to return the shirt.

But he had a feeling Rohak intended for him to keep it, and actually, he kind of liked the way it fit.

It made him feel taller, somehow.

COME GET ME

GRACE JARVIS

Eleven pm. I'm watching *Daria*. I'm watching *Daria* at the lowest possible volume because my family is sleeping and I left my headphones on the back seat of Chelsea's car. It's late and it's cold. The lights are off. My pants are off. My electric blanket is on. I can see the dull red glow of the dial between the blankets as Daria says something wry from the laptop on my chest. A dog from down the street barks what I believe to be approval of my choices and I'm considering attempting sleep when my phone rings. Its cheerful jingle is loud and abrasive against the silence and I scramble to answer before the tone wakes my sleeping family.

'Hello?' I whisper, praying the person on the other end also understands the sanctity of silence and the time of night at which they are calling.

'Hey,' the voice responds. My breath flickers. This is a very important voice. I haven't heard this voice in over a year. This voice is fucking hammered.

'Are you okay?' I ask, inciting concern as my primary

emotion and avoiding the others enacting a fight to the death to exhibit in my voice.

'Yeah, I'm drunk in town,' the voice slurs, cheerily. 'Come get me?'

This invitation prompts an increase in my heart rate that feels dangerous. I think I might be better off hanging up on this drunken voice and calling an ambulance. As the two scenarios spin faster and faster around my skull, the heart attack option seems to hold less potential trauma and before I can set out upon my journey to A&E the voice comes again.

'Please, Laura?'

Yeah, alright.

'Come outside to meet me, okay?' I say, pretending to be aloof while silently panicking. 'Outside the movie theatre in twenty.'

And I hang up.

It occurs to me that there must be a plethora of reasons to get out of bed at 11:15pm on Saturday night and drive to the main street of a regional Queensland town really too small to have a nightlife. Many of them might even be acceptable to relay to one's sleeping mother. I can think of none of these and as I swing open the door to my sleeping mother's bedroom, I rely on an old classic. Throwing a neutral party under the bus. My poor friend James.

'Mum?' I whisper at the lump in the bed. 'James is drunk at a party,' (probably true)

'and his ride has bailed on him,' (unknown levels of true)

'and he needs me to pick him up.' (false)

Silence. Moan of approval.

Nice.

This moan is all that's required for me to jangle my car keys into the pocket of my jacket and supply my bare legs with jeans in aid of the mission. My butt hits the driver's seat of my parents' Mitsubishi and I take three deep breaths.

'Be cool,' I whisper to myself, as my heart beats out a tattoo against my Little Miss pyjama shirt. It's going very well so far.

I park behind the theatre in my usual spot. Secluded enough, but not serial killer territory—I sit in this car, in this spot, a lot. I come here to think.

It's windy when I get out of the car, colder than I was anticipating. There's a snail travelling slowly across the footpath and I stand and watch it for a while, before growing impatient and moving it aside. Nobody has ever had enough time to wait for a snail and I am no exception. The street outside the theatre is empty and silent, but I can hear the music leaking out of the clubs and bars a few streets over. I battle the wind and walk towards the noise, attempting to keep my upcoming cardiac arrest at bay.

He's standing in front of the cinema, his lanky frame buffeted by the wind and unsteady from the gallons of gin he's consumed. I smell fumes from across the road. As I get closer they're mixed with a familiar cologne. He's wearing an American football jacket with sunglasses tucked into the front pocket. Apparently, there was a dress code—1960s dickhead.

He sees me and cracks into a giant lopsided grin. I hear my name escape the gaping chasm in his face and I black out momentarily. I awake to the sensation of his hand holding mine through my jacket pocket. It's a weird gesture. There's fabric between our palms, but his fingers grip tightly between mine. The jacket, now personified, becomes an awkward third wheel to our digital groping and I look up at his beaming countenance only to be infected by the enthusiastic smile. I laugh and my heart returns to normal.

'You're drunk,' I say, hand still trapped in his affectionate vice.

'Yep!' he enthuses, pulling me into an embrace. 'Can we get McDonalds?'

We walk away from the noises of the main street, still entwined in our awkward three-way handholding. Me, him and my jacket. His raucous drunken babbling pierces the silent car park as we walk through it and he attempts to catch up on a year's worth of invasive questions.

'How was Year 12?'

Hell.

'Been on any dates?'

No.

'What, none?'

None.

'Kissed any boys?'

No. I had glandular fever twice.

'Girls?'

No.

There are other questions. I'm not paying too much attention. I'm looking up at his peculiarly shaped head and examining his face. Full lips, bushy eyebrows, pleasingly crooked teeth. Has anything changed since the last time he acknowledged me? Lines have appeared, perhaps prematurely for his nineteen years and I can see poorly shaven stubble under the streetlights. He looks older, sadder—despite the grin. I look over his arms for new scars.

'Have you had sex with a man yet?'

I stop, just past the theatre and pull my hand away.

'No.'

'But you're so oooooold!' he mocks, walking further up the street without me.

I am seventeen. I don't feel old.

'Yeah, well it's not for lack of trying,' I huff, unsure of how much comedy to put into my tone.

He turns back to me, gleeful. I roll my eyes and back away.

'Who have you been trying with? Who have you been trying with?' he pesters, backing me toward a nearby wall.

'Nobody!' I laugh and look at my feet. I'm wearing odd socks. I hadn't noticed. 'It's just something you say.'

He's silent, but I know he's grinning down at me. I look up. His giraffe-like frame attempts to bend into a position where our faces are easily accessible to one another. He kisses me, pressing my back harder against the rough brickwork. I had forgotten how much mouth he has. How much mouth he uses when he kisses. I feel somewhat as though my lips were being enveloped by a gaping wet, crater—like he was somehow trying to suck them off. I try reaching around him to touch his butt, but my arms are too short and too trapped to traverse the great distance of his torso, and besides his butt mostly disappears into his extensive legs anyway. I had forgotten how awkward we were, two people completely incapable of becoming one. I love this feeling. I kiss him back and then move my face gently out from under his. He draws away and holds my hand again, this time without the unwanted third party.

'You're drunk,' I say, softly.

'I'm not that drunk,' he exclaims, attempting to prove it by wobbling to the gutter and back with his arms out. He looks like a demented scarecrow. I laugh and he pulls me toward him again.

'Where did you get this?' I ask, fingering the jacket he's wearing and noticing the embroidery of his name on the chest. Wanker.

'When my mum was young and pretty, boys used to buy her things,' he says, swaying slightly in the wind.

'You think she named you after this boy, as a thank you for the jacket,' I murmur, my face against his chest.

'I think that's exactly what happened,' he replies solemnly.

We make out in the backseat of the car. He takes my top off and we start a cycle of him unbuttoning my jeans and me distracting him, before buttoning them back up. He's too drunk to notice. He tells me that he's never had sex drunk before. I think that this is a lie. He tells me that he has had sex high before. I hope that this is a lie. He puts his hands down my pants and I tell him that we are not having sex. We lie next to each other and I listen to his rapid heartbeat through his translucent chest. He wants to get pizza. I scoff at the lack of change in his appalling diet. I tell him that at this rate his heart attack is scheduled for his thirtieth birthday. He kisses my forehead.

We get pizza.

I drive him home, Domino's box perched precariously over the canyon his gangly legs provide. Halfway there, he insists we pull over and I watch him heave gin and cheese onto someone's front lawn. The lawn belongs to a very pretty house and is full of porcelain figures, which seem to frown with disgust at the undignified ejection of his stomach contents. I see lights go on across the street and hope no one comes out to remove us. You really shouldn't rush a vomiting drunk.

'Are you okay?' I ask, as he clambers back into the passenger seat.

'Yeah, all good,' he replies, smiling at me.

I squeeze his knee and leave my hand on his thigh.

I pull into his driveway and he kisses me goodbye. He tastes like sick. I don't mind. I read somewhere that love is getting dog poo off someone's shoe without being asked and with no disgust. I feel like kissing someone who has recently thrown up is equivalent. He leaves the leftover pizza in the backseat.

When I get home, I disturb my dog who is curled up in the corner of my bedroom and notice that *Daria* is still playing.

AN ABSENCE OF GRANITE

JESS M. MILLER

In the middle of a cemetery, on a day that has bled into the others by mid-morning, the last man on earth runs into a girl he knows.

This is unexpected.

He can't remember her name, so instead of calling out, he walks over. Tries not to scare her; does terribly. When she overcomes the shock she reminds him that her name is Asher, and he says it's ironic that he should forget, because remembering names is his life's work.

The last man on earth's social skills have, understandably, been in decline, so we can forgive him for misinterpreting her silence. You or I might notice that the grave is her grandmother's, and deduce that she just wants to be alone, but what he sees is a window shaped perfectly for storytelling. He's never had anyone to tell his story to before. It comes out like bits of a build-it-yourself racetrack straight from the box: good in parts but going nowhere.

He asks if she remembers what priests used to say at

funerals, that the dead live on for as long as their loved ones remember them. 'My problem is this,' he begins. 'What happens when *those* loved ones die? We don't tally up the people for whom we're responsible; we don't pass our ancestors' memories on to our children like family heirlooms. We just let them go. And a few generations later, we ourselves are let go. But what about if we held on? If we remembered every single name?'

'We'd get a headache,' says Asher. 'Trying to remember everyone who ever lived? Do you have any idea how many people that is?'

'One hundred and fifteen billion, and two hundred thousand,' he promptly replies. 'And I'm on about fifty-five.'

'Fifty-five people?' she snorts.

He shakes his head. 'Fifty-five million.'

You see, the last man on earth has a house in his mind, but it isn't his childhood house or any sort of cherished memory— no, he's not built it for himself. Three years ago the man was flung out the other side of the apocalypse somehow still intact. Naturally, for a while, he didn't quite know what to do with himself. So he began small, by wandering into the nearest cemetery and reading the tombstones. After a time he realised he would need a better system than simple lists, and so he built himself the house. He takes names, holds them for brief delicate moments of tribute, then folds them into filing cabinets. One room in the house for Australia. A room for the unknown victims, mostly the more recent ones with no-one to bury them—these filing cabinets he's filled with every first name and surname he can think of, hoping that it's enough. The rest of the house so far is empty, but he's begun construction on the New Zealand room next door.

The last man on earth asks, 'Are you wondering how I'm going to get there? To New Zealand.'

Asher shakes her head. 'I'm actually wondering what else you're lying about.'

'I'm telling the truth.'

'But even if you are—what's the *point*? Everyone's dead.' She reaches out to the top of her grandmother's gravestone, then pulls back quickly. 'I'd like to just forget I ever loved anybody.'

'I can't do that.'

'Why not?'

'It's too much to lose,' he says firmly, and leaves her there.

When he is halfway to the cemetery's entrance, a patter of footsteps falls in time with his thudding ones. A sidelong glance brings her eyes to him and suddenly he can remember her, under a dim light in a lounge room, saying something. Drinking wine. Laughing.

'You were a pilot,' she declares. 'You told me at the party.'

Sometime later, she asks about all the Ashers he's remembered. 'Humour me,' she adds. 'I'm bored.'

So he goes into his house, rifles through some cabinets, and tells her that Asher Hillary was a convict in the nineteenth century; that Asher Prince was a radio host in Brisbane in the eighties; that there's been Asher Johnston the jockey, Asher Stuart the lawyer, and then Asher Keddie the actress.

'I feel incredibly un-extraordinary,' she says, and then asks him about *his* name. It's more common a name than hers, so he is able to rattle off his counterparts in quicker succession.

'There you go.' She smirks. 'I bet that made you feel pointless too.'

'No, it makes me feel part of something.'

Time passes, as time often does. When he has folded the very last of Sydney into its cabinet they find the old airport, asleep under the blank screens and the frozen escalators. He resuscitates one of the smaller planes.

'Well,' Asher shrugs, 'at least I know you weren't lying about that.'

He grins broadly and leans down to blow the dust off the controls. In the window's reflection he catches her smiling.

'If you wanted me to,' he says, 'I could help you build your own house. You could help me do this.'

She regards him, motionless. It's only when they're off the ground that she mutters, 'You know, for someone who's trying to memorise the world, you've got a terrible memory.'

And she smiles again, but it only reaches halfway up her face.

After a few weeks, the last man on earth realises that the process is still quicker whether Asher shares the work or not. He assumes it's because dialogue between two people is helpful when committing things to memory. Even if all she does is skip ahead of him, calling out wrong names, backwards names, non-existent names: 'Bethany Tull, forget her! She was useless! Charles Faulkner—he was a serial killer, he doesn't deserve it. Charles Fulton, Charlie Foulter, Harley Coulter...'

'I was slower before, because my technique was wrong.'

He says this out loud. And then he goes inside his house, down the hallway and into the Australia room and past the Perth cabinet and the Adelaide cabinet, and he sits with his chin on the top of his knees and he says, 'I was slower before, because I was lonely.'

In China they come across a seesaw. And because there are now two of them, and because they can, they run to it with the joy of children. The wind comes and unfurls Asher's hair like octopus tentacles reaching out underwater, and it makes her laugh, and it makes him laugh too, to see her like this. His feet push off the ground and every time, at his highest point, he wonders what would happen if he just refused to land.

In Russia, to celebrate his one billionth person remembered, Asher cracks open a bottle of red and they go to a shop that once sold formal wear. They salvage the coloured silk from the dust, and she remembers how intimate it is to have a man zip up the back of your dress; to have his eyes seek out the 'you' under the 'it' even when you're twirling. She shouts out, 'My name is Aleksandra Kurosev—will you remember *me*?'

'That's not your name!' he giggles, flicking a top hat onto his head.

'Yes, it is! I'm Aleksandra Kurosev and I am here and *you*,' she points, 'must remember *me*! Because I was *here*!'

In Germany they share a bed and, out of sheer boredom, they do what neither of them have done for thirty years. In Belgium they begin to depend on these moments.

'I am getting slower because I am happy,' he says, to the inside and the outside.

In Ireland eighteen months later, she plucks the first grey hair from his head and holds it up to the light. But it's too close to focus on, and so he just keeps on looking through it, at her.

When he is sixty-five years old, the last man on earth walks into his Australia room and he just *knows* something is wrong. On the outside he is staring at a tombstone in Cairo but on the inside he is in the first room he ever built and there's a cabinet missing. A patch of discoloured carpet stares up at him, the shadow of ten million people, of vowels and consonants, of plans and fears and first loves.

Asher's hand touches his shoulder and he whispers, 'It's genocide in my head.'

'No,' she says, 'it's just dementia.'

He stops collecting new memories, and starts to write out his old ones at the front desk of an office building. Over a thousand pieces of printer paper, he empties his house. But for every filing cabinet he drains, two slip away—from the New Zealand room, then the China room, then the Egypt room still warm from yesterday's touch. He thinks of America and of Canada. Mexico. Other places they will never reach.

They go on like this for three years until one day he puts down his pen and says, 'Enough.' Names on tombstones, they are not people. They are not even memories; he never knew any of them and he can't bring them back. They are nothing but what they are. Letter-shaped holes in granite and bronze and marble. An absence.

He says, 'I don't want to be an absence of granite.'

She whispers, 'No.' She takes him by the shoulders and tells him, 'You will be a memory.'

He sighs and looks up with a word on his lips. But then the letters start to reel backwards, down his throat, away from his vocal chords. New letters take their places.

'I can't remember your name,' he chokes out.

She smiles a halfway smile, and reminds him.

They walk to Giza, his feet dragging like anchors. Out of nowhere, he looks at the desert and the sky and he says to them both, 'I am the last man on earth.'

'I know,' replies Asher. 'There's nothing here at all, let alone people.'

'Everything is here.'

I am the last man on earth, and this is the last sky on earth, and the last desert, and the last sun. And this sky, don't you see—it is carrying the memory of all other skies, as is the sand, and the sun, and the pyramids. The world has followed us here. We are the only place the absences can go to exist.

At the bottom of the pyramid he looks up and says, 'Let's climb it.'

'But you can barely see the top!'

'You can't see it at all. It's perfect.' She looks over and some part of her must understand, because she takes his hand.

Halfway up, he collapses into her arms. She curls herself around him in the shade and some time later, with a great gulp of air, he wheezes, 'There was no point.'

'Of course there was.'

'Then what was it?' The dust is climbing into his mouth. 'What was the point? We could have tried—we could have rebuilt the population, we could have—cleaned up—we could have *tried*! Too many people. Too many. So much to lose.'

'Ah, but darling,' she whispers, 'it was so much to keep. Not even the earth could do it.'

'Not even the earth?'

'Not even the whole wide world.'

He gazes up at her and he thinks that she is better and wiser and more beautiful than every Asher who came before, and he decides on a marvellous whim to build a room in his house just for her. He will paint the red of her Russian dress, the blue of the seesaw, the beige of that couch from forty years ago. He will paint Asher and Aleksandra Kurosev and the name of her grandmother and everything she has ever been. And when he shows her inside for the first time, he will make the smile go all the way up her face. Yes, that is what he will do.

'It'll be beautiful,' he gasps.

The last person on earth looks to the top of the pyramid and murmurs, 'I'm sure it will be.'

crush

noun

4. a crowd of people pressed closely together

'I was afraid I would lose him in the crush.'

THE CASTLE, THE TOWER AND THE OTHER CASTLE

RYAN SCOTT

Evan hadn't noticed the small café, right on the corner, just across from his hotel when he arrived yesterday. It would look great on a postcard, so he snapped it with his phone and posted the pic to Facebook.

Now that he thought of it, he fancied a coffee.

At the outside tables, men smoked, played chess and spoke with excited hands. Chess pieces and espresso cups scattered. It was good to finally be in Europe. Evan stepped over a knight, which had come to rest in the grooves of the cobblestones; a waiter on his way out with an order swept down to collect it. He added the piece and then two dainty liqueur glasses to one of the tables. Each glass contained a green liquid, the colour somewhere between mouthwash and a teenage punk's first dye job.

Evan wanted to try it without knowing what it was. At least he could tick it off the list of experiences, though he'd have to add it to the list first.

Inside, the café's interior was split down the middle by a thick line of blue grey cigarette smoke. It was certainly authentic, he thought, and swatted his way to the bar where in his best French, he ordered a coffee.

'You vood like zum tink to drink?' the barista replied in an accent Evan couldn't place.

Evan nodded and, without asking for anything in particular, a coffee arrived. He brought it to his lips. The drink was hot. Hot and bitter. Hot, bitter and—that was it, hot and bitter. He would ask for the liqueur next time.

Something or someone tugged on his sleeve. An old man, slightly bent over, stood at his elbow. His grey beard was trimmed to a point over his chin. He wore a black felt hat, which matched his black corduroy trousers, though the vest was closer to the colour of his beard. Over his eyes sat a layer of tears thick enough to magnify them.

'Ah yes, this reminds me of the time I met my dear Mathilde,' the man said with an accent less pronounced but no more curious than the barista's.

'Do I know you?' Evan asked.

The old man looked around. Evan wasn't sure what he would be able to see.

'You are American, aren't you?' the man asked now in an accent, which wouldn't have been out of place on the BBC.

'Well...'

'Foreign, at least? From abroad?'

'Yes, though...'

'So listen,' he said brusquely, returning to his original accent. 'This reminds me of how I met my dear Mathilde. We used to come walking here.'

'Here? You met a woman in this place?' Evan asked, looking at the various patrons shrouded in the smoke.

The old man rolled his dry eyes and headed through the smoke cloud, beckoning Evan to follow. Once they were outside, the old man said, 'Would you prefer it if I met her here?'

'Sure. Why not?'

He still had no idea who Mathilde was or why this man was talking to him. But the decorative facades, ornate cornices and windows with wooden muntins were more suitable to any story.

'We would walk here and once she came up to my studio where she let me draw her…or sculpt her… I forget now. Afterwards we stayed up until the sun rose over the city. Have you seen the sun rise here? Over the castle, and the tower and the other castle.'

Castle? That was where Evan planned to go today. In fact, what the old man said was his itinerary exactly: the castle, the tower and then the other castle. He wanted to catch the changing of the guard at one and guard's procession at the second. Or the other way around. It didn't matter.

He looked for somewhere to place the espresso cup he was still holding. At that moment, a waiter came by; in one fluid motion, he took it from his hand and strode back into the cafe.

'Sorry. I have to go,' he said. 'I have a full day ahead. But thanks for the story. It has certainly made my trip more… memorable.'

Evan fondled his phone and wondered if it would be rude to take a photo of him.

'Yes, you go to her, lad. You go to her before it's too late,' the man said. 'Don't let her get away from you like I did with Mathilde. Oh, Mathilde. How could I have been so foolish?'

Evan released the phone. Perhaps a photo was not the best idea. But he would like to know who he was nattering on about.

'Who am I meant to go to?' Evan asked.

'Why her,' the old man said pointing in the direction of a young woman in a red duffle coat and green stockings. With one hand, she twirled a loose coil of her chestnut brown hair. In the other she walked a ferret.

'She's the one you have been telling me about. The one you came here to search for. Don't miss this chance now.'

'There's clearly been some mistake. I never mentioned anyone and I have no idea who that is,' Evan said as the man pushed him toward the stranger. He knew himself too well. He wouldn't choose someone with a pet. Least of all a ferret owner; those things required a lot of care and could smell as bad as skunks.

Yet there was a sudden ache in his stomach that wasn't the coffee.

The woman continued toward them. Evan had turned back to ask the old man who she was, but he was gone. He watched her as she approached, unsure if she was smiling at him. At the last moment, she veered abruptly and walked into him.

'I'm so sorry,' she said. Evan was no more certain of her nationality than anyone else he'd met this morning. The voice was…Russo-Mediterranean? Was that even a thing?

'I was not watching where I was going,' she added.

'What do you mean? You did that on purpose. I saw you. You were walking there and then you just turned suddenly and crashed into me.'

The woman was not listening. She had her hands up to her face and was looking around in a startled way.

'Oh my god,' she trilled, almost panting out each syllable and shouting them to the street. 'Jacque-Louis. I 'ave lost Jacque-Louis. 'As anybody seen 'im?'

Now, she appeared to be French.

Weren't the people here also French? Wouldn't the French language be of more use than preposterously accented English?

The men at the tables called back that they 'adn't seen 'im.

'Who is Jacque-Louis?' Evan asked.

'Ee iz, 'ow you say, my pet. My pet, *mon dieu, comment dit-on le furet in anglais?*'

'Ferret,' the men at the tables called out in unison. At that very same moment, one man at each table, always the one on the outer edge, won his game, causing the other's hands to become more animated than usual.

'So we are in France,' Evan said, looking around.

'Does it matter?' the woman said in a drawl that sounded almost American. 'Paris, Rome, Barcelona—it's all the same to you guys.' Then switching to an accent that sounded more Spanish, she begged Evan to help her find her lost pet.

He wanted to say he couldn't help her when he noticed the animal dart under a parked cheese delivery van. It was behind a croissant delivery van and in front of a wine delivery van.

'Your ferret is over there. Under the van. No, the other van,' Evan said.

'Oh my god,' she pouted again. 'I 'ave lost my ferret. You will 'ave to help me look for 'im. Ere I 'ave a map.'

She shoved a map drawn on brown paper, translucent as of onion skin. The details could have been done in crayon or lipstick.

'We don't need a map. He's over there under the croissant delivery van. He's chewing on the transmission fluid cable.'

'No. I 'ave a map. We will look for him all over the city. See I already 'ave drawn a route. We will start at the castle, go past the tower and finish at the other castle. Who knows what may happen?'

She blushed when she said this.

'But your ferret is right there. Look. He's under the van. He's coming out now. If you're quick, you'll catch him. See, he's coming toward us. Quick, there, quick… Oh. Oh, dear.'

'No matter, we can still follow the route. It will be—'ow you say?—whimsical.'

'I think a kid saw that.'

Once again Evan felt a tug on his sleeve. The old man had returned, his eyes once again goggled with melancholy.

'This is how I met my Mathilde,' he said. 'It was 1923. She had lost her pet turtle.'

'1923. But that would make you…'

Before Evan could do the maths, the woman grabbed him and kissed him. She tasted of liquorice, wine, dark chocolate, garlic and cigarettes, though the latter could have been a residue left on Evan's tongue from the cafe.

The feeling in his stomach returned. He no longer cared

about his plans or the ferret. He would go on this journey across the city with her. They would simply search for something else.

Suddenly, the sky darkened. The sun, which had been there a moment ago, dropped from sight, and stars were again strung across the city. Almost as quickly, it began to brighten, the black going from violet and then to blue.

'Just as I remember when I was with my Mathilde,' the man said.

'Oh my ferret. We found Jacque-Louis,' the woman said, crouching down as the animal, which Evan was sure met its end under a taxi, scampered toward her.

Evan was struck by an idea. He would stay in this city, in this European city, whichever one it was, and write the novel about how he met this woman and the journey to the castle, the tower and the other castle they had not taken but which he felt he already knew. He would call the book *Mathilde*. Perhaps the woman with the ferret would even let him call her that too.

The men at the café tables stopped for a moment, looked to the sun rising again and checked their watches. They all agreed they would have extra time for another coffee and maybe fit in a rematch.

THE LOVE THAT ATE PARIS

KATHRYN HUMMEL

Florian and I edged around the big issue; the *mot* of the moment, of the city we were in. Love. It was what we had come to Paris for. Love and sex. Or was it sex and love? I asked him casually, as though I was ordering coffee, understanding that we'd both rather affect cynicism than admit to shattered hearts. Sex first, Florian assured me, then love. He even said *fucking* and love. *Vucking*, really—the word came out half-swallowed and unconvincing. Everything else we laboriously covered in that conversation—pollution, racial tension, the absence of old men with Gallic noses playing liberty songs on the accordion—registered low on the scale of tragedy compared to our personal misfortune. We talked, fed up with the Paris of our reality and all it had to offer, except for the toasted *pain passion*, which we consumed insatiably (to fill the void) and appropriately (because we both agreed we had no passion left).

'What's your hotel room like?' I asked.

Florian sipped his coffee, narrowing his eyes. 'Was that a line?'

'I can't possibly tell,' I said, 'until I hear about your room. Go on.'

'White walls, sloping ceiling with exposed beams. The floor slopes in the opposite direction. There's a tub of lavender growing on the windowsill.'

'With the dust of Provence clinging to it,' I suggested.

'Exactly. What's yours like? Any better?'

'I moved out yesterday,' I began, 'but it had striped wallpaper, peeling with yellow patches, like long underwear you'd find in the back of grandad's wardrobe.'

Florian grimaced. 'I can't picture a more romantic setting.'

'Not my first choice,' I said, 'but he thought it had character.'

'And he was the one who left you?'

We both reached for the butter. I began feeling courageous.

'I'll tell you one thing,' Florian went on, 'she knows how to split scrupulously. A parting that'd do her mother proud. Did he leave anything behind?'

'Just a shirt, drying in the bathroom. I threw it out.'

'Out? Of what? The window?'

I shook my head. 'With the rubbish. I didn't think about the window. Imagine the closure I'd have got, sending it sailing down from our grimy attic into the streets of the Latin Quarter.'

'Ah,' said Florian, 'but this isn't the weather for catharsis.'

I hadn't noticed the pounding of the rain on the awning above our heads.

Through rainy streets, black underfoot and fading to an ashen beige at each side, the lovers walk to the hotel where

Oscar Wilde had breathed his last. They stand at the discreet entrance next to a small man with a yellow umbrella and an eclectic grasp of the English language.

'Fat man with epigram,' says this man to no one in particular.

The man turns to his darling. 'Do you think we handled it well?'

The woman tilts her umbrella and her chin to the same angle as she reads the inscription high on the wall near the doorway. *Poète et Dramaturge*—over and over, her eyes trace the carved letters. She has a feeling Oscar had not died in a nearby room but in some highly beautiful place forged together from the scraps of Art not quite wrung out of him, aided by absinthe and the cerebral part of his meningitis.

'I know there's no good way to have done it. We couldn't avoid causing them pain. I just think—'

The man with the yellow umbrella turns to them to interrupt: 'Died 30 November 1900, age 46.'

The lovers nod, their smiles as thin as water. The man snaps a photo of them.

'What do you think?' asks the woman.

'That I should have talked to her, face to face. Not left a note. Only cowards leave notes.'

'In this situation,' the woman replies, her voice strained with longing, 'we couldn't have waited.'

The man stumbles over his own ego. 'How do you think they took it?'

'She's devastated. So is he.'

'Devastated?'

'But not for long. By now they'd have found each other

in a café and traded quips and had a good meal. Then they would have gone back to a hotel room with sloping ceilings and pulled down the covers and got into bed.'

'Buried at Père Lachaise!' interjects the yellow umbrella man. He hands his camera to the woman and walks over to the door, striking an Artistic pose with one hand on his hip. 'Take me, please?'

The camera swoops and catches. The lover, fed up, thumbs through his guidebook. 'The supreme vice is shallowness,' he reads.

If Florian and I hadn't recognised each other from that day on the Champ de Mars, we would never have spoken to each other. If we hadn't been aware of those details of each other's lives, the kind of knowledge that creates intimacy from necessity, we wouldn't have chosen to remain in the same neighbourhood—walking the streets, drinking at outdoor tables—in case we saw them together. Neither of us knew where they were, whether they were still in Paris or had gone off to somewhere like Vienna to check if the Danube was blue. If we came across them, Florian said, they'd already proven how good they were at running away. In the meantime, we would sit and wait and watch time rush about our ankles. This attitude attracted the attention of a master *raconteur* who roved through the streets, narrating in different languages histories short and tall for the small fee of a carafe of wine and a little fresh company. 'You are not ordinary,' he told us. 'You are not sealed against romances.'

He performed for us:

'My mother raised me well, by hand. We lived in a caravan

and she worked with her cousins at the fish factory washing the floors of cement. My father was a strange man with a long grey beard. He did not send me to school. My first words were the objects I saw around me. I learned about these by running my tongue over them. With my tongue I acquired taste and feel and smell and from this, I found I could say the objects and draw them better than badly, though I could not spell them. I was taught to look at objects from a close distance, my eyes separated from the surface by only the length of my tongue. I grew to know things deeper in this way than by touching them with my fingers simply.'

'And the tongue is vital. A man can survive without fingers, my father told me, showing me his right hand. He had been a thief in the War—and a spy, they say, and a traitor. They had cut his fingers and saved the hand. A generous punishment, perhaps? From others they cut the tongues. Then, it would have been more difficult to force prisoners to form the words: 'Our enemies were hard and good and they were just. They were an idiom, like the entire Old Testament.'

'The penitent kept their fingers,' said the storyteller's father. 'The defiant kept their tongues and were made to break them.'

They sleep tonight with a valley between them.

'Darling.' The woman turns to speak low into her lover's back. 'Do you believe in God?'

There is a drowsy pause. 'I need more time to answer,' the man replies.

'We're going to the cathedral tomorrow, aren't we?'

'There was no plan, but yes.' The man sighs out his

answers. 'Yes, we can go…which cathedral?'

The woman looks up towards the ceiling. The walls around it are papered in white and yellow stripes, peeling in places, damp in others. 'Any cathedral,' she says. 'It doesn't matter. I want to go to confession.'

It was Florian's idea to improve our French by reading children's books. From Monoprix we bought flimsy glossy stories and at flea markets we found several antique schoolbooks, shedding their leatherette covers and smelling vaguely of fried lamb chops. *The Little Prince* was conquered without either of us learning anything new: we had both read it as children, remembered the story and invented woolly translations to fill in the gaps. Florian sat close with his elbow on the table, watching the stout candle peel down its wick on the table between us.

'Do you think the Rose really cried when the Prince left her?' I asked. 'The story was written by a fascist pilot—all that flying must have gone to his head. And you can never trust a French man to write or speak the truth.'

'You're forgetting I was born here,' said Florian.

'I'm not. I never said I trusted you.'

'Except with the most profound intimacies of your healing and fragile soul.'

'Unimportant things are easy to share with strangers.'

Florian pushed his face forward over the heel of his hand. 'You're about as delicate as a beefsteak, did you know that? I can see where you're going.'

'Where am I going?'

'I haven't cried, if that's what you mean. Not one single

tear on my pillow or in the bathtub or anywhere.'

Our copy of *The Little Prince* is preserved in a box, together with a shirt I had kept long after its owner had departed; a sheath of matches from a café; a paper napkin stained with a ring of *kir* and an old man's autograph; a velvet-soft label from a beer bottle; a piece of broken string. The book has a broken spine and Florian's handwriting in the margins—lines of his terrible poetry, sketches of grinning cats and the Eiffel Tower, and timeless quotations like *Je t'aime* and *Voulez-vous couchez avec moi, ce soir?*

We did it all, of course, but not in the expected order.

The lovers walk without touching, yet they think of touching. They remember the first night after the first afternoon when they met on the Champ de Mars and reached for the same balloon. The memory is overpowering. They wonder about going back to recapture the desire that first seemed so effortless, so easy to secure. They cannot find the words to discuss what is happening or ask each other about the value of their brief history.

Picasso drew in blue for such a long time it was afterwards known as a Period. His blues were final—the final goodbye—a tribute to a lost friend—a friendly farewell—a well of sorrow. Was it because he was floundering in blame?

For a while, the lovers talk without meaning. They then move from the Musée Picasso to the Musée Carnavalet without speaking a word.

It started off with a *Mort Subite* apiece at a communist bar along the river. Sudden Death, the beer was called, since a single bottle was potent enough to inflame the blood of the world's fattest man and large enough to drown him. Florian and I sloshed out of the bar at the end of the afternoon to discover that most of the one and a half litres we'd poured into ourselves had dammed at our knees.

'Let's do a grand tour,' Florian said.

'I can barely move.' To prove my point, I bent forward at the waist and let my arms hang slackly, my fingertips skimming the cobblestones.

'Come on come on come on, we haven't done the sights. We're in Paris in the springtime and we've spent most of the time licking our wounds.'

'I thought you hated tourists.'

'We're not ordinary, remember? We're magnificent.'

'It's raining.'

'It's clearing. Come on, let's do Notre Dame, the Bastille, the Arc de Triomphe, the Louvre!'

'Half of those places'll be closed.'

'A speedy grand tour, then. *Très vite.*'

'We could do the Moulin Rouge,' I said slowly, straightening up.

'That's it.'

'The Mona Lisa.'

'Well Freud might have an objection, but I don't.'

'The Eiffel Tower!'

We had both looked up the Tower's absent skirts, along its phallic lines, with our absent lovers—long ago. It was just another item on the list that had come to nothing: sex, love and the Eiffel Tower. Why mourn it? Here, there was a universe of emotion in one city. People caged and released their passions, drank wine, got bored, drank more, became inspired. Ours was just one more romance lining these vast walls. Twisted, ravelled, it had become another part of Paris; the city had no story that was not our own. Homage should be paid to this place that didn't cast us off but let us drift— if not into its heart, then into one of its hospitable outer chambers. We should, we would return to the setting of that scene of betrayal, where our lovers had reached for the same blue balloon, their eyes filling with startled recognition. They had come to Paris to fulfil their desires with entirely the wrong people; they ran away together to fully realise the former dearth. Were they blameless—were we guilty? The city revolved, the earth moved: every second spun and was lost. What would we find there? We decided to leave it up to Paris to decide.

I was sure, only Florian needed further persuasion. When I took his hand and looked at him, he returned my gaze without blinking.

'I'll buy you a balloon,' I said.

Cleared of cloud and sharpened by starlight, the sky held itself apart from the city. The night applied its balm after the rain; the air was like wine and cream, the best of French sensation. Small glittering objects stirred and noises erupted from below, layered over with the silence of distance. We saw Paris as a spread of dark patches, threaded with light.

Florian wondered at the view. 'Now it's different,' he said.

'I wish I could stay.'

'When do you fly out?'

'Saturday. You?'

'The day after.'

We grasped each other. We began feeling courageous.

'Do you think they're down there?' I asked.

'Do you think they're down there?' asks the man.

Despite her penitence, the woman is exhausted by this conversation. 'They've gone home,' she tells the man. 'Their friendship lasted until the taxi pulled up to take one of them away. It lasted through the exchange of phone numbers and email addresses and then dissolved. We weren't one of those disasters that ties people together.'

The city calls to the lovers. To purge themselves, to replenish their hearts, they hold each other and look out over the dark squares and lit streets of the city.

'Look,' the woman says.

A blue balloon dangling a short string bounces across the crowd and over the edge.

A blue balloon dangling a short string bounced across the crowd and over the edge.

'Look,' said Florian.

The man who sold me the balloon at sunset had looped the string around Florian's wrist and tied it, noticing our tipsiness and perhaps sensing our desire to unburden ourselves. The tenderness of the act, confirmation that the city was looking after us, had subdued us during our ascent to the Tower's viewing platform. Florian was right: it was different. The desire for liberation had grown strong.

'After you,' I said.

'After you,' he says.

The woman shakes her head and is silent—beautifully silent.

'Shall we?' the lovers ask.

'Shall we?' Florian and I asked.

It was, after all, what we had come to Paris for.

At the beginning of your holiday in Paris, you went to buy a balloon for your lover from a man on the Champ de Mars. You wanted the last remaining blue balloon; so did another traveller, but because it was your first day in Paris and because you were in love—both of you, as it happened— you decided on the green balloon instead; the other lover, on the violet. Like all anecdotes, it began as comical but utterly unromantic: one that emerges in every traveller's repertoire, especially if the traveller happens to be starring in a film, especially in a romantic film about Paris. It is a story easily forgotten until recounted, years later, for an apathetic dinner party crowd.

'You never told me!' your constant lover exclaims. 'I just thought you'd muddled my favourite colour.'

Then later, away from the table and the smeared cake plates, slightly drunk:

'Was the traveller, the one who wanted the blue balloon, beautiful? You could have run away together. All three of you. You and the lovely one and the blue balloon. It could have been the start of a true romance.'

With a kiss and a glass of wine, your lover would be placated. But anyone in the room looking on would notice that you didn't answer, would know that the truth is rarely pure and never simple.

You know that what happened is something to be kept, pressed between the vellum of memory. Instantaneous attraction, then sex, then love—the possibilities of these are not easily forgotten. Even if you didn't grasp it that day on the Champ de Mars, you could not have mistaken it the next time. You saw the same beautiful traveller again—in a café, of course, since memorable meetings in Paris rarely take place in any other setting. You were sitting undercover, on the terrace; the object of your desire was only one tabletop, one arm's length, away. It was raining, and even now there are images that flicker across your mind.

There is the matter of betrayal, of coffee and bread, of magnificence, damp paintings in fat frames fissures in hearts, and two terrible lines of poetry pencilled in the margin of a little old book, fraying at the edges—

They met at once, the virtuous strangers / Who ate Paris with their love.

BEER-N-BUBS

VAHRI MCKENZIE

Frankie heard about this course to prepare men for being 'birth partners'. They held it in a pub to put the men at ease, she said, so I agreed to go and give up Friday drinks at the Prince. It was interesting actually, they got us to talk a bit and so I got to check out the other blokes there. I was surprised how good I looked in comparison. Quite a few having kids for the second time 'round said they were going to do better this time, starting with the labour. You got a little clap for that.

'I've known Frankie, my woman, forever, and we're having our first,' I said when it was my turn, feeling quite pleased with myself. I began to feel up for it, up to the job. I had no worries financially but I hadn't really thought much about the rest of it before then.

The Friday after that first Beer-n-Bubs I went back to the Prince. I told Frankie it was so I could tell everyone about the baby, but probably it was just habit. Usually the men with families go home after a couple and the others stay longer. So

I let it be known that as of the next week I'd be joining the ranks of the pikers. This led to another round of drinks, and another; the fathers went home and the others encouraged me to stay out for one last time.

Actually some of those guys who stayed on were fathers, but divorced and in the market again. They're mostly decent, but after a few drinks things sometimes get a bit ugly. There was one, Alex, who was a complete wanker. He'd cock-sucked his way to the top at work so I never called him out on anything, though I knew he wasn't as smart as he thought he was. He'd started seeing someone new a couple of weeks before, Tracey. He'd met her there at the Prince, in fact. Another stayer, Michael, was fat and practically a fascist, with no redeeming features. Somehow that night I got stuck with these two at the bar.

Alex said, 'Tracey's a single mum. Got a fourteen-year-old and a seven-year-old. Can't seem to get anything else these days.'

Michael said, 'There's a certain age I won't do—three-to-six-year-olds. Can't stand 'em.'

And Alex added, as if he hadn't heard Michael, 'But her daughter's hot.'

It went on like that, a routine between them. I knew it was pretty sick to talk about women like that but I didn't comment, because, well, it was just their thing. Not mine. Not me. It wasn't the kind of last night out I wanted to remember, sneering Alex and leering Michael, so the next Friday I skipped Beer-n-Bubs and went to the Prince again like normal.

In the early days of me and Frankie getting together

I'd sometimes meet her at the Prince on Fridays as a way of letting the others know about us without having to get all deep and meaningful, because I knew we had this kind of glow between us, these taut lines of something that you couldn't see but everyone knew was there.

She'd stopped coming, even before she got pregnant, though she never had a problem with me going out to blow off steam.

But when she freaked out over me missing the course I wasn't too surprised. They'd talked about that, hormone changes and whatnot. I told her I loved her and would go back the next week. But that wasn't the end of it; she wouldn't let it go. We fought all weekend and when I got home from work on Monday she wasn't there. I called, she didn't answer. Cold text message: Staying at Mum's for a while.

Fuck you then, I thought.

We'd always flirted, me and Frankie, and I'd wanted her forever. But I'm just not husband material, I've figured that out by now. It was me who introduced her to my brother, ten years back, and I'll admit I felt ripped off when they decided to get married. I know why she did it: she's smart. At least I used to think she was smart, I thought she saw it all, knew everything. I got over it and we went back to flirting. Ben didn't care, or didn't notice. We had mucking around in common, me and Frankie, always up for a laugh, while Ben just looked on and smiled. If you do it out in the open, it's okay, right? There's no secret.

One time we were having a pool noodle fight. This was after Frankie and Ben started seeing each other but before they were engaged. If I'm honest, I thought I might still win her back. We'd never fucked, you see, and I thought, if we did, she'd choose me, no question. But I was also pissed at her for never letting me in her pants. So we had this weird thing going on. We'd muck around, play rough, laugh and look at each other in this weird way that reminds me now of the way I talk to dogs. The kind of communication that happens without words, just the push of muscles and skins, the eyes. In the pool that time we both went under together and, instinctively it seemed at first, she grabbed me. Just for a second she held me and pushed her mouth over mine, blew air into it. Maybe she said something, but who knows? When we came up, laughing, gasping, there was nothing. Ben was at the barbecue, chatting with some guy from his work.

They never had kids. I reckon that for her, that meant it was never a sealed deal. Sure, there was a big wedding, standing up in front of everyone they knew, all the parents. I was best man, I made the speech, and did a bloody good job too: not crude but cracked the right jokes, showed just enough envy to make Ben feel like a winner.

There was a moment between me and Frankie that night that got stuck inside me somehow. She asked me to dance, a slow number, not the first but not late in the evening either. She put her head on my chest; I stared ahead without looking at anything. Every so often she'd slowly turn her head the other way, sweeping her eyes past mine, as if drawing me in. One time she paused and I was right there, she held my gaze, I felt exposed and I had to look away. It was like I was saying, right now I'll do whatever you want, go wherever you say, and she read me, I know she did. But what was she saying? I had to look away.

I moved on, worked in Brazil for five years and learned to speak decent Portuguese, though that was just for the women, not for work. But somehow that thing, fuck it, I don't know what to call it, Frankie planted something that took root and I could never shake it off, no matter how many women I had and how much money I earned.

On one of my trips back to Australia, Ben told me they were separating. He was light on the details, but gutted for sure. Mum told me it was entirely Frankie's decision, but she never could see Ben clearly. Because he was quiet and I was always in trouble it was easy to think he was the sensitive one, good to his women, and I was a shit. But that's too easy. I can see how Ben would piss her off, Frankie I mean. He was so fucking *cool*. When we were kids and I was spoiling for a fight, needing to get things out in the open, just the small stuff that builds up between brothers, I'd poke him, provoke him, even hit him a bit, just a punch on the arm. To any of my mates that was enough to signal a yelling match, to say everything that's on your mind and even a bit more that you make up in the heat of the moment, then we'd pick up again in an hour, the next day, next week, whatever. But with Ben, *nada*. I'd heard mates, men and women, call him a decent guy. I guess they meant he never drank too much, never yelled, never did any crazy shit that left someone out of pocket or upset. But he never said what he meant, either, which means he's either a compulsive liar or a total dick. I don't think he's got enough imagination to lie.

I didn't seek her out but when she got in touch I agreed to meet up with her at a place we'd wasted too many nights, back in the day. I didn't tell anyone, not that it was any of their fucking business, I wanted to hear it from her, whatever it was, her story I mean. I was nervous. It had been a couple of years, and we weren't the kind to 'keep in touch' over Facebook or whatever, what a joke.

I came a half hour early and tucked away a bourbon. As I waited I remember thinking that I didn't know what would be worse—that she'd be a complete bitch and do nothing but complain about Ben, or that she'd somehow have become like him, an ice queen. I'd tried not to think about her those last years, she'd made her decision, I expected to hear about kids and if I had, maybe I'd have come home sooner, or maybe stayed away forever. But it wasn't like that, she was neither of the things that worried me most, and in a way that was worse.

She smiled when she saw me, kind of sadly. She was wearing jeans and a shirt, not dressed up, and she was still incredible, just older. There were lines around her mouth I'd never noticed before, a groove between her eyes even when her face was still, like she was thinking about something difficult.

She told me she was sorry about Ben, and sorry for my family, especially Mum. It was her decision, she said, Ben didn't do anything wrong. She was sorry, not that she'd married him, just that she'd married. She was so young, too young, what did she know? She hadn't thought it through and she was sorry for being stupid, wasting Ben's time, wanted to make a clean break before kids came along and made it a whole lot worse.

I understood, I told her so. Told her that's what your twenties are for, right? No hard feelings.

But that wasn't all.

'It's not okay,' she said. 'It was a big mistake.' She took a deep breath, looked me in the eye, and I felt something shift in my guts. I needed a shit. 'It should have been you. It's always been you. I thought Ben was like the grown-up version of you.' She laughed, hard and sharp.

I didn't look away, but she did. Apologised again, and left. 'Here's my number,' she said. 'I'd like it if we could be friends, though I understand if that's not possible.'

Things moved pretty quickly after that. I got in touch and told her how I felt. We decided to keep it a secret at first, for our families' sake. Frankie was embarrassed, whereas I felt like justice had been done, everything coming together. It had always been Frankie, and now here I was, here she was, I was working in Australia and about to turn thirty-three.

Frankie was living in a shitty apartment since she'd moved out of her and Ben's place, so we spent a lot of time at mine, which was big and new. Gradually she made it more comfortable. I'd not really thought about how long I'd stay there and had rented it unseen. It was the right price and the right postcode. I could see what was going on, nesting I guess, and part of me liked it, wanted it. Suddenly there were cushions and rugs everywhere and we fucked on each one. I felt like a king, couldn't imagine wanting anything else. If there was a small part of me where alarm bells were ringing I drowned them out at the Prince on Friday nights.

She got pregnant and 'moved in', a technical distinction she insisted on though we saw each other just as much and all the stuff she cared about was already in my house. She insisted we tell our families and I agreed. I went to see Ben first, took him a bottle of the scotch he likes. I said my piece and ended with, 'You can't go silent on me, mate, don't do what you normally do. I know this is a big deal so if you feel angry say it to my face, right now.'

'No, it's okay,' he said. 'I always knew. I'm happy for both of you.'

Mum cried and just kept saying, 'Oh Adam! Oh Adam,' and I didn't know whether she was angry with me for hurting Ben or happy to be becoming a grandmother.

Until I'd talked to Ben and Mum I couldn't really think about what was happening. I'd never spent so much time with a woman as with Frankie during that period, but that was the point. I'd never done it before. She had.

I thought things were going okay but one time I fucked up. We were in bed, had just had sex, not the most amazing ever but our regular good thing. I wasn't prepared for it, I think that was the problem.

'I love you.'

I hesitated, stared, held eye contact. That was our language. She smiled, kissed me, said, 'You'll see,' and it passed. I thought it was okay. But her voice kept coming back to me. I couldn't accept that there was only one thing I should have said to her though I knew I'd made a mistake. I wasn't clear on what it meant, I love you, and I felt frustrated that there weren't other words in between 'like' and 'love'. I knew 'like' was inadequate for what I felt. But 'love' was an absolute, a risky move, a no-way-back kind of thing. Was that what this was?

Over time I came to think so, and as Frankie got closer

to giving birth and we weren't fucking so much as in the beginning, I started to tell her I loved her, occasionally at first and then all the time. She smiled, sometimes she said it back, but it was never like that first time, when I missed my cue.

She didn't come back from her mum's, said she needed the support and I was at work all day. That pissed me off, because I was saving a lot of money, for us, I thought. I said her mum could come over to my place; our place, I meant, but that just made her go off again.

'What do you want?' I asked her. 'Just say it. I'll do it.'

'I'm not sure,' she said.

'Do you want the baby?'

'Of course! How can you even ask that?'

I didn't ask the next question because I was afraid of the answer.

She stayed at her mum's; I kept going to Beer-n-Bubs, and tried to drop stuff casually into our conversations on the phone so that she knew I was ready. 'When you go into transition…' stuff like that. I was sick of dancing round so once I said, 'Look Frankie, do you want me there or not? I'm doing this course, do you even want me to be your birth partner?'

'Yeah…' she said, in a way that made it sound like 'no'.

We worked out a plan, she'd call me when it started and I'd come and collect her from her mum's, unless it was an emergency and then we'd meet at the hospital. I felt ready.

It turned out I wasn't. Frankie went into labour at three am. I picked her up and we went in together. I got her started on the exercises, the breathing and stuff. Eight hours later nothing much had changed and she was exhausted, just fucked, and I was starting to worry. The nurses said it wasn't unusual, her first child. Perhaps a walk in the park across the road? Yeah, right.

By three in the afternoon things were moving faster, she was fully dilated and finally getting some proper attention, midwife on one side, me on the other, her yelling and me just holding, pushing, whatever they told me to do. I'm not sure what happened, I was looking at her face the whole time, seeking out her eyes, sending her the message I was here and I'd be doing it for her if I could. But at some point more people came in and I was pushed aside, then out of the room. Emergency C-section, they said. You can stand here, behind this, they said. Frankie was pulled around like meat on a hook, there was blood everywhere, a fucking train wreck. Nothing beautiful about it.

When they got it out and passed it to me it took a few seconds, at least, for my arms to work. Like I'd forgotten there was a baby involved. Frankie had been cut open and half her insides pulled out, it seemed, and now she was being put back together. I leaned against the wall, they pushed me into a chair. I looked at it, purple skin smeared with white, vernix, that was, and piles of slimy dark hair on top. I looked at Frankie and this time she didn't look away. She was talking but it took me ages to understand.

'Is she alright? Is she alright?'

I looked at the thing in my arms and cried like a baby.

THE SILVER SANDWICH NIGHT

JANEY RUNCI

I lived once in a house that backed onto a school. Just a small school, and a small house. I was newly married at the time, it was the 1970s and although the house was only rented it felt like my own little realm, my first one, apart from a corner of a bedroom I'd shared with my sisters, and then a dormitory with boarding school girls. I know it is said that some women marry a house, and although I would have found that statement puzzling and even offensive at the time, I can see now that I was in love with that house.

It was really only half of a whole house, what's called a semi-detached. This meant that if you could have cut it down the centre like an apple there would have been laid open two identical houses. But the two halves were joined by a solid brick wall. On each side of the wall a short passage went through to the kitchen with two doors to bedrooms on the way.

I came to know the distinctive footfalls of my neighbours. The woman wore loose slippers that shuffled along the floor to the kitchen in the morning to prepare food for her husband and son. Later when she left for work her high heels tapped along as if in eager expectation of the day outside. The son who was aged about ten often went barefoot in the house, his bare feet slapping on the boards and nearly always running. His father's footsteps were measured, but not his hands. He banged his hands on the wall when he was angry.

'We're hardly detached,' I said to my husband.

'What?'

'You know how they call it semi-detached.'

'Oh yes.'

He was tired in those days, working long hours.

.

In order to recreate some of the more idyllic aspects of our courtship I decided one day to clear a space in the back yard and fashion what I thought of as an outdoor area where we could cook and eat on warm evenings.

The back yard was a narrow strip of land bisected by a concrete path leading to an incinerator at the back fence. On the left side of the path a succession of leaning sheds housed the laundry and the toilet and what had once been a woodshed. On the right side there was a sprawling lemon tree, unpruned for years, and various other shrubby plants and weeds.

I began by clearing a space under the lemon tree. Apart from weeds and rubbish I uncovered a packing case that made an outdoor table and some old bricks for a barbecue. I removed a rack from the oven in the kitchen for the grill.

With the help of kerosene on the fire and a glass of wine from a cask for myself I managed to coax a small fire into being by the time my husband arrived home. We sat there feeding the fire with dead twigs we snapped from the unpruned lemon tree and drinking wine. Eventually we ate the charred and half-cooked chops and the potatoes that were still hard in the middle and we laughed about this.

Just as we were about to go inside, right beside us was a scrabbling sound. I grabbed my husband's arm but he just pointed. There on the fence were two bright eyes. A possum. My husband put a piece of apple on the railings of the fence. The possum moved warily, and then boldly to take the apple. It sat there then, nibbling.

We sipped our wine and watched and talked quietly, and I thought at the time that I was very happy and that that would continue.

When I think back to the semi-detached house in the 1970s the first thing that comes to mind is the animal life.

Apart from the usual cats and dogs that roamed fairly freely in those days, there was the possum we saw that night, and later I saw its mate and their young.

A lizard lived somewhere in the wall between the laundry and the toilet. Sometimes when I sat on the toilet seat it would appear between me and the door, its small pointed head raised, its tongue moving in and out. The boy next door said he had once seen a black snake in our woodshed. I never opened that door and I never saw the snake.

I first saw the rats along the back fence near the incinerator. It was usual in those days to burn parcels of rubbish in an incinerator and I found this soothing, especially with the sound of the school children calling and playing on the other side of the fence. I had just tipped in the rubbish and applied a match when I saw something moving on the ground beside me. And then something else. Rats. I stepped back and just as I did something came through the air and landed at my feet. A half-eaten sandwich. One of the rats darted forward and tried to drag the sandwich away. A banana, gone a bit brown, came over next. The children were laughing, egging each other on. I saw then, that in the long grass and weeds lining the fence there were many items of food in various stages of decay.

'Stop it!' I called.

There was silence on the other side of the fence, and then whispering.

'You should eat your lunches,' I said.

The children were quiet. Perhaps they'd moved off from the fence, and then I wished I'd told them about the time I'd stuffed my own unwanted school sandwich into a hedge I passed on the way to school. I began to fashion a story about that, about fish paste sandwiches, about not knowing that fish paste would reveal itself no matter how invisible it seemed in the thick foliage of the hedge. There was the owner of the house with the hedge, the fingers of one hand dangling the stinking sandwich, the other hand firmly gripping the scruff of my dress and dragging me home.

I hauled myself up on the fence and peered over. There was only one girl, about nine years old, in a narrow passage, sunless and silent, at the side of the school. The others had gone. The girl had an open lunch box in her hands.

'Were you getting rid of your lunch?' I smiled and spoke in as friendly a voice as I could, but the girl just stared back at me. I wasn't sure if she'd been crying.

'Are you alright?' I said.

For a moment her eyes flickered and I thought she was going to tell me something, but then she turned and walked slowly towards the large playground.

The landlord came unexpectedly the next day for an inspection. He paused as he stepped from the kitchen into the back yard. He tipped his head, sniffed.

'Fire?' he said.

'Pardon?'

I was behind him, still in the kitchen, and at that time the smell of rats from the unused kitchen chimney was all that I could detect. Outside the air was fresh from the recent rain.

'Perhaps the incinerator?' I said.

He stepped forward, into the weedy long grass that had grown up again under the lemon tree. He moved the grass aside with his foot. I had all but forgotten the old cooking spot we'd made back in the summer, but now I could smell the charred odour that must have been released by the rain.

'Just a little barbecue,' I said.

'You could have burned my house down!'

Grass had grown up through the bricks and feathered over the rack. I froze. It was the rack from the stove in the kitchen, but the landlord didn't seem to realise.

'There are rats in the roof,' I said, partly to distract him. Sometimes I lay in bed listening to them pattering over the ceiling. When I got up for a glass of water their smell filled the kitchen.

'You must be leaving rubbish out.'

'No.' I pointed to the back fence. 'The school children throw their lunches over.'

'Clean it up,' the landlord said. 'Okay?'

As soon as the landlord left I went down to the back fence and poked among the rubbish in the wet grass. There were orange peels and ice cream sticks that had survived the rats and the rain, and various bits of sodden paper and indistinguishable items of rotting food, but nothing that was clearly a recent sandwich.

A sound came from the schoolyard and I climbed quickly on the cross beam of the fence. A man with a bucket was walking past.

'Children all gone?' I said.

He didn't answer, only looked at his watch. Of course they were all gone. It was early evening.

'I'd better keep moving,' I said, as though he was the one who'd been talking and I was the one with the bucket, on my way to do some useful task, instead of looking for children in an empty playground, or searching for a sandwich that would already have passed through the digestive tract of a rat.

The man nodded and turned to go. I ducked my head behind the fence and waited for his footsteps to move on and then I raised my head again. He was almost at the big playground but he was twisted right around, watching. I gave a little wave and climbed down from the fence.

Just after this I heard something about a silver sandwich, and later I came to call that night the silver sandwich night. It happened like this.

My husband had suggested we have a man he'd met through work and the man's wife over to our house. My husband was keen for me to befriend this woman, to play tennis with her, even though I had no racquet and I'd never played tennis in my life. He often had to work on the weekends by then. The woman had invited me to go to her club the next weekend. The thought made me sweat with fear.

We'd had a meal together before, at a pizza café, and I had been shy, found it hard to make conversation, but my husband said it would be different in our own house. I had a couple of preparatory drinks before they arrived. I planned to tell amusing stories about the wildlife in our back yard.

The conversation dragged. The other couple had come to the city a year before us. They were buying a house. They spent their Sundays visiting display homes and new housing estates. That was what they talked about in the beginning, but at some stage the man stood up, said he needed to stretch his legs. I thought he was going outside to the toilet.

'Watch out for possums,' I said. 'Plus lizards, snakes and rats. The school children throw their sandwiches over the fence.'

The man leant over my chair and smiled.

'Urban wildlife,' he said, and my husband and the tennis woman laughed.

I was ready with the sandwich in the hedge story, but it was then that the tennis woman said she'd just remembered something about a sandwich, a silver sandwich.

'Silver?' I said.

The woman wore a deep red lipstick that night and some of it had smudged on her teeth so that as she smiled her mouth seemed full of blood. I had to turn away.

A silver sandwich? To bite into silver. I shuddered. It would have to be silver foil, a layer of thin foil between the slices of bread, and then the sharp dagger of pain through the teeth, through the nerves to the brain, the body pinioned by this pain.

'How awful!' I said.

The woman shrugged. 'It was just that cheese that used to come in foil. A bit got caught in the cheese.'

Her husband smiled fondly. Even my husband smiled.

'It felt odd,' she said. 'And I remember saying to my classmates that I had a silver sandwich. They all thought it was funny.'

I waited, but it seemed that was all. My husband was still smiling at the woman.

'Let's move over to the comfortable chairs,' he said.

It was as though we were in a ballet then, our moves pre-ordained, choreographed. My husband took the woman's arm, they rose from their chairs, glided to the couch. The man rested his hand on my shoulder and then moved it smoothly to my cheek, held it there. Gentle in one way, but firm as well. It was as though I was a beat behind, a whole bar behind in following the music, the steps. His face came down, his lips seeking mine.

Even now, so many years later, I cannot say I was not stirred by that softest of kisses, and I let my head drop back slightly, opened my lips wider to take his seeking tongue. There were murmurings from behind us where my husband and the tennis woman were on the couch. I put my hands up to cup the man's face.

'You're good,' the man whispered when we first took breath, but I didn't want him to stop, and then I heard the music. Just a strain first, so faint that I thought it might be from next door, stringed instruments, but then more insistent, growing, expanding in a way that I knew and loved. The music was the soundtrack from a film my husband and I had seen when we were courting. I'd chosen it especially for that night, to give myself courage.

I pushed back from the man.

'What's wrong?' he said.

My husband stirred from where he was on the couch, the tennis woman on his knee, her blouse undone, his face rising from her breast, his eyes glazed with that look I knew so well.

'What's happening?' I said.

I ran out into the night and locked myself in the toilet. By the time I went back inside the tennis woman and her husband had gone.

As might be expected my husband and I argued that night. He was placatory at first, said I was new to the city and had led a sheltered life. The man and his wife had been concerned for me.

'I thought we were happy,' I said.

'We are. But we can have friends.'

'I don't want that tennis woman as a friend.'

'I wish you wouldn't call her that.'

I threw something then, hard against the wall that divided our house from the identical one next door. My husband grabbed my hand. 'Stop it!' he whispered.

'That stupid story she told, about the silver sandwich.'

My husband frowned. 'What?'

'You thought it was funny,' I said. 'That's when it started, when you all started…'

I couldn't continue, couldn't find the words. I pulled my hand away.

'Don't be ridiculous!' my husband said. 'It started before then. Don't pretend you didn't know. When I said we could have them to the house you agreed.' He paused. 'And you seemed to like it, anyway.'

A sound came out of me then, a wail, as I ran up the passage. My husband came after me and his large hand went over my mouth and I let that happen. I didn't struggle. What was the point?

My husband worked longer and longer hours after that night, and some nights a phone call came, summoning him to fix something immediately.

Gradually I became used to the nights on my own. The rats in the roof kept me company, and the sounds of my neighbours on the other side of the wall. Sometimes I sat on the floor of the passage in the dark, my head pressed against the wall just to hear the sound of their radio, their voices speaking softly in their own language.

I knew the rhythms of their lives and I knew when the man's voice became more clipped, his wife's more wheedling and then the boy running and the hand banging on the wall and the gasps from the woman. She never ran. Why didn't she run like the boy? But the father always cornered him in the back yard that was the mirror image of mine. The boy would wail as he was beaten and then suddenly go silent.

Sometimes I saw the woman and the boy the morning after. We greeted each other in the usual way. Perhaps a slight sign passed between us, a momentary locking of a line of vision, and then a blink, a shift, an agreement to say nothing about what we each heard from the other side of the wall.

Around that time my husband called the rat man. The rat man closed gaps, leaving only one, and set baits. He said the rats would swallow the baits and this would bring on unbearable thirst. They would leave the house to find water. We could expect to see dead rats in the drains. Once we'd seen one we were to call him and he would come to close the last gap.

The rats died their agonising deaths, the rat man came as promised and closed the last gap. My husband thanked him.

The rat man shrugged. 'They'll find another way in,' he said. 'It's only a matter of time.'

I left that house shortly after.

CROSSING THE LINE

RITA TOGNINI

'What time is it now?' Nina asked for the third time since they had come on deck.

'Just after three,' Adele replied.

'Another three hours before we disembark in this—Fremantle.'

'At least,' Adele said. 'You heard the steward at lunch. Probably sometime after dinner.'

'This low, grey sky, I hate it. I wish the ship would start to move.' Nina pushed herself against the rail as if the liner only needed her weight to set it in motion.

'Why don't you go down to the cabin,' Adele said, stroking Nina's shoulder. 'Try to have a nap. We'll be up late tonight.'

'Might as well. Promise you'll come down soon.'

'Promise.'

Adele watched Nina cross the deck and disappear down the companionway. She turned back to the port with its low slung, tin-roofed wooden buildings. How different it was from her hometown of Trieste, with its fine, old limestone buildings. She sighed and tried not to feel disappointed.

'Old-fashioned' was how Adele saw Nina when she first appeared at the cabin door almost a month ago. Her dark hair was braided into two heavy plaits and wrapped around her head. She wore a dark blue, long-sleeved dress with a white lace collar, carried a grey coat over her left arm and a small suitcase in her right hand. *So she's my cabin mate*, Adele thought, propping herself up on her elbows.

'I think this is my cabin. 76B.' Nina's voice was tentative.

Adele sat upright and swung around so her legs dangled over the bunk. 'Yes, that's right. Come in, I'm Adele.'

'Nina,' the young woman responded, stepping inside the cabin.

'The bottom bunk is yours, as you've probably worked out.'

Nina placed her coat at the foot of the bunk and her suitcase next to it. 'I think I'll lie down for a while,' she said in a small voice. 'I'm tired.'

They lay on their bunks. The engine throbbed and the sea slapped against the ship. Snatches of *Vola, colomba bianca, vola*[1] drifted down from the main deck. Adele wished they wouldn't go on playing it. It always made her feel tearful. She listened carefully for any sniffles from Nina, but heard only her breathing.

Nina spoke first. 'I'm going to Australia to join my husband. And you?'

'Yes, me too. Well, sort of.'

---

1 *Fly away, white dove, fly*, a love song, was the winner of the San Remo Festival in 1952.

'Sort of?'

'We were married by proxy.'

'So, have you met him—like in person?'

'No—that'll happen when we get to Fremantle.'

'How did you get to know him?'

'A friend of mine gave me his address and suggested I write. I thought, well why not?'

'And one thing led to another and now you're getting properly married. That's very romantic.'

The next day they showed each other photographs.

'This is Claudio,' Nina said, carefully taking a large silver-framed photo from its velvet cover and holding it up. 'We're from the same village. Edolo. You probably haven't heard of it. It's in the mountains near Switzerland.'

Adele gazed at a dark-haired young man with a prominent brow, large eyes and a sensitive mouth. 'He's very handsome.'

'Yes. It was taken just before he left, almost three years ago now.' Nina placed the photo on the table next to the bunk, facing her pillow.

Adele took the small photo Sam had sent her in his last letter from her purse. He was posing in front of a palm tree with a group of mates. 'I'm the handsome one in the middle,' he had scrawled on the back.

Adele's finger hovered above the man at the centre of the group. 'This is Sam.'

Nina peered intently at the photo. 'How long have you been writing to him?'

'About a year and a half.'

'But—well, what if you find you don't really like him when you meet?'

'I hope that won't happen.' Adele put the photo back in her purse. 'Claudio might have changed too, you know,' she said. 'Three years is quite a long time.'

Nina looked panicky for an instant. Then she said firmly, 'No. I don't think he's changed. He's always been—how can I put it—very solid.'

'How can you be sure?'

'For one thing, he still wants me to keep these.' Nina sat on the bunk and unpinned her plaits. They hung long and heavy down to her breasts.

'I'd decided to cut my hair before I left,' Nina said. 'Everyone was telling me it was going to be so hot in Australia and there wasn't much water. I thought short hair would be more sensible, and easier to manage. I wrote to Claudio suggesting this. He wrote back saying no, and asked me to promise I wouldn't cut it short.'

'Did you?'

'Yes…and no.'

'Yes and no?'

'I wrote a letter promising not to—'

'And?'

'I was really busy.' Nina pulled her plaits together under her chin, tied them together. 'I didn't get around to posting it.'

At Port Said, Adele, Nina and a group of other passengers went ashore with Don Tarcisio Perego as their guide. He was travelling to Sydney, to a parish where many Italians had settled.

'A priest shouldn't go around like that, wearing only his bathers,' Nina had whispered to Adele the first time she'd seen him strolling along the deck on the way to the swimming pool, stopping to chat to everyone. 'It's not respectful to God.'

'What should he be wearing, then?' Adele had asked. 'His soutane?'

'No—but he could wrap the towel around his chest, at least when he's talking to women. You can see all the hairs.'

'He's going for a swim, Nina.'

'He should be properly covered up—wear a dressing gown or something. And when he gets in the pool, he'll be parading his backside to the public, won't he? My mother would be horrified.'

'Even though it's well covered?

'Yes, even then.'

For their Port Said excursion Don Tarcisio wore his soutane, and his biretta as well. Adele noticed that Marco, a young man who had come on board in Naples, made sure he was close to Nina as they lined up for the motorboat taking them from the ship to the Suez Canal Authority building.

'Don Tarcisio,' Marco called when they were all settled in the boat, with Marco sitting next to Nina. 'You're going to be hot in those heavy clothes. And that biretta doesn't give you much shade.'

'My son, we're going among Muslims, as you know.' He brought the cross that he wore around his neck to his lips and kissed it. 'It's important that I bear witness to Christ.'

'Or just make a point, because Nasser is threatening to take over the Canal,' Marco replied and smiled at Nina. The motor was revved up and the boat swung away from the ship, towards the port.

'What did you say, my son?' Don Tarcisio shouted. But the noise and the blustery breeze made conversation impossible and they all sat silent, watching the approaching shore.

Once disembarked at the Canal Authority building, Don Tarcisio tried to persuade the group to walk to the end of a long jetty to see the statue of the French engineer who had designed the Canal. Ferdinand de something—Adele didn't catch his surname. But the group didn't share Don Tarcisio's passion for monuments and they headed for the city and markets. Adele and Nina wandered about arm-in-arm, excited by stalls selling unfamiliar fruits, vegetables and sweets, sparkling trinkets and brilliantly embroidered fabrics. The stallholders, all men, wore loose, long robes and held out their goods, beckoning them to buy. Adele bought bananas and oranges and Nina purchased two cushion covers with desert scenes, oases and camels, bordered in silver thread. Later, they sat in a café and sipped iced tea. Marco appeared and asked if he could join them.

Nina's face, already pink from the heat, turned even pinker. 'Oh yes, do please.'

Adele watched Marco as he settled in his chair. 'Marco, you've lived in Australia for a couple of years, right?' she asked, hoping that if she watched and listened to him carefully, she'd find out some of those things about Sam that she didn't know.

'Yes. My uncle migrated there in the thirties. After the war jobs were scarce at home. I'd just finished my mechanic's apprenticeship when he wrote saying there was a job for me in his garage in Fremantle—if I wanted it. I packed my cases straight away. My mother was against me going, so I promised to come home after a couple of years.'

'And she couldn't persuade you to stay there?'

'She tried very hard. Wanted me to get married. But, I'm not ready to settle down. I really liked Australia. I wanted to come back.'

'Tell us about it,' Nina begged. 'Are there wild animals, crocodiles?'

'Yes.'

Nina looked horrified.

'But only in the zoo—in Perth at least,' he added, grinning.

Adele smiled and Nina laughed. 'Is it as hot as here?' Nina lifted the heavy skein of hair tied loosely at the nape of her neck and patted the skin with a handkerchief.

'Hotter—sometimes.'

'I'll just have to do something about this hair, then.'

'Let me see—just turn to the left.' Marco studied Nina's profile with mock seriousness. 'Yes, short hair would definitely suit you.'

'You really think so?'

'Would I lie?'

Nina laughed. 'Claudio, my husband, doesn't want me to, though.'

'But if you do it on the ship—'

'Look, isn't that Don Tarcisio across there, waving?' Adele interrupted. 'I think he wants us to head back.'

Nina cut her hair the day the ship crossed the equator. She asked Adele to go with her to the hairdresser and help her choose a style. Adele suggested a gamine, Audrey Hepburn crop.

'Excellent advice.' The hairdresser held the length of Nina's hair in his hands. 'So beautiful,' he murmured. 'Could I suggest, madam, that I make two plaits and cut them off whole—so you have a memento—for your husband maybe.'

Nina looked uncertain. 'We don't want to be late for lunch. The steward said that's when we're going to cross the equator.'

'It won't take a minute, madam. And I'll put the plaits in a nice box for you.'

'Alright then, thank you.'

The first course had already been served when Adele and Nina finally arrived in the dining room. As they sat down there were cries of, 'Nina, you've cut your hair,' and, 'Oh Nina, you look wonderful. So modern.'

Marco walked over to Nina and took her hands. 'Nina, you look—astonishing,' then bent and kissed them. Nina blushed but looked happy.

'The celebrations this afternoon,' Adele asked Marco. 'Tell us what happens.'

'It's an old tradition. Sailors crossing the equator for the first time had to be presented to Neptune, King of the Sea.' Marco responded. 'The captain dressed up as Neptune and the new hands were given a drubbing by the crew, before being thrown overboard. It was pretty rough.'

'And now?'

'It's entertainment for the passengers. Everyone dresses up and passengers can be presented too. In case you're worried, people just get tipped into the pool. I hope you're all coming to watch,' Marco urged, looking at Nina.

As Nina opened her mouth to reply, the ship's horn boomed several times. 'We're crossing!' the steward announced.

Everyone at the table stood up, cheered, hugged and kissed fellow passengers, then toasted the new hemisphere. And after, led by Marco, Nina's new hairdo.

After lunch, Adele, Nina and Marco found deck chairs close to the swimming pool. Vola, colomba bianca, vola, which was playing over the loud speakers as usual, suddenly stopped.

'Hooray!' Nina shouted. 'I don't think I want to hear that song again—ever. Even if it is Claudio's favourite.'

There was a drum roll and King Neptune strode out on deck, holding his trident. Wearing a false beard, crown, white toga and red mantle, Neptune still looked remarkably like the captain. He walked to the pool's edge, followed by a hairy-legged Persephone in a yellow wig and a grass skirt. Neptune sat on his throne.

Two new crewmembers were dragged before Neptune and Persephone. Their hair, face, chest and limbs were lathered with soap and shaved with outsized razors. Then they were tipped into the pool.

'It's Don Tarcisio,' Nina cried when a stocky man wearing large black bathers tied high above his generous waist was one of the passengers presented to Neptune. He screamed and shouted melodramatically for divine intervention to rescue him from his 'ordeal'. Nina laughed helplessly at his antics, and at the huge splash he made when he landed in the water.

Marco had been invited to a 'crossing the line' party and insisted that Adele and Nina join him. There was a band and dancing. Don Tarcisio was there too, with the captain's party. To Adele's surprise, Nina waved to him and smiled.

At first, Nina was hesitant about dancing with Marco. Once on the dance floor and relaxing in his arms, she beamed with pleasure. Watching them, Adele realised she didn't know if Sam liked to dance or not. There was quite a lot she didn't know about him.

'I'll be joining you—in a while,' Nina had called from the dance floor when, not long after midnight, Adele signalled that she was off to bed.

'Don't worry, she's in safe hands,' Marco added, his arm firmly around Nina's waist. They looked at each other and laughed.

Adele was woken by what seemed to be a heaving and pitching of her bunk. She lay still, trying to remember where she was. This must be the storm the captain had said they'd run into beyond the equator, she thought. She peered over the edge of the bunk. Nina's was empty. She had the cabin and the storm all to herself.

Nina's having a good time with Marco, Adele thought. 'In good hands,' as he had quipped. Somewhere, far below the cabin, the engines strained against the waves that rose ever higher around the ship. Adele dozed. A sound of retching brought her back to wakefulness. Adele levered herself down from her bunk with care. She saw Nina bending over the basin in the bathroom and put her hand to her mouth as she inhaled a sweetish, sickly odour.

'Nina,' she called softly.

Nina turned around and burst into tears.

'I've been sick and the basin is all blocked. Oh, this is disgusting. I'm sorry.'

Adele wiped Nina's face with a towel and steered her back

to her bunk. 'Lie down, Nina. You'll feel better.'

'Stay with me,' Nina begged. Adele lay next to Nina on the bunk. Nina was crying quietly.

'Don't worry about being sick. They'll clean it up later.'

'It's not that. It's Marco. It all happened so quickly. I didn't mean to let him go that far. But he was so sweet.'

Adele lay silent.

'And Claudio? What will I say to Claudio?'

Adele held Nina tight. 'Nothing,' she whispered. 'In a few days you'll be arriving in Fremantle. Claudio will be there and you'll start your new life.'

'Nothing?'

Adele held Nina's face close and kissed her cheek. 'Nothing.'

It was dark, and a fine rain was falling when the ship finally docked. As the ship edged to the wharf, there were tentative waves from individuals in the crowd gathered in the best-lit area below.

'I hope Claudio's there.' Nina pressed against the railing

Adele squeezed Nina's hand. 'Of course he'll be there.'

And Sam too, Adele told herself.

A heavy man with a tanned face and black hair combed back from his temples seemed to be waving in their direction.

'Look Nina, down there. Isn't that Claudio?'

'No,' Nina replied irritably. 'He's too dark. And fat.'

Everyone in Australia is tanned, Adele was going to say, when the man started waving energetically and shouting, 'Nina, Nina. Here!'

TWO MINUTES

C. J. MCLEAN

He arrived two minutes late. Dressed in a plaid shirt and torn jeans, he wasn't a vision of beauty by any means. He was pretty ordinary, all things considered—a huge lanky thing really—and in any other situation Tony wouldn't have looked twice at him. But their destinies had become entwined from the moment they'd matched on Tinder, and cemented by the fact that as he crossed the street to meet Tony he was flattened by an eighteen-tonne bus.

Tony didn't move. The suddenness of the event—the accident, or *death?*—seemed to make time stop too. He searched the street for another soul but found no one. And all he could think was *oh god, who do I call? What do I do? I can't…I can't even remember his name. What the hell was his name?*

Keegan arrived two minutes early. Tony liked that. Dressed in the same plaid shirt as his Tinder profile, he looked every bit as delectable as he'd hoped. There was something about him—maybe in the cheeky grin he gave and the way he wiggled his fingers at him as he crossed the street. He quickly checked the traffic before jogging across to him.

'Tony?' he asked.

'You know it's me, you twat. Lovely to meet you.' Tony pulled him into a massive bear hug, and Keegan responded by gripping him back tightly.

'It's good to meet you too!' he gasped when Tony let go. 'That's a really confident greeting.'

'I think it probably pays to be confident straight off the bat. Helps do away with any potential awkward moments.'

'What, like if I got flattened by a bus or something?'

'I mean, maybe. Oh look!'

Tony pointed down the street at the approaching 541 bus.

'I think that's your cue to jump?'

'Jump out of the way kid!' the paramedic bellowed in Tony's ear, pushing him against a metal cabinet. The tiny doors swung open and band-aids cascaded all over him. Tony rubbed the sore spot on his shoulder, trying not to look at the supine body of his date on the gurney.

He was like a piece of paper that had been crushed by a fist. His bulky frame was curled and bloodied, his wrists wound into themselves, his legs wrapped underneath him. The other paramedic tried to stem the bleeding, working calmly while his colleague rushed about, falling to the floor every time the ambulance violently turned a corner.

'What was your relationship to him, mate?' the calm one asked Tony.

'I...'

'Spit it out!' the other one shouted.

Tony sputtered something incoherent. The words couldn't leave him properly, because there were none. He frantically tried to run through any information he might have gleaned from his profile; but nothing came.

'I just met him online.'

'Not too bad for a Tinder date then, hey?' Keegan licked at his ice cream, a playful grin splayed across his face.

'Look—ice cream, hot guy, who can complain?' Tony joked. 'Ooh look! Ducks!'

They'd walked all around the park, finally coming to the edge of a great, deep pond at its centre. Close to the banks, a mother duck paddled lazily across the surface, trailed by five bizarrely fluffy chicks.

'They're so adorable aren't they?' Tony cooed, kneeling down by the water.

'Too cute.' Keegan licked his ice cream and looked away.

'I love ducks.'

'Hmm? Oh yeah, me too.' He patted Tony's back. 'What do you want to do now?'

'I don't know.' Tony straightened up and, as boldly as ever, took Keegan's hand. 'Let's just see where the day takes us?'

'You've got no plans then?' he joked.

'Nope. It's more fun that way though, yeah?'

'Agreed.' Keegan flashed his dopey grin again and Tony melted a little inside. 'Once more 'round the park?'

Tony wasn't family, so when the paramedics rushed his date through into the emergency ward he was roughly held back and told to wait if he wanted. Blood was coursing through his body, and he found himself cursing the attendant, about to kick a chair over before he stopped himself. He was worked up, that much was sure—the high-speed ambulance drive had set his adrenaline going, but now he had nowhere to send that emotion. And for who? Some guy whose name he couldn't even remember?

Some guy. It was cruel, wasn't it—that he was nothing more than a stranger to him, but they'd shared a weirdly intimate moment together. Seeing someone splayed out on the pavement by a bus is not a common sight, and as morbid, as *sick* as the thought was, in Tony's mind he was sure they had shared something special.

He took himself down to a small park, adjacent to the hospital, and sat by the edge of an algae-coated pond. He jiggled his foot impatiently, waiting for his temperament to cool so he could take stock of the situation and decide—leave and pretend this never happened, or wait until he wakes up? But then, that wasn't even a guarantee. Before that, then, Tony decided to wait and see if he lived.

'Stop it!'

'Make me.'

'I'll scream.'

'Would it be the first time?'

'Give it here!'

Tony chucked the box marked 'Wine Glasses' he'd been dangling out of the second story window at Keegan. He leapt forward and grabbed the box with two hands. Tony chuckled and made to throw another box at him, but he disappeared behind the door and shouted, 'Can you take this seriously please?'

The removalists were late arriving, so they were two hours behind Keegan's immaculately planned schedule. While he directed which boxes were to go to which rooms in the house, Tony joked with the movers and wound Keegan up. Later, as Tony was sharing a joint with both of them behind the water tank, he revealed they'd only been together seven months. They exclaimed in genuine surprise; they could have sworn they'd been together five, six years old at least.

'Nope,' Tony said handing the joint back as he let out an immaculate cough, 'but it feels like it sometimes.'

Once the movers had gone and all they were left with were boxes covering all of Tony's furniture, they made love on the living room rug. It was more passionate than ever before; something about the newness of the situation, the prospect of a life properly shared. At least that was what Keegan had garbled afterwards. They started to make plans—about when their parents would come and see their new life together, when they would have the housewarming, when they'd have to expect…but maybe those plans were a little *too* much to think about. Tony stroked his chest, wrapped up with a blanket he'd pulled out of a nearby box.

'That's what we have to look forward to,' Keegan sweetly whispered in Tony's ear. 'We'll be closer together than ever.'

Tony circled some of Keegan's chest hairs with his finger, and felt a pang as he thought about how menacing that sentence could have sounded.

Tony visited once every month. It was all he could stomach.

He had become quite pally with the receptionists, and every time he visited they stopped him on his way out to talk for at least an hour. Two, if Bill was on. The young man had even asked him out, quite matter-of-factly after Tony had come back from sitting with Keegan all day. Tony politely refused, and Bill teased that he was saving himself for someone else.

It had been seven months since the accident. In all that time, no one else had come to visit Keegan. Tony approached the receptionist's desk, not expecting to see any other name next to Keegan's on the visitor's pad. He almost did a double take when he saw 'Jeanne', scrawled in curly script.

'She finally made an appearance,' Bill said.

'Who did?'

'Who do you think? His mother.'

Tony glanced down the corridor towards the open door of Keegan's room. There she was, sitting next to his bed, dressed in a starchy woollen coat and a sequined beanie. Tony had learned months ago from Bill that after they'd identified Keegan and contacted his next of kin—his mother—she'd slammed the phone down immediately upon hearing her son's name.

'Ashamed, my guess is. That her son's a homo.'

'So why's she shown her face now then?' Tony said through gritted teeth.

'Guilt probably. Gets us all in the end, a thousand times over. And it hurts more than what he's going through. At least he gets to sleep through his pain.'

Tony politely knocked on the door to Keegan's room, though he felt she ought to be asking his permission to be let in. She turned, looked directly at him, and quickly looked away as if Tony were the sun.

'You're Keegan's…*friend* then, I suppose.'

Tony's mouth dried. 'I'm…I'm no one. I was just there.'

'Don't worry. They've already filled me in on all that.' Her hand lay still on her son's chest. Tony could see the fine hairs poking through his pyjama shirt. 'I suppose you think I should thank you.'

'No.' Tony sat down on the other side of Keegan.

'Good.'

Tony avoided her gaze, but by the sound of her stifled tears he guessed that Bill was right, and guilt had indeed 'got' her.

Keegan's mother had turned down their offer to dinner, so Tony's new domestic bliss was christened with an awkward double date with his parents.

'How've things been going?' Tony's dad asked Keegan. 'This one hasn't been boring you to death, has he?'

'Dad!' Tony barked.

'I mean, fair's fair Tone.'

'It's been fine,' Keegan said soothingly, placing a hand of truce onto the table between them. 'Your son is surprisingly easy to live with. He doesn't even snore.'

Keegan winked at him, and everyone but Tony laughed. 'I don't snore!' he protested.

'You do!' Tony's dad laughed. 'I could hear it down the hall, nineteen years of it. Oh you should've heard it Keegs…'

Tony starting to rub his neck, visibly squirming in his seat. Keegan straightened up suddenly. 'Why don't we change the subject?' he suggested. He rubbed Tony's thigh pacifyingly, but Tony brushed it off immediately.

Bill watched Tony and Keegan's mother play cards from his desk. They started laughing about something unheard; a secret joke passed between them. They'd been visiting twice every week since their first encounter. Bill shook his head, mildly irritated at the newfound friendship, and returned to his work.

'You love it don't you?'

'What?'

'Making fun of me in front of my parents. You can't get enough of it!'

'Are you hearing yourself? Go to bed Tony, you've drunk way too much tonight—'

'Don't *you* tell me to go to bed, fuck you Keegan!'

'You're looking to pick a fight because you're drunk. If you still feel this way in the morning we can—'

'I'm not gonna stand here and let you talk down to me, like I'm some pathetic fucking kid!'

'Fine.' Keegan threw the dishcloth into the sink and walked out of the kitchen. Tony heard the front door slam and the car start up. Without thinking, he grabbed the nearest bottle of red and sloshed some into a glass. Once he'd drunk it, he smashed the glass down onto the kitchen floor and went to bed. *Let him clean it up in the morning*, he thought.

She wasn't there when he woke up. Tony had fallen asleep on Keegan's bed, his head nuzzled up against his hip, when he felt the slight movement of his hand and bolted upright. A nurse rushed in and checked the equipment by his bed, and called for the attending doctor.

'Is he…?' Tony asked. The nurse just smiled warmly at him and nodded.

Keegan's eyes took a while to open; but when they did, he immediately locked his gaze onto Tony.

'You….' he started.

'Bet you weren't expecting to see me here, were you?' Tony asked thickly. He found tears clotting his vision, brought up from relief—that the man he'd never spoken to while he silently fell in love with him had finally woken up, and that he remembered him, even now.

'Fuck!'

Tony was woken by Keegan's strangled cry from the kitchen—and all of a sudden he remembered the shattered wine glass, and stifled a laugh. 'Tony, you fucker!' Keegan screamed upstairs to him.

When Tony descended, feet clad in thick wellington boots, he found his beloved partner sitting at the dining table, picking glass out of his foot with a pair of tweezers.

'Having fun?' Tony smirked.

'You….' he started. But he stopped himself.

Tony blinked, suddenly unsure. 'I'm sorry. Ok? Sorry. A word you've never heard me use.'

'Sorry won't fix this.'

'No…' Tony slid down the cabinet, pushing glass aside with his boots. 'Let me have a look at it.'

Keegan grudgingly offered up his foot. The sole was bloody and slick with blood. The small shards sparkled in the morning sun; Tony swallowed down a sudden urge to sing 'Diamonds On The Soles Of Her Shoes'.

'It's bad isn't it.' Keegan wasn't asking him; they both knew. He lifted his foot higher, practically shoving the slivers into Tony's face.

'Yes,' he murmured, 'but a Band-Aid—maybe more than one—should do the trick—'

'I don't mean my fucking foot.'

Tony left the hospital with Keegan in a wheelchair. He didn't need it, he was sure, but the hospital staff were insistent. Bill blew a kiss to the pair as they wheeled past his desk. Tony mouthed a quick 'Thank you,' to him; not quite sure what to thank him for, it just seemed appropriate in the moment.

'Thanks for meeting me,' Tony said.

'Sure.' Keegan sat down opposite him, and grimaced at their surroundings. 'Why here though?'

'You don't remember?' Tony gestured out towards the pond, towards the ducks.

'Have we been here before?' Tony let it slide, holding his anger down in the face of Keegan's ignorance. 'Anyway I don't have long, so what's this all about?'

'I…I wanted to see you. To talk. I feel like we've left a lot of things unreso—'

'No.' Keegan's voice was brusque. 'Nothing's unresolved for me. I'm very, very certain we've made the right decision.'

'You did.'

'What?'

'You made the decision. I just had to follow.'

Keegan settled back into the awkward silence.

'You know, in another reality we were probably someone's

idea of a sick joke. Like, let's stick two people together who couldn't be more wrong for each other and see what happens.'

'Couldn't be more wrong—?' Tony arched up. 'Is that what you think?'

'Come on. Don't tell me…what, we were *meant* for each other or something?'

'Maybe, yeah. I felt that, ok? And sure, there were more than a few moments that gave me pause for thought, but I never fucking regretted it, and I *never* wanted it to end. I never regretted you. And if I could have those days back to do it right with someone else, I wouldn't. They'd make *me* worth nothing.'

'What do you mean?'

'I wouldn't be as happy as I am now, if you hadn't broken me so goddamn much and made me realise I deserve so much better than you.'

Keegan was speechless. 'Broke you?'

'In a roundabout way, I guess.'

He slumped against the bench, seething with disbelief. His gaze settled on the ducks, and he suddenly stiffened.

'You love ducks.' He turned to Tony, grinning like a nerve had been pinched inside him.

Tony looked back at him blankly. 'And?'

'What do you want to do now?' Tony asked as they exited the hospital. The park with its little duck pond lay before them.

'I don't know.' Keegan gingerly took Tony's hand. 'Let's just see where the day takes us?'

POMEGRANATE

PHOEBE CANNARD-HIGGINS

We lie on the grass in the park opposite the commission flats. The redbrick walls and grey concrete balconies glare out at us. Pigeons crouch along the window-ledges, their shit splatters beneath them. The sun is warm for once. I watch Lach roll a cigarette with one hand, then chuck me the pouch. I line up the tobacco that looks like pubic hair, lick the paper, roll it in-between my index finger and thumb, run my nail along paper, then lift it to my mouth. Lach reaches out and lights my cigarette for me and we laugh because he knows I hate it when people light my cigarette. In the sky there's a cloud that looks like a flamingo with its head stuck in the sand. Lach starts telling me about his recent trip to Mildura, about the arid land, the Australian bush. He wants to be a botanist.

'*Punica Granatum*,' he says slowly, being careful with the words, 'or Pomegranate.' He leans over to show me a picture on his iPhone. I see a brown and yellow tree, withered, crinkled, and heavy with round red fruit.

'Something mysterious is wiping out all the pomegranate

crops up there. The fruit still goes red but it doesn't mature inside. When you break it open, all the seeds are shrivelled.' He gestures with his hands as if breaking open the fruit, and then rubs his fingers together to symbolise the seeds that disintegrate between them.

For some reason, maybe because I am thinking about the bush, or the shape of his hands, I am reminded of a time on school camp. How we fought on a log that had fallen across a billabong to become a battleground. How when we both fell off, our limbs erect and entangled in each other, when we hit the blackness of the water, the coldness, he had groped my pubescent breast. A sharp sensation, a violent pinch of swollen flesh. As I came up for air he was already swimming away from me, climbing the muddy bank and looking over his shoulder with a smile that said 'prove it'. I don't remember saying anything. But I had forgiven him, for something he never knew how to feel sorry for.

I look up and see Miff crossing the grass with a six-pack under her arm, a beer already open in one hand. She has long runner's legs that stick out of blue denim shorts. I find myself admiring the muscles in her thighs as she strides towards us. The afternoon sun makes her glow.

'Ask, and the universe shall provide,' she says, standing before us and tearing the beers from their cardboard packaging.

'Legend,' I reply. She unties the jacket from around her waist and lays it out on the grass before sitting down.

'So what's up?' Lach's eyes are fixed on her. She takes the cigarette from my fingers and puffs, letting the smoke trail from the corners of her mouth.

'Just telling Anna about Mildura.'

She nods, handing me back the cigarette, 'How was?'

'Yeah good,' Lach is suddenly shy. 'How've you been?'

'Good.'

I let my eyes slide over her because I know that she is lying.

We had been walking up MacArthur Street past Parliament station together; the spot that the Right to Life protesters have claimed as their territory.

'They're so old.' I brought my palms to my cheeks, pushed my skin forward around my mouth and eyes to look like wrinkles. 'Like, don't they just want to live the rest of their lives doing something nice, rather than standing in the freezing cold and protesting this bullshit?'

A woman in a t-shirt that read *Helpers of God's precious infants* waved a sign saying STOP THE ABORTION HOLOCAUST. I rolled my eyes at her. Miff's pace quickened. She seemed uninterested; she was not indulging me in my humour like she normally did.

'Are you okay?'

'Yeah.'

But she kept walking just in front of me so that I couldn't see her face. She walked all the way to the corner of Smith and Johnston Street where she took a seat at the tram stop. I could see she was crying. For two hours we sat there smoking ciggies, watching the day turn into night. The ramen shop illuminated her head from behind. We sat there until it was too cold to sit there and so we walked home and I slept in her bed trying not to say, *but we could raise it together?*

'I was just showing Anna this.' Lach holds out his phone to Miff. She takes the phone and looks at it, expressionless.

'The pomegranates are dying,' he says.

She looks at me with her dark eyes. I look down at my beer, into the bottle. The amber liquid sloshes from side to side. I had sat in her bed trying to figure out how far along you could be to have an abortion without actually using the words abortion or pregnant.

I typed into Google *baby development* and an article came up on the screen. *How big is Your Baby: week-by-week fruit comparisons.*

'Week four,' I read aloud as she lay beside me, 'poppy seed.' She listened silently.

'Week five: peppercorn.' I looked at her trying to gauge a reaction. Was it a poppy seed or a peppercorn? Or neither? How far along was she? What was happening in there? How did she feel? What did she want me to say?

'Week six: pomegranate seed.' She sat up on one elbow to take a closer look at the screen. I waited for a moment, and then went to click the next button but she reached out her hand and softly stopped me. We looked at the small, bulbous pink seeds. I could almost taste them, their juice bursting, splattering on the roof of my mouth.

'I'm a pomegranate seed,' she said, 'I mean, I have.'

'I know what you mean.'

'It's mysterious,' said Lach, draining the rest of his beer and flicking his fringe out of his eyes. 'Anyway, enough about that stuff, it must be boring for you guys. How's Jack going, Anna?' he looks at me with a cheeky smile.

'He's gone,' I say, melodramatically. 'Like all the others.' The truth is I had stopped replying to Jack's messages as soon as I found out Miff was pregnant. He suddenly seemed unimportant. Something inside me had changed, I wasn't sure what exactly, but I knew I didn't want to have sex with him, not at a time like this. I couldn't picture him beside me anymore.

'And you Lachlan, any foibles with women?' he blushes and Miff takes a steep sip of beer. An awkward silence lies stagnant between us. Suddenly I realise who has planted the pomegranate seed in Miff's belly. I wonder if he knows. If she had found the words to tell him, the words she couldn't find with me. If he had paid for half of the operation or if he even knew how expensive it was. If he could even, for one moment, conceptualise what it is like to have something else inside you and moving. What a dick. Best friends don't fuck each other and then fuck off to Mildura for a month to go study dying trees. I hate him.

'You're a prick.'

'What?' he looks surprised and tears another beer from the six-pack. Miff's face is turning red. She doesn't like confrontation.

'You're a bastard. You don't even know what you've done to us.'

Lach's mouth falls open. 'What the fuck?'

'Look at you, so fucking smug.' His face is yellow and blurry.

'What the hell have I done?'

I stand up and brush the grass off the back of my jeans and begin to walk away. I feel the heat in my cheeks. I must keep walking, I tell myself, or everything will fall apart. I imagine an earthquake, the footpath opening up right before me, losing my footing, crashing down through the layers of earth, being pulled under, torn apart until I am only tiny particles at the core of the world—molten rock.

I walk up Nicholson Street, past the tennis courts, through the warm evening and into the Carlton Gardens. The first of the stars become visible against the pink sky; shiny, white dots—half a frosted moon. I pass the three-tiered fountain, remember the time Lach had stumbled drunkenly through the water and climbed to the top of it. I'd taken a photo of him, one hand clinging to the marble breast of a mermaid, one hand waving.

It was me who took Miff to her abortion. Drove her through the peak-hour traffic to the other side of the city. All the other cars on their way into the world, slowly. What was their way? We arrived at a set of green metal gates, passed the dry birdbath standing alone in the middle of the gravel yard. In the waiting room, the TV played some yellow morning show with a blow-waved blonde and a man with a small face. The room was full at eight am, heads turned to the screen. In the corner, an older woman wept silently onto the shoulder of a man. We read the fashion magazines first. Then the food ones. When they still hadn't called Miff's name, I read the paper. Another air strike in Syria. Another car crash in Broad Meadows. Pauline Hanson/Halal Snack Pack/Abbott/ Malcolm/Marijuana as medicine. I fell asleep in the warm sun that came through the window, my head against the waiting room wall, my hand resting on Miff's knee. When I woke up

Miff was being led down the corridor by a nurse, my hand on an empty chair. When she came out I walked her slowly back to the car. Words had been too clumsy to use, and the silence was too unformed. I turned the radio on, and we took comfort in the instant clattering of background noise. Miff was still hazy from the anaesthetic, but she said in a broken voice, as I turned the key in the ignition, 'You're a good friend, An. You're a good friend.' I drove her home and she fell asleep, her head resting heavily on the windowpane. I heard it thud as we turned the corner into her street. It was done. And I had been the one who was there for her, not Lach.

It is getting dark and the bats begin to leave their hiding spots in the trees and fly away, to some other home. There is nothing to do but copy them. I walk home, listening to the clap of their small wings above me. When I get there, I realise I am starving. In the fridge there is an old pizza box with a couple of slices inside. I take it to my room and eat the cold pizza in bed, my back slowly slipping down the wall until I am almost entirely horizontal. My eyelids become heavy, slow. I am still fully clothed under the blankets.

A small tap comes at my window. A familiar sound, made by a familiar long-nailed friend. I open my window and Miff throws one leg over and climbs through, landing heavily beside me on the bed.

'What the fuck?' I can tell she is a bit drunk because one of her eyes is lazy.

I pull the doona up to my chin, ignoring her question. She slides her long body down beside me and puts her head on the pillow. Her breath is smoky.

'What the hell was going on with you and Lach?'

'He's the one who got you pregnant, isn't he?' I sit up on one elbow. 'And he hasn't even been there for you, plus he's a creep—he once groped me when we were young.'

'What are you talking about?'

'Yeah he groped me underwater on school camp once.' I grab my boob violently, demonstrating.

'Wait? What school camp?'

'I don't know, the one by the river.' She looks at me, raising one eyebrow.

'So you're angry at Lach because he groped you on school camp ten years ago?'

'No,' I roll away. 'I mean that's just a demonstration of how he's a creep.'

'He's not a creep, Anna.' Her voice is getting louder, it always does when she drinks.

'Well look what he did to you.'

'Are you serious? We had sex, get over it. Shit happens. He didn't force me to do it. What do you think, he raped me?'

'No, I just mean, he probably manipulated you into doing it.'

Her mouth opens and I see her pink tongue. I've said the wrong thing. 'He didn't manipulate me into anything, Anna, I can look after my own fucking body.'

'Then why the hell would you do it with him?'

She shakes her head in disbelief. 'Because I wanted to. Just because you don't want to, doesn't mean other people don't.'

I collapse into my pillow. The room around me distorts.

The shadows in the corners grow larger, flicker in and out of focus. *How could she want to with him, and not me?* She softens, slings an arm over my waist and pulls herself into my side.

'If you and Lach have issues because he groped you or whatever, that's fine, but don't bring me into it, okay, I have enough of my own problems at the moment.'

I nod, feeling her breath on my neck. She leans over me further, reaches out and turns off the lamp on the bedside table.

'I'm going to sleep.'

'Okay.' I lie awake, letting my eyes adjust to the darkness. I can tell she is still awake too. The way her body is next to mine, her hips making slight movements up and down. I feel her breasts push into me from behind. She lets out a small sigh. I close my eyes, feel her hand brush my leg. I turn to her and she turns the other way, sticking her bum into the hollow my body creates. I lift my hand up and let it hover over her neck, should I touch her? Finally I let it fall softly and stroke the hair off her skin. Everything is silent. Her body is still. She is either asleep or pretending to be. Her breath deepens. I hear my housemates stumble through the front door and their noise, their presence in the other room, makes me wiggle away from her, and roll over. In the darkness my desk chair looks like the silhouette of a child.

I am woken by Miff tapping out a message. She holds her phone above her face in the bed, still horizontal. A wedge of sunlight falls across her.

'Lach wants to go to breakfast.' She drops her arms, letting the phone fall into the creases of doona between us. I look at her, waiting to see if I'm invited. Not sure if I would want to go either way.

'Well?'

'Well, what? I'm sure he doesn't want to me to come.'

'Don't be stupid. You should come and apologise to him for calling him a dick.'

'Prick.'

'Whatever, same thing,' she laughs, flinging back the blanket and jumping onto the carpeted floor.

'Come on, you guys need to sort your shit out, and I'm starving.' She pulls out a pair of jeans from my bottom drawer.

'Can I wear these?'

'Sure.' I watch her put them on. They're a better fit on her than me. She turns in the mirror, admiring her own arse.

'What top can I borrow?' She opens the top drawer, begins to rummage.

'Whatever.' I find the jeans I was wearing yesterday scrunched up at the end of the bed. I stand next to Miff by the drawer. She pulls out a yellow t-shirt.

'For you?'

I take the t-shirt from her, 'Thanks.'

She slips into my silk cami and tucks it in to the top of the jeans.

'So you're coming?'

'Only cos I'm hungry.'

'Yes.' She prolongs the 'sss' sound like the snake from *The Jungle Book.*

Lach walks towards the café and I can tell he is trying to pretend like nothing happened. Miff and I are already sitting at a round table, out the front, sipping coffee. There is a brown bottle with sprigs of purple flowers in it and small sugar-bowl in the middle of the table. I rearrange the items to busy my hands and eyes.

'Hey.' Miff jumps up and wraps her long arms around Lach, kisses him. I sit sullen, raising my cheek to meet his lips as he bends down cautiously to kiss me too. He gives me a sideways glance, not sure how to act. What I will do, say? A homeless man approaches our table with an extended hand. I see the dirt in his palm lines. We shake our heads slowly. The waiter is behind him.

'Coffee to start?'

'Long black, please.' The waiter trots off. Lach takes a seat. Miff is between us, leaning back in her chair. She seems to have decided not to push my apology. I read the menu silently, aware they are making small gestures to each other with eyes and shoulders that say 'I don't know what her problem is.' The cool breeze whips my hair.

The waiter comes back and I realise he looks a lot like Lach. Same brown fringe, bony body. He is admiring Miff, I can tell by the way he lifts his chin up, his lips pulled into a polite toothless smile. I want to punch him in the face, yell at him for trying to look down her top. I look around at the tables, through the window. The barista looks like Lach as well. He bangs a porta-filter loudly against the rubbish bin, his eyes fixed on Miff over the coffee machine. There is a table of Lachs in the corner, all pretending to eat their bacon and eggs, while sneaking sideways glances at her. Behind me another Lach feeds his baby in a highchair, he drops the baby's spoon so he can peak at Miff's legs under the table. My eyes dart over all the Lachs. My heart is pounding in my chest.

'Are you okay?' says Miff, touching my arm.

The waiter is still standing there.

'You guys ready to order?'

I butt in before the others. 'I'll have the pomegranate porridge.'

Miff shifts in her seat and I can see Lach's hand is on her knee.

'I'm sorry,' the waiter taps his pen on the notepad, 'sold out.'

AN EXCELLENT RESPONSE TIME

RACHAEL MEAD

When people think about ambulances they tend to imagine adrenaline-rich lights and sirens work; traumatic road accidents, industrial disasters and ambos dangling out of helicopters to save people who've fallen down cliffs. Don't get me wrong. We love the romance of this paramedic stereotype and do our best to hold up the façade. But our days are far more likely to involve mundane asthma and abdominal pain than glamorously de-fibbing cardiac patients. You didn't hear this from me. Six months ago I would've been the first to tell you that in both life and work, romance is dead. That was before I met Mrs Bickle.

Nothing proves the relative nature of time like an ambulance. A patient calls 000 and minutes can feel like hours. Time stretches to breaking point. We arrive and they are beside themselves with stress, convinced we've sat around finishing our Sudoku before hefting ourselves into the truck.

But when those serious jobs come in and it's clear the caller is not someone wanting us to sit down for a chat and a sandwich, we are working those cases from the minute we receive the call. As I hear the patient's information I'm mentally running through the variables, analysing the symptoms and considering possible diagnoses, treatment options and drug dosages. We're getting our game faces on, not talking about where to stop for dinner. So I'm always pretty taken aback when we're greeted with, 'You took your fucking time. I called you at least half an hour ago!'. This person may've experienced an ambulance-generated time-bend, but that kind of attitude makes me wish we *had* spent the drive debating Savvas Yiros vs Dumpling King.

In a job where time is everything, I find it curious that I only wear a watch for work. I need one with a second hand to take heart and respiratory rates but if left to my own devices I wouldn't wear a watch at all. As a kid, I wore one religiously and winding it every night was the closing act in my bedtime ritual. Back then, I was also afraid of blood and seeing any kind of injury would make me all shivery, the inside of my mouth dry and metallic. In fact, this about-face on blood and watches supports my recent theory that people's characters are much like the concept of time. On the surface they both seem totally consistent, but when their essential nature is questioned they turn out to be unreliable. Capable of distorting reality so drastically it's as if you never knew them at all.

These days, I have a phone that keeps me from being late, which used to be my only concern with the passing of time. I've never been one of those women who lie about her age. I'm forty-three and I look it. There's nothing I can do about that and I couldn't care less. As a girl, I was the opposite, addicted to my own reflection and *Dolly* magazine with equal intensity. God, if I met my thirteen-year-old self today she'd probably take one look at the green uniform and lack of make-up and die of embarrassment right at my feet. I like to think of myself as useful, not ornamental. While my mum describes me as having taken an early retirement from sex, I'd much rather be comfortable in my own skin than trotting around, as her mother used to say, like mutton dressed as lamb.

Worrying about age and the inevitable passing of youth has always seemed a guaranteed way of triggering a midlife crisis and these are rampant right now among my friends and colleagues. Sports cars. Plastic surgery. The tree-change. The man you thought yourself happily married to for twenty years leaves you for some woman half his age with a full set of clichés. Until six months ago, I'd always felt torn between finding these people courageous and ridiculous. What I know now: I was limiting myself. There are many, many more options.

I met Mrs Bickle in November. I remember this because the jacarandas were in bloom. John and I had been tasked to a call in Burnside, one of Adelaide's affluent eastern suburbs where the council had invested ratepayers' money matching the rubbish bin lids to the exact purple of jacaranda blossom.

The call had come from a medic-alert necklace, so straight away it had the hallmarks of a forgettable job. Relatives of elderly people love these medic-alert necklaces. The idea is that when grandpa falls out of bed he presses the button on the necklace and an ambulance is immediately dispatched.

Unfortunately there are flaws in the system. First of all, it is incredibly easy to set the necklace off accidentally, so many of these jobs end with the person you expect to find writhing in pain on the floor answering the door with a perplexed expression. Another issue is that elderly people are often very security conscious and have houses that are harder to crack than a penitentiary. When the call comes in, the occupant is usually curled into a foetal ball on the lino with a broken hip, so the way we get in is by using a house key that is hidden in a secure box for which the ambulance service has the code. Easy. The real problem lies in the fact that elderly people hate wearing the necklaces. Really hate them. Hate to the degree that they refuse to wear them. Or they do what my grandmother did and leave them on the bedside table. Then, when they fall out of bed, they have to spend a cold night and the following day on the floor with help lying just beyond arm's reach.

We pull up outside Mrs Bickle's 1940s bungalow on a quiet street lined with jacaranda trees that are almost fluorescent with intense purple blossom. John heads straight for the deep veranda to knock on the front door just in case Mrs Bickle has accidentally set the necklace off, while I detour to the garage to find the box and grab the key. There's no answer to John's knocking, but there are lights on inside and as we unlock the heavy wooden door and dump our kits in the hall we can hear running water.

'Hello! Mrs Bickle? Ambulance Service.'

The only answering sound is the running water that we can now tell is coming from the back of the house. We make our way down the narrow jarrah boards of the hall, calling as we go. No answer. This is not a good sign. By this stage we are past the assumption that this is an accidental call.

'Mrs Bickle? Hello!'

We move deeper into the house, checking each room as we pass for the unconscious form of Mrs Bickle. The water we can hear is now clearly the sound of the shower. We stop outside the closed door of the bathroom.

'Mrs Bickle?'

There is still no response. My gut registers a sinking feeling that is not exactly dread. It's just that I've done jobs like this before and I'm expecting to find Mrs Bickle on the floor of the shower, slippery, in pain, and if she's been there a while and the hot water has run out, possibly hypothermic. So it's not a difficult job but it is awkward for all involved, especially for Mrs Bickle having to confront two strangers in her bathroom while she's naked.

I open the door. I needn't have worried about the hot water. The room is thick with steam but I can see a walking frame propped in the doorway of the shower. Through the fogged glass I can just make out the form of a large body slumped forward over the walking frame. The weirdly contoured mass is jerking as if having a seizure and I can just make out a mix of grunting and laboured breath over the sound of the shower.

'Mrs Bickle?'

There is a short shriek. The odd shape resolves itself into two figures as Mrs Bickle and her companion spring apart. The shower door is open far enough to see the couple are wearing only startled expressions. I pivot, wishing I could find a way to politely gouge out my eyeballs. My eyes meet

John's. He's hanging back in the doorway, struggling to keep a straight face and with a surreptitious sweep of his hand he lets me know the floor is all mine. I mouth a sarcastic 'thanks' in his direction.

'Ambulance service. Someone used a medic-alert necklace?'

'Young lady, you could've knocked! Just a second.'

'We did ma'am. And called several times. Do you need help?'

Behind my back I can hear the walking frame and the slap of wet feet on tiles. I study the exhaust fan as if considering undertaking a thesis on this particular model. There's a pause and a deep chuckle that doesn't seem to hold a hint of embarrassment. I'm desperately hoping that they are wrapping themselves in towels.

'No, you can stay where you are for the moment please. I wasn't expecting you so soon. I had a bit of tightness in my chest and thought I should have it checked so I pressed the button. That's what it's for, isn't it? But I thought you'd be a while so Ralph and I decided to have a shower while we were waiting. We weren't to know you'd be straight around. I thought you ambos were meant to be busy and always running late. That's what I hear on the news.'

Maybe it was the embarrassment but she phrased it like this was our fault for being too efficient.

'Mrs Bickle, I think I can safely say that if you are happy to jump in a hot shower and elevate your heart rate you are probably not having a cardiac episode. But I'll need to check you out just in case.'

There's another chuckle from Ralph. 'I'll just put the kettle on, shall I?'

'Thanks, my love. We shouldn't be long. My heart feels fine now.'

'Good.' Ralph, thankfully now clad in a terry-towelling robe, leans in to kiss her damp temple then edges past me as he heads towards the kitchen. I only see him out of the corner of my eye but I'm pretty sure his gait has an element of strut to it.

I manage to make our introductions without meeting Mrs Bickle's or John's eyes.

'I don't know what you're so uptight about. I would've expected you'd pretty much seen it all, doing what you do.'

I let Mrs Bickle lead the way with her walking frame to the lounge room where she flops into an armchair and gives herself over to me to start work. I roll up the sleeve of her robe and wrap her upper arm with the blood pressure cuff.

'So I guess you were expecting to find me sitting here, watching whatever crap passes for entertainment these days on the idiot box, knitting something for some great-grandchild or other? Isn't that what old people are supposed to do?' She looks at me, clearly expecting an answer. I try to imply in a non-verbal way that I'm concentrating on calculating her blood pressure but there's no avoiding it. I have to answer.

'Well, I'm not really sure I was expecting anything, I just wasn't expecting *that*.' I say it with a smile but Mrs Bickle's face tells me she's in no mood to be taken lightly. She glances down at my name badge then looks me straight in the eyes.

'Natasha, I don't know how old you are but I guarantee that you feel much younger inside than you look. I'm eighty-one and I can tell you that it's the world that starts to treat you like you are old and tells you what being old should be.'

She plucks at the wrinkled skin hanging from the underside of her forearm. 'This is just the vessel. Everything else is the same. The way I feel about him—the same.' She nods towards the kitchen then leans back, looking at me in silence.

Feeling intensely uncomfortable, like I'm being challenged and found wanting, I fluff it, losing track of the pressure reading. I release the tension on the blood pressure cuff and, mumbling an apology, re-inflate it. The skin of her wrist is papery and I can feel it moving loosely over the flesh and bone beneath as I search for her pulse.

With her free hand Mrs Bickle reaches under my chin and gently tilts my face to meet her eyes.

'That's not me. I'm in here.' Her gaze locks on to mine. I can't look away. Her irises are pale blue and so clear it is as though I can see right through them.

She holds my gaze for a few more seconds, then her eyes move to the door where Ralph has reappeared, holding two steaming mugs. Her look softens and she reaches toward him, taking one of the mugs and smiling her thanks. He touches her cheek and she turns to kiss his hand, their gestures so swift and natural that in this moment they are ageless, no more and no less than in love.

Once we're out the front door, John can't stop laughing. He's Kenyan and has an incredible, full-bodied laugh. Usually, I can't help but join in. Not right now.

'Elevate your heart rate. Heehee. Fabulous! Just fabulous. Tash, you just got woke by an eighty-year-old. Total slap down. Bickle 1: Tash 0.'

John cannot let it go. And I don't blame him. If he had been the one to open that bathroom door I would definitely be making sure that John and the entire crew back at the station would not soon forget the libidinous Mrs Bickle and her Ralph.

Walking back to the truck the footpath and street are carpeted with bright purple blossom. Even though the bells have fallen and begun to decay they still hold their intense colour. I climb into the driver's seat and while John clears the job on the radio I adjust the rear-view mirror and look deep into my own eyes.

The mirror is instantly crowded with the disappointment I see hunkered in the frown lines, the crow's feet chronicling more sleepless nights than laughter. I reach beyond this instinct to only see the physical, searching for what I saw in Mrs Bickle's eyes, that vital spark burning within the ageing shell.

The radio crackles to life with our next job. 'Parkside 72 - chest pain / shortness of breath at Skye.' Readjusting the mirror, I pull my focus back to the road ahead.

'Parkside 72. Acknowledged.' I check my watch. My shift is only half over.

TINDER TALES

REBECCA STRATTON

But what do you do after the ding?

Ding—it's a match!

Someone you found attractive at first glance also found *you* attractive at first glance.

I guess that's why Tinder puts those prompts above their photos.

Because what *is* the point if you don't send a message?

Validation? Validation in the ding?

08:43pm

'Guten tag!'

Often it's good to throw them in the deep end. Or at least entertaining.

He opened with 'Hey Cutie' and a winky face, so he may not appreciate my deliberately confusing reply. Then again, he is wearing a Birkenstock in his second photo. You never know.

09:02pm

Hamish: What

Jesus Christ. It's not looking good. I really hate giving up on them so easily, though. I'll reply.

Me: What, you mean you don't speak German? So that Birkenstock photo is in fact cultural appropriation?!?!! OOOO

Fuck it, he'll either bitterly disappoint me or redeem himself.

Hamish: Haha na that's just October fest! Do u know a fair bit?

Sigh. He continues to walk the line.

Me: Not anymore, but I got through Year 11 German, so that's something! And I've never culturally appropriated a Dirndl ;)

Now we'll see. I can hear Amanda: 'Unmatch, unmatch! You've gotta keep your standards high!' She's probably right, but I can't help giving people the benefit of the doubt.

I hadn't planned to, but somehow we did it three times. Luke's naked torso was confusing; it didn't match his limbs or his head, which were made of long and slender lines. Knobbly fingers, bony feet.

No, his torso was all lumps and curves, and in surprising places, too. I can only attribute the repetition of the act to the eleven barren weeks preceding that night. He left in the morning, and that's when my troubles truly began.

Luke: Last night was great

(It was average.)

Me: Yeah, it was pretty good :)

Luke: Have you ever completely shaved your pussy?

Me (stunned, but trying to be polite): Yeah, but it's a lot of effort and it can injure unsuspecting penises when it starts to grow back, so I haven't in a while.

Luke: Would you consider shaving it again

Luke: Cause that'd be hot ;)

This was the first of many attempts by Luke to rekindle the dead flame of my desire. Despite my communication of what I considered a gentle but firm 'no thanks', he continued to contact me every couple of days. Today, it has been four weeks.

I am feeling good. I have had better (and worse) sex since then, and feel I have mastered the etiquette of Tinder. I have decided that by now, he really should have given up, and that it is reasonable of me to block him on the two social media services through which we are connected. He is on Tinder, after all: plenty more fish in the sea.

Yes, it's a good decision.

In the afternoon, I receive a friend request: Luke Reynolds. It's him. By now I am angry. What part of my actions has suggested to this man that further attempts to contact me will be in any way successful?

I delete the request. If necessary, I will take things further.

Message request from Luke Reynolds: Blocked :'(aww

I consider how to respond. I ask my female friends, who say to tell him I'm sorry but I'm not interested. I ask Tim, who says to tell him to fuck off or he'll pay him a visit. I go for something in between.

Me: I. Am. Not. Interested. In. You. Or. Anything. Relating. To. You. Take. A. Hint. Stop. Contacting. Me.

Luke Reynolds: Ok, thanks

Luke Reynolds: Can I ask why?

My female friends say to just use the boyfriend excuse, as anti-feminist as it is. Tim says to say the sex was bad and I'm not attracted to him. I disagree with both of them. I don't think Luke is actually a terrible person, just a bit of an idiot. Minimum pain but maximum finality, I decide.

Me: I don't need a reason to not want to see you again, buddy. The sex was fine, you're not a total arsewipe, and I don't want to see you again.

Luke Reynolds: Noted. All the best

I sit back down on the lawn and pull out another stalk of wheatgrass.

The cat stalks a sparrow.

08:55pm

My bedroom door swings shut behind me. I collapse onto the bed, shove my head into the blankets and let out a long groan. I feel like the most disgusting piece of shit, but at the same time, I really need to tell someone. It was just too, too good. And *baaad*.

I rip out my phone and call Amanda.

'Hello?'

'Amandaaa,' I moan.

'Oh God. Was it that bad?'

I shove my face back into the pillow and let out a whine that ends in crazed laughter.

'Dear Lord, what've you got yourself into this time?

Did this Koby guy propose?'

I explode into laughter, manic. 'No, no...he just...arrrgh!'

'Just what?'

'He, ah...' I wince. 'He voted One Nation.' Amanda's scream dissolves into uncontrollable laughter. I join in—it was either laugh or cry. 'Oh, shit Amanda, it was just so awful! He w—he was telling me—about how' (I lowered my voice into a blokey drawl) "it's only fair to stop Muslims coming to 'Straya, cause if you look at the stats almost all the terrorist attacks are done by them" and I was like, mmhmm...trying to be all reasonable and shit, cause if I'd just given him my opinion he wouldn't have listened, I was like, "don't you think though, that it might just be that when white people perform an act like that, the media don't *call* it terrorism?" and he was like— get this, he said, "nah no way, that's just wrong, and I should know cause *I subscribe to News dot com*." The Murdoch press!'

Amanda sounds like she is almost in tears at the other end of the phone. 'Jesus, Bec! You sure can pick 'em!'

'He didn't talk about anything but politics for *two hours*. Like, what the fuck, mate! How is that appropriate first date behaviour?'

'My god, this date was worth it just for the story!'

'There's more...'

Amanda is silent. Then, 'Mmmmm?'

I swallow. 'I, ah...just got home from his place...'

'WHAT THE FUCK! *REALLY?!*'

'I know, I know! I don't know what came over me, I just...' I groan. 'Okay, just hear me out! I need to tell you the whole story.'

'I need to *hear* the whole story! What the hell happened?'

'Well, we kept talking…and it was still just as awful, but I had another drink just to be polite and then he was like, do you want to come back to mine. And he offered to pay for my taxi home afterwards, and—fuck—I seriously have no idea what came over me. There is literally no excuse except my hormones or something, 'cause…well, I'll get to that later.'

'Rebecca…' said Amanda dangerously.

'Okay, Okay! Just let me tell you the whole thing. So we went back to his place, I have no idea why, and we started doing it, and then—' No, it was just too much. My god. Myyy god. What had my life come to? Tears of sheer embarrassment sprung into my eyes and I let out a long, high squeal.

'*And then??* Tell me, you horny fool!'

'And then my body must've been like, "fuck this, Bec's brain is gone, we need to take control here." 'Cause out of nowhere, with absolutely *zero* warning, I got my fucking period all over his sheets. Like, *everywhere*!'

The noise coming from the other end of the phone was instant and deafening. 'OH. MY GOD. That is fucking GOLD!'

I cry and laugh and moan, punching the pillow. 'You know what the weirdest part is?' I gasp. 'My period isn't even due for another ten days! My body totally hacked itself!'

'What the hell! What was his reaction? Did he freak out?'

'He was actually really good about it! He stripped the bed and rinsed the sheets himself, didn't make a big deal about it…*not* what you'd expect from someone who's anti-gay marriage and doesn't think women need equal pay!'

'Ohhh my god. Rebecca, you've made history. I will tell

this story at your funeral. And if you don't tell it to your grandkids, I will be extremely disappointed.'

Still laughing, still crying, I realise Amanda is right: this is Tinder gold.

'I totally will. I feel like the worst person on the planet right now, though. Like, *what* was I thinking?'

'It's okay, I'm sure it was just your pre-period hormones making you insanely horny.' She snickers. 'Horny enough to sleep with a One Nation voter, even.'

'I really, really hope you're right. But hey, at least I know I can trust my body now! It has wisdom that the brain knows not, and the power to instigate a full-on goddamn period if need be.'

My body feels encrusted with other people. My face is rough from the scratch of stubble. My skin, my hair—they don't smell right. The bedroom smells like sex, and the sheets are somewhere in between. I feel dirty: over-touched, over-used, clotted.

I wash the sheets. I run a bath. I scratch my nails over my whole body and shed dead skin onto the bottom of the tub. I read a book. I write some notes, things to do. I make plans for the week, none of which involve anyone else.

He told me that I had come. He could feel the difference as my muscles relaxed.

It took someone else to prove to me that those heights of good-feeling were orgasms. I had assumed, based on a great deal of research, that I was failing to climax. The internet described a rush of dopamine and a sense of deep physical release/relief. Galaxies exploding behind your eyes.

Apparently I had set my expectations too high.

I wondered if I should call my ex-boyfriend, like you would upon discovering an STI:

'It's me. They were orgasms, after all. Kind regards.'

2:56 pm

Kevin: Hey how are you:-)

Me: Hey! I'm pretty good, having a nice lazy day :) you?

Kevin: I just chill on the beach with a few mats

Me (willing to pass 'mats' off as a typo): Nice :) which beach?

Kevin: Glanelg :) Do you have any plan's for the rest off the nice day

I have no answer for that.

11:31 am

Kevin: Hey rebecc

Me (mildly pissed): Hey Kevi

Kevin: what's up?

I don't need to tell you that's as far as it went.

I have had Tinder for two months and twelve days. According to the internet, if I were a medium-sized, mixed-breed puppy, my Tinder age would already be two years. That's not so bad, right? I can still count my intimate partners on both hands— just. The statistics at this point are interesting to consider, although difficult to analyse due to the myriad factors at play behind the final result of sexual intercourse.

Perhaps the most surprising result of my studies thus far is penis size. Of the ten male penises that I have personally witnessed erect, six have been above average in overall size (if one estimates both length and circumference to calculate a mean). Of the remainder, one was on the small side and three were roughly average. Seven were circumcised, and three have been accompanied by a set of testicles large enough to slap against me in certain positions. While the sample size is still small, I feel it is safe to conclude that there is no one shape or size that delivers optimum sexual pleasure. Granted, an above average penis can give penetrative pleasure to my vagina more easily, but I am in no position to speak for all vagina-possessors on this matter. A stronger conclusion is that it is not the penis itself but the individual's style and skill that is most important in determining the amount of penetrative pleasure experienced by both parties during intercourse.

At this important chronological marker—two dog years, ten partners—it is important to look to the future. Further study should focus on seeking explanations for this proportional anomaly, which is not parallel to the global or indeed national average. Perhaps Adelaide is uniquely gifted in this respect—only time, and further data quantification, will tell.

Epilogue: Four Months Later
9:32 pm
Luke Reynolds: How's it going?

11:52 pm
Me: Dude
　　Me: No

Seen 11:52 pm

THE TRAPPER'S CATCH

SUZANNE MCCOURT

It was Dolly who put a stop to it. She set the tea things on the floor and glared all around. 'All right,' she said, 'who's got Alf's eye?'

By then her brothers had cut the power and plunged the shed into silence and their sniggers were loud in the lull that dizzied Alf's head.

'Who's the stupid cow?'

The guilty stood like foxes in a spotlight, the others watched.

Alf hated being noticed, hated the glass eye that made him a focus. When a tail of fencing wire stabbed into his eye, the doctors said he was lucky. *Glass comes in more shades of blue than brown*, they said. *Remember the marbles you had as a kid? Be grateful you've got blue eyes or there'd be no look-alike eye for you.*

Alf didn't stay grateful for long. Glass eyes were not made for comfort. He hated the itch in the crevice, the gritty-sand feeling. He always took it out before he went to bed, carried it along in his pocket when setting his traps, put it back only if he saw the boss or one of the SOBS heading his way.

You had to be careful of SOBS, he'd learned that long ago. Sons of bosses were lily scared under all that strutting and bluff, and just itching to test their unearned authority on you. Too trusting, he'd been when they offered him work in the shed with three meals a day but no bed in the shearers' quarters for him. After lunch, he had laid down on the race and taken out his eye, lodged it safe on a ledge above his head while he had a five-minute kip. When the gong went, his eye was gone. He knew it hadn't rolled off without a helping hand, knew it wasn't Snorkie, Patsy or Bear. Grins and winks pinned it on a McCartney. But which one?

'Seein' alright?' asked the eldest as he threw the next fleece on the table. 'Not missing too many dags, are we Alfie?'

Noise from the diesel and the crank of the press made it easy to pretend he hadn't heard. Head down, he skirted the table, pulled off sweats and fribs in a frenzy, ignored the whole shed until Dolly arrived with the tea things and set them on the floor. When she stumbled on the top step, he reached out to help, only remembered his eye when she thanked him. But she didn't seem bothered, seemed to look right into the socket, into his head, and see more than he wanted.

'Who's got Alf's eye?' she repeated. And waited.

Eventually the young one reached into his pocket. 'A bit of fun, Alf, no harm meant.' He slapped the eye into Alf's hand and grabbed Dolly around the waist. 'Trouble is, Doll, you've got no sense of humour.' He tickled her under the arms and lifted her high off the board. 'Need to lighten up a bit, Doll.'

Setting her down, he tried to tickle some more but she

turned and kicked him hard on an ankle, hit at the solid mass of him with her tiny hands. Dancing around on one leg, he laughed and hollered and egged her on as only a brother can. Red in the face, she left the tea things on the floor, left the shed. When Alf looked out, she was stomping back to the house, her little dwarf legs bouncing off the ground as if the earth itself was heating her up.

That evening, Alf took his usual place at the table on the veranda. Old Girl McCartney ruled the roost from the other end while Dolly ate between fetching and clearing. Alf saw the way she jiggled on her chair as she ate, as if every mouthful pleasured her. Saw the way she tuned out farm talk and stayed somewhere inside her head. Like him. There were plenty who thought she was a bit loopy. Probably thought the same about him. Dolly caught him looking and waved her fork.

Right then young Bear Williams leaned back and patted his belly. 'Great stew, Mrs Mac. Thank you.'

'Thank Dolly, not me.'

'Cook like that, Dorry McCartney, you'll make someone a darn good wife.'

'Doris won't marry,' said the Old Girl, quick off the mark. 'She'll be here looking after me in my old age. Won't you Doris?'

Dolly didn't answer.

Later, Alf stood beneath the pines near the rubbish pile before turning full circle to check no one was watching. There was stealing. Then there was souveniring, which is mostly what Alf did. A sort of payment to make up for what the boss didn't give. And other things: like whether the boss or missus or SOBS could look him fair in the face without their eyes wandering south. He tallied it up. Then looked around for something to make it right.

It still amazed him that no one missed the turtle shell from the saddle room at *Tingala*, up near Coomandook. When he lifted it off the wall and ran a thumb under the dust, he found golden brown circles underneath like reptile scales, like a slice of Tassie Blackwood that had taken ten lifetimes to grow a grain of lines around a tiny core.

On his last night, he cleaned the shell by lamplight. At sparrow's fart, he tied it on his back with a length of twine, then draped a blanket on top to stop it being scratched by the jiggling weight of his traps. Keeping away from roads, he padded through saltbush pans and tea tree stands, until he came to the tracks that ran north and south. And just to be sure, he walked a whole day further south before he caught the train; then he knew he was safe.

Until then, he'd only ever taken something small: a spoon from a tea tray, a knife from the meat shed that might have dropped in the grass, a salt shaker sitting too close to a window. It was all he intended taking from the McCartneys but as he searched the rubbish pile, Dolly came trotting down the path to the hen house. The sun was already dropping in the west, the spoggies quietening and settling for the night. Alf slid behind a pine: it was his nature to hold back, step back; it went with trapping, the watching and waiting.

In the cage, Dolly upended a pail of scraps—apple cores and eggshells, pumpkin and potato peelings. And as the chooks fought around her feet, he wondered about them eating their own shells. Wasn't that chook cannibalism? He'd once seen a rabbit eat its own kittens to save them from a fox plaguing the burrows. And he'd heard of rats doing the same, given enough reason. Then Dolly lifted a bantam into her arms and stroked its red feathers into a silky coat. He wondered how it would feel to stroke her soft round shoulders, to feel the ball of warmth within her woman's body.

He stepped out then, bold and forgetful. She wasn't scared, or surprised; she shucked off the bantam, closed the gate and came straight over. He didn't give her a chance to talk. He took off his jacket and spread it on the pine needles, took her hand. She watched him wide-eyed the whole time, squealed like a rabbit when he pressed through. But when he took his hand off her mouth, tasted her lips and licked her armpits, she giggled with pleasure.

Afterwards, he helped her clean up. She was like a doll, a woman's lush curves and the limbs of a child. But she could look after herself: she pushed him away and straightened her dress, clipped back her hair and dusted off the pine needles. And when the Old Girl yelled from the house, 'Do-o-ris,' she giggled with guilty delight.

'Wait for me,' she ordered before running off. 'I'll come back tonight.'

And later still, with barely enough moon to slice through the stars, he stood beneath the cypress, never thinking she'd come. But a wisp of white nightdress passed the hen house and then he was leading her down the slope to his camp, cursing for not cleaning out the tent, not believing enough. Then he wanted to reward her for coming, for wanting him, wanting so little, and as he pulled open the tent flap, he quickly spread rabbit skins on the ground sheet to make a fur bed. And lost himself in her softness.

Each night he walked her back to the house, skirted along the fence to the main road so the dogs wouldn't bark up a racket, then crept through the garden. Each night it grew harder to let her go. Under the walnut tree, he held her clamped in his arms for so long that a sooty owl in the branches above might have mistaken them for a garden statue. And it was only when they were both limp with tiredness, that he crept onto the veranda and helped her through the window.

There was risk enough meeting at night, but when the shearing finished and he was back to trapping, she raised the stakes, came running down the slope in broad daylight. On the fence, skins with outstretched arms and pegged legs were drying in the sun. 'She's gone to town,' she said. 'I can come with you.'

He was not too welcoming. 'Come where?'

'To check your bunnies.'

'You don't want to do that. Killing. And gutting.' And as she slithered under the fence, he scanned the paddocks. 'And what about your brothers?'

'If they come, you cover me with a rug. But they won't.'

He wasn't so sure. And he wasn't sure he wanted her watching him wring rabbits' necks. But before he left, there was time together in the tent and later he decided there was no harm in it, not this once.

He drove south where the swampy ground near the lake was planted out with strawberry clover, so lush and green beside the summer grass that it looked as foreign as she did sitting next to him. He pointed to the flash of sun on galvanised iron that was Curtis Point, thirteen miles away. But towns reminded her of her mother and time running out so he cut inland across a paddock of yellow turnip weed to the ridge where his traps were set.

At first she wouldn't watch him wringing necks. 'They might look cute as Easter bunnies,' he told her with each quick twist of his wrist, 'but the damage they do's something awful. A wonder the whole country doesn't collapse with the burrows they've built. As for that rabbit-proof fence up north, whoever thought of that was a right dill. Didn't they think rabbits could burrow underneath?'

On the sandy soil, he showed her how to read the ground for paw prints, dung size, the scratching of mickey rabbits still learning how to burrow. Soon she was helping reset the traps, scooping out the earth with her hands while he bared the teeth. He told her each trap had a name. 'What's this one?' she asked each time. Baron. Wolf. Devil. Stumpy. Bigtooth. Snapper. Satan. He made them up as he went along. And she laughed like a kid. Then she balanced the paper scrap on top and carefully dusted dirt over the lot. He hammered in the pin and smoothed away their tracks, they moved on and did the same again.

By the time he'd collected twenty pair, she was looking tired. He made her wait in the shade while he finished off the final few. Then he had to gut them. 'You don't want to see this,' he told her. But she said it wasn't much different to chooks, so he showed her how to slit the back legs and twist them together in pairs, how to string them over the wire in the back of the ute. And while he threw guts to the wind and fed the circling hawks, Dolly quietly sized them for sale.

Finished, he drove to the stand of she-oaks that shaded the fresh water soak near the creek. There he made her wash up with soap from the ute and he did the same. He hated the stink of guts, the fresh blood smell that he could never get out of his nose, hair, clothes, that he tasted in his sleep. And he didn't want the Old Girl getting a sniff of it on Dolly. Afterwards as they sat on a log and dried off, he wanted to tear at the itch in his eye, turned away to wriggle it about in the socket.

She pushed between his knees and examined his face up close. 'You should wear a black eye patch like a pirate.'

He laughed. 'That'd sure get me noticed.'

'With it covered, everyone'd see how beautiful blue the real one is.'

He told her she was the one who needed her eyes checked. And in one quick swoop, lifted her off the ground and carried her back to the ute.

It was late when they hit the main road. He could see she was nervous, bouncing on the edge of the seat, jiggling her feet. When he stopped, she scampered off like a rabbit herself, afraid that her mother was back. He strung his catch by the side of the road for the Rabbitto and drove back to camp where he washed up again, this time in the turtle shell that he used as bath and basin.

He was surprised they got away with it for so long. When summer shortened into an early autumn and leaves flew at them like bats as they walked back to the house at night, he knew inside where knowing hides that it couldn't last, that nothing did. He wasn't surprised one morning when the Old Girl came beating through the grass, rifle over her shoulder, Dolly running ahead.

'She says you won't marry me. Alfie. That I can't have a baby. Tell her you want me, Alfie, tell her.'

But the Old Girl was doing the telling. 'You're an animal, Barnes, used a poor, dumb girl for your own ends. Now she's in the family way and only a kid herself. No brain. What hope's she got when she can hardly mother herself?'

He helped Dolly under the fence and pulled her under his arm. 'Says she's twenty-three. And her brain seems fine to me. Maybe you don't want to see.' The Old Girl sighted the rifle. He stood his ground. 'Not gunna be much good to her dead, am I?'

'You're no good to her anyway, Barnes. Get your arse outa here.' She loosened the catch. 'Out of the way, Doris. Move!'

But Dolly didn't move. They stared along the barrel and time lengthened into a senseless silence. 'I'll pay you,' said the Old Girl, lowering the rifle. 'Five quid to get out of the district and never come near Doris again?'

'Make it a twenty and you got a deal.'

Dolly bucked against him and he tightened his hold. The Old Girl told him he was a bloody rogue, offered ten and not a penny more, told him to come up to the house, then clear off for good. 'Come on, Doris,' she ordered.

He squeezed Dolly's shoulder and she wised up fast. 'I'm staying. I'm saying goodbye to Alfie.'

The Old Girl half raised the rifle then lowered it; her shoulders slumped. She waded into the high grass and was swallowed up before she reached the house.

With ten pound in his pocket, Alf drove out to collect his traps. Coming back, the sky turned slowly black and an eerie light bleached the lake white. Soon it looked as if a great sweep of charcoal crayon had swiped earth and sky, reversing day and night. He was in the tent barely minutes before the horizon smudged and a rain cloud raced over the paddocks like a beast running on water. With skins piled around him like a warm coat, he rolled a smoke and watched the rain come down, heavy and drenching. It filled the hollows that shallowed into the swamp, filled his turtle shell and flooded over the edge before trickling away in long rivulets like eels wriggling back to the lake. He eased his eye from its socket and put it safe in his shirt pocket, waited for the rain to stop.

That night he parked the ute far down the road, out of sight and sound, behind a clump of boobiallas. He walked back to the gate and hid in the shadows, cursed the full moon that appeared as the rain cleared away. On the horizon, the range crouched like a row of fat rabbits. Down the homestead drive, the white walls of the house glittered through the trees, taunted, teased. Close by, a mopoke called: *Slow-poke. Slow-poke.*

Would she come?

As he felt in his pocket for his smokes, something fell to the ground. He felt around, knew it couldn't have rolled far. He widened his reach, found twigs, leaves, pebbles, struck a match and circled low with the flare, still couldn't see it. Squatting there, he thought of Dolly's pirate patch and wondered if he'd be game enough to wear one. He shook out the flame and waited.

In the distance, a dog barked, once, twice. Then he heard

her feet ringing on the hard clay track. The sound of her steps seemed to tremor the ground, seemed to run through him like a long sigh. 'On the grass,' he willed her, 'on the grass, so no one will hear.' He moved from the shadows. Stars spilled from a milky sky and he could see mist was already whitening the road. And then he was running too, running towards the soft bruised shape of her running to him.

CLOSE TO THE PEOPLE

MARIAN MATTA

It started innocently enough, and could almost entirely be blamed on that sweltering afternoon when the air oozed sweat and the city skyline across the park shimmered and swayed and threatened to slither into a molten puddle. Downstairs, the fridge was fighting a losing battle with the atmosphere; upstairs, the bedroom ceiling fan shuddered in its death throes.

'Bit of a cool breeze coming up,' Hal said, stepping back through the tall French doors into the darkened bedroom. Shards of white-hot light entered with him. 'Least it's fresher.'

He hauled a protesting Goldie up off the crumpled bed and together they huddled on their narrow upper balcony, where the neighbour's liquidambar tree cast a meagre patch of shade. The tessellated tiles burned like beach sand in February but Hal had been right about the breeze. They laid down a blanket and sprawled out their limbs, trying to trap coolness in armpits and elbows, around necks, behind knees. Trucks and cars stop-started just below them, feet pounded the pavement as commuters raced for the train station, the freeway, the air-conditioned sanctuary of home.

The tiny breeze, with its scents of salt and bilge water, gradually revived them. Fingers stretched and touched, an arm tangled with another arm, a leg found pleasure in a nearby leg, and soon enough their thoughts were turning to other matters. Hal paused long enough to pin a sheet to the wrought-iron railing with bulldog clips. The sheet rippled, its corners lazily lifted and flapped with an erratic rhythm; a steadier rhythm was coming into play behind its modest cover. Then an errant gust of wind flung modesty skywards.

Oh! mouthed a long-haul driver, high in the cab of his prime mover.

Oh!! gasped Goldie, her eyes making a surprised, skewed connection with the driver's.

O-o-o-h!!! Hal groaned as it all came together in one perfect moment.

And for the rest of that hot summer the balcony became their favoured spot, until an autumn chill drove them back inside.

For a while the front room sufficed, with its window—and curtains—open onto the pocket-handkerchief garden, its high Victorian ceiling recoiling from the wanton sights below, but they both agreed that it lacked a certain *frisson*. Hal eyed the long hallway, flung the front door wide, turned to look at the kitchen down the far end.

'How do you fancy the kitchen table?'

She fancied it.

They scrutinised eBay for important yet small items that

could be cheaply couriered or mailed by registered post. They invited the neighbours around more than they'd ever done before. Hal reawakened a long-dormant interest in chess, joined the club down at the Community Centre, told the other members he was always up for a game if any of them wanted to drop around. Goldie made it her business to introduce herself to the new wave of aspirational homebuyers in their street, those glossy magazine readers who'd recently discovered the charms of inner city living. 'Don't you think that's going too far?' Hal asked her and she almost agreed. And every day, by inches, they crept further and further down the hallway, clothes abandoned in the distant kitchen.

'I ordered the wood to fix the back steps,' Hal said one day, glancing up through the beaded flyscreen to the street beyond. 'Should be here sometime this morning.' He paused to catch his breath, and the carpet settled against Goldie's shoulder blades. 'And remember them god-botherers that came the other day?'

'Yes! Yes!'

'Told 'em to drop by again on Saturday.'

She had never owned a fur coat, had never wanted one, but in her imagination the sensation of slipping the finest mink coat over naked skin would be a pale ghost of the feeling that surrounded her now. She moved in a bubble of warmth and light, her feet barely touching the ground through the damp and chilly months as she danced, basket in hand, on her daily visits down to the local shopping strip. Bare branches, filigreed against the lowering sky obligingly arranged themselves into entrancing shapes and patterns; there was new delight in the way leaden light caught and illuminated veranda posts, chimney pots, parked cars, puddles, everything; sweetness returned to the stale city air. She stopped to chatter to each and every neighbour, gleeful in the knowledge that she had a secret.

'Good morning, you two!' she trilled over a fence, 'what a wonderful day to be alive! Fabulous day, hey? Makes you glad you're not dead.' The Bensons, cold and disconsolate as they tackled winter weeds, glanced skywards and muttered about threatening rainclouds. Goldie heard her own voice high and excited like a cartoon mouse and firing off platitudes as if she were paid by the dozen; the joy within was impossible to contain. Her hands caressed a newel post as she prattled, and her basket just *had* to rat-tat-tat against the metal bars when she finally moved away, calling back over her shoulder, 'Don't forget, drop in any time!' *Poor old things*, she thought, *looks like their life could do with some spicing up.* As the first drops fell she whistled 'Singin' in the Rain' and swung around a lamppost.

As had become his habit, the greengrocer slipped some free seasonal extras into her order that day, handed them over with a wink. And when she bought flowers—*for the house*, her mouth said but her heart said, *for Hal*—the florist added a few more sprigs of baby's breath because Goldie's beaming smile, he assured her, always made his day.

Down at the butcher's shop, young Gerry in his smart navy and white stripes was grinning with the almost obscene jollity which so often accompanies working with animal flesh.

'Hello there, Mrs B. Looking good. Hubby must be doing

something right, I reckon. What can I tempt you with today?'

Goldie eyed the thick steaks, the plump sausages with their parsley trim, the swelling legs of lamb, the pinkly perfect pork and rich, red mince, and the world swam before her. She swayed a little, grasped the treacherous display case, whispered faintly, 'Just this once, Gerry, could I get you to deliver?'

Summer drifted around again and the heat demanded a new solution. Standing out on the footpath and trimming their sparse box hedge, Hal contemplated the situation, his smile getting wider and wider as the answer dawned. That afternoon he angled a couple of bamboo curtains across part of the front porch, a fragile shield against the busy road, and they had a quick test run while the dinner vegetables were steaming. From behind their screen they might, if they chose, easily wriggle their arms through the low hedge and between the iron posts, and what would an unsuspecting passer-by think if his shins were thus assaulted? The very idea was delicious. The traffic's rumbling masked their soft laughter. And other sounds.

A virulent late afternoon sun squeezed through the bamboo, snuck around the beaded flyscreen, sent orange diamonds dancing down the hallway, patterned the thin, unsmiling face of the woman as she leaned, tired and wilting, against the kitchen wall.

'Don't know how you can stand it. Gets worse every year. The air stinks, the trucks shake the place, no room to move—'

'There's the back garden,' Goldie interrupted equably.

'More tea, Julia? Something cooler perhaps?'

'That's hardly a garden. Tea.'

'Well, it's keeping Tilly happy enough.' She glanced out of the window to where Hal and the little girl were busy picking blackberries, and shooing cabbage moths away from the tiny vegetable patch.

'You could come out and live at our place, Mum, you know that, don't you? Fresh air, sunshine that isn't this putrid colour, a veggie garden as big as you like. The birds actually sing the dawn chorus, they don't cough it.'

'You wouldn't want us under your feet all day—'

'There's space for a kit home up near the orchard, as you know very well! You could have real live air-con. And Tilly would love the company now that the other kids are at school.'

'True, true. But she'll be away before you know it. Kids, they shoot up like bean stalks. Anyway, she loves coming here to stay with us. It's exciting down in the big smoke. So much happening, the beach, the zoo, everything within arm's reach.'

'You're incorrigible.'

'But we're not like you, Jules. This squashed-together city living has its charms.'

'None that I can see.'

The back door opened and Tilly tumbled through, lips purple with berry juice, holding a plastic tub in her outstretched hands.

'Look, Nanna! Me and Grandpa found lots and lots!'

'That's wonderful, my lovely girl! Shall we have them with ice-cream later?' She retrieved the tub and gathered her smallest grandchild into her arms, watched as Hal knocked the dust from his boots. 'Julia's been trying to talk us into shifting up country, love.'

'Has she now? And what did you tell her?'

Over the top of Tilly's curls, Goldie beamed a smile at her beloved husband and dropped just the faintest wink in his direction.

'Oh, I told her we could never do that. We like to be close to the people.'

DETERMINING POST MORTEM

LYNETTE WASHINGTON

Prenatal

Unformed things to clutch at, as vague as skittery moths. Songs are written about this faraway place of yearning and unfinished knowledge. Solitude was an enemy and a refuge, a place that became filled with anxiety and hope. *Will he like me when I find him?*

Birth

It began with a glance, truncated and revisited. A quickening in my chest, in places I didn't yet understand, in nerves awakening and synapses forming.

That glance became a brushed hand, toes playing in secret under the table in summer, breath-holding and dreams unhinged. Nothing was fathomable anymore. Everything with you felt like the first smile.

Infancy

Vulnerable words, written in ink, sealed and pressed into

your hand. You revealed more about me in a few months than all the preceding years unveiled. You seemed different to the rest. You were a love letter. You were an alien. You were a prince. You were a mystery. You were a storm and a shelter. You held me tight and held yourself back and I held onto my breath again, wondering, wondering…what could this be?

Childhood

You made a mistake. It was out of character, but you told me about it, which was *in* character. Forgiveness wasn't even a question. Your promises, so earnest. Your regret, so grave. Like a child caught playing with matches, your long face, bent spine and fear were intoxicating. Temporarily empowering. With your frankness, there was no option other than to forget.

Adolescence

Discovery, exploration, plunging desperately for more of everything, more, more, more. I was your teacher, never realising I had such knowledge. You taught me *that*. I knew my body better than you knew yours. You had mud maps, I had satellite images. The back seats of cars, pizza boxes pushed aside. The park on a chilly night, just out of the floodlight. Our bedrooms, parents sleeping next door. Dark corners, parties, clubs, bars, houses, yards, everything stolen from the public space. There was a force field around us, then. We were invincible and locked together.

Adulthood

How did I get so tired? How did we become such a cliché?

Why do I do the dishes while you mow the lawn? Why do we argue about money? We have enough. Enough dishes, enough lawn, enough of everything except what we need. The castle has been replaced by an anthill. Hollow inside. Scraps of light peeping through. Scraps of me remaining in the darkness.

Livor Mortis

Blood flow stopped. Feelings pooled at low points, gravity drawing them away from vital organs and towards the extremities of skin—calves, heels, shoulder blades—places where feeling is not truly required. Places that did not argue back. And places as irrelevant as my lips, eyes, stomach—the places where I used to feel you—were forgotten. When pressure was applied to those body parts, a void appeared. Nothingness where once there was the tingling promise of everything.

Rigor Mortis

First it was my jaw. I could no longer talk. There were no words for this thing that I only understood somewhere in my body, some long lost place. Heat hastened the process. It wasn't long before the muscles and therefore my limbs ceased operations. They tightened and clasped. They refused to even walk away. They shackled me, holding me to the ground, telling me to stay. A desperate motherbird, stuck in 1965.

Algor Mortis

The cooling stage. Thank goodness for this. A moment to breathe. Clear-headedness for just long enough.

Decomposition

Decomposition occurred more quickly in places where there were injuries. My heart went first.

Larvae

The lawyers came. They favoured moist places to breed. The tissue boxes in the office prove they have a preference for teary eyes. They bred in us, they fed off us. We made them fat. We couldn't walk away because our muscles were wasted, our sinew was food. So we sat at the table of this once great love and stared into space until the day was done.

ABOUT THE AUTHORS

Danielle Angelli is an Adelaide based writer with an obsession for travel and history. She's a student of professional writing at the Adelaide College of the Arts and is currently writing her first novel, a young adult fantasy.

Katherine Arguile was born in Tokyo and is Anglo-Japanese. In 2008 she emigrated from London to Adelaide where she now lives. She has published short stories, won first prize in London's Momaya Press competition, a Varuna Writing Fellowship and completed her first novel, *The Things She Owned*. She has a creative writing PhD from the University of Adelaide.

Chelsea Avard is a writer and teacher from Adelaide. She is co-editor of the short fiction and poetry anthology *The Body*. She holds a PhD from The University of Adelaide, and teaches Creative Writing at Flinders University. Her short fiction and poetry has been published by Sleepers Publishing, Wakefield Press and *Verity La*.

Lauren Butterworth is an emerging writer with fiction and essays in *Wet Ink, Libertine, InDaily* and *Verity La*. She podcasts at Deviant Women, and is co-director of The Hearth. By day, she teaches English Literature and academic writing at Flinders University.

When not doing her real job, **Elaine Cain** is a writer, traveller, hiker and tea lover. She has dipped her toes, all the way up to the knee, into the world of dating. She swears not all her dating stories are true. This is her first story to be published.

Phoebe Cannard-Higgins is a writer from Melbourne. She has been published in *Voiceworks, Fead Magazine* and the *Sumtimes*. In 2015, she won the Future Leaders short-story prize. She has recently completed her undergraduate with Honours in Creative Writing at the University of Melbourne and will leave to complete her Masters in Creative and Life writing at Goldsmith's University London later this year.

A. Marie Carter is an emerging writer from Adelaide. Her short stories have appeared in venues such as *Seizure*, the *Review of Australian Fiction*, and *Tiny Donkey*. She has won, or been highly commended for, the Imprints Booksellers' Short Story Award, the Salisbury Writers' Festival Short Story Award, and the Langhorne Creek Writers' Festival Short Story Award. She currently teaches English Literature and Creative Writing at Flinders University.

Carla Caruso has had romance novels and women's fiction published by Penguin, HarperCollins and Harlequin. Her background is in magazine and newspaper journalism. These days she juggles fiction writing with co-editing Romance Writers of Australia journal *Hearts Talk* and wrangling twin three-year-old sons. She lives in Adelaide. Visit www.carlacaruso.com.au.

Melisabeth Cooper Fell's stories have been shortlisted or commended in the Hal Porter, Grace Marion Wilson, notJack Writing From Place, and the Newcastle Short Story prize, and been published in *SALA* short stories 2016. In 2014 she started the Sheila Malady Short Story competition with the Shakespeare on the River Festival. She occasionally tweets @ mellybee542

Simone Corletto is the Communications Officer at the SA Writers Centre, having freshly graduated with Honours in Creative Arts (Creative Writing) from Flinders University. Her stories have been published by *Double Helix* and *Empire Times*. She spends her spare time crocheting lumpy hats, writing about teenage superheroes, and telling people about her science degree. Sometimes she's funny on Twitter. @ SimCorWrites

Jennifer MacKenzie Dunbar lives between the hills and the sea on the margins of Adelaide. She has a BA in English Literature and worked as a Social Worker in the justice system. She believes in the restorative power of storytelling, nature and music, all common themes in her writing.

Rowena Edwards is a country-raised, vegetable-growing, grammar-policing hippie with uncommonly gifted eyebrows. She graduated from Flinders University with a Bachelor of Creative Arts (Hons) specialising in Creative Writing. The most influential person in her life lives in a paddock and whinnies romantically at feeding time.

Michele Fairbairn is a freelance writer, playwright, visual artist, performer and community health and arts worker. She has a passion for story-telling and hybrid theatre practices, with a particular penchant for working outside the square and taking risks by deviating from the well-trodden path into the quirky and sometimes, downright absurd.

Lauren Foley is Irish/Australian. She won the inaugural Overland/Neilma Sidney Short Story Prize, was shortlisted for the @Writing.ie/BGEIBAs Short Story of the Year for the same story: 'K-K-K'; also published in *Award Winning Australian Writing*, 2016. She lives in Skerries, County Dublin, and has Systemic Lupus Erythematosus. laurenfoleywriter. com @AYearInSouthOz

Rebecca Handler is from San Francisco and currently lives in Perth. She has worked in the philanthropic sector for many years and writes the blog www.onewomanparty.com. She is writing a novel about grief. Some of it is funny.

Christine Hanolsy is a science fiction and fantasy writer who cannot resist a love story. She serves on the editorial staff of the online writing community *YeahWrite*, where her primary portfolio includes microprose, flash fiction, and poetry. She lives in Portland, Oregon, USA, with her wife and their two sons.

Kathryn Hummel is a writer, ethnographer, poet and the author of *Poems from Here*, *The Bangalore Set* and *The Body That Holds*. Her diverse new media/poetry, non-fiction, fiction, photography and scholarly research has been published and presented worldwide and recognised with a Pushcart Prize nomination and the Dorothy Porter Prize at the 2013 Melbourne Lord Mayor's Creative Writing Awards. Kathryn is the current editor of 'Travel. Write. Translation' with *Verity La*.

Grace Jarvis is a second year university student in the throes of an arts degree based existential crisis. She was the recipient of the Queensland Theatre Company's Young Playwright's Award in 2015 and feels she needs to mention it constantly as it's the most impressive thing she's ever done. You can find her on Twitter @grace4jarvis.

Riana Kinlough is an Adelaide-based emerging writer. She recently completed her Honours in Creative Writing at Flinders University, and now spends most of her time shifting her cat off her keyboard.

J. R. Koop is a recent Creative Writing graduate from Flinders University. Since she began writing at age twelve, she has compiled a total of fourteen novels, along with novellas, short stories, and hundreds of poems. A fantasy writer at heart, this is her first romance story.

Marian Matta began concentrating on short fiction after being inspired by Annie Proulx's 'Brokeback Mountain'. A

Victorian hill-dweller, grandmother and circus student, she claims Heath Ledger as her muse. Her stories have appeared in Award Winning *Bush Verse & Stories, AWAW 2014*, and Spineless Wonders' *Amanda Lohrey Selects* e-anthology.

Amy T. Matthews is an award-winning novelist who also writes under the name Tess LeSue. She has published short stories in collections including *Best Australian Stories*. Amy is a Lecturer in Creative Writing at Flinders University, a member of the JM Coetzee Centre for Creative Practice, the Chair of the SA Writers' Centre, and was the convener of the RWA/Flinders 'Ain't Love Grand' conference in 2016.

C. J. McLean is a writer and playwright. His work has appeared in *InDaily, Buzzcuts* and *Rip It Up*, and his dramatic work has been produced by Australian Theatre for Young People and ABC Radio National. He has twice been commended in the State Theatre Company's Young Playwright's Award. In 2017, he produced and sold-out a cabaret show for the Adelaide Fringe, *Love & Anger*.

Vahri McKenzie is a writer and Senior Lecturer in the School of Arts and Humanities at Edith Cowan University in Western Australia. She publishes research about creative arts, writes short fiction and makes performance works: interests that inform her fiction writing.

Suzanne McCourt's debut novel, *The Lost Child*, (Text, 2014), was longlisted for the 2015 Miles Franklin Award. Her novella, *The Last Taboo*, shared first prize in the 2016 Griffith

Review Novella Competition. She is currently working on her second novel, set in Poland and Russia. Suzanne blogs at 'The Essential Mirror', www.suzannemccourt.com.au/blog

Rachael Mead is a South Australian poet, short story writer and arts critic. She is the author of three collections of poetry: *The Sixth Creek* (Picaro Press 2013) and two chapbooks. You can find more of her work at rachaelmead.com

Susan Midalia is the author of three collections of short stories, all shortlisted for major literary awards: *A History of the Beanbag, An Unknown Sky* (written with the assistance of An Australia Council grant) and *Feet to the Stars*. Her first novel will be published by Fremantle Press in February 2018.

Jess M. Miller is an emerging writer and PhD candidate at Flinders University; her work has been published in *InDaily* and *Lip*, and in 2016 she was a VIP-Fellow at Europa-Universität Viadrina in Frankfurt (Oder). Her research interrogates the absence of empowering female protagonists in time-travel fiction.

Michelle Ogilvy lives in Adelaide. Her first publishing credit was in a medical journal, due to her day job, but stories are her real passion. 'Cold blue to warm brown' is a prequel to her novel, *Coming In*. You can follow her on Twitter @ MichelleOgilvy.

Sonali Patel is an Adelaide-based writer and visual artist. Her writing and art is inspired by places she has lived in including Mumbai, Edinburgh and San Francisco. Her short stories have been published in *The Role of a Lifetime Stringybark Twisted Anthology* and the *Food, Wine, and the Fleurieu Anthology*.

Sue Robertson is a Melbourne-based writer. Her stories have appeared in *Best Australian Stories 05, Melbourne Subjective, SALA 2015, Shibboleth and Other Stories,* popular magazines, have been presented on RN Short Story and in 2010 she won the Limnisa Prize. She received a Special Commendation in the Scarlet Stiletto 2013.

Janey Runci lives in Melbourne. Her short stories have been published in literary journals, magazines and anthologies, including *Best Australian Stories*. She has won prizes for her short fiction in a number of Australian competitions, and also in the international Bridport and Fish competitions.

Ryan Scott has had stories published in a few websites and journals, including *B O D Y, Indigo* and *Fail Better*.

Bernadette Smith studied Creative Writing at Monash and Adelaide University. She has published short stories in literary magazines and anthologies, and is currently seeking to publish her first novel.

Rebecca Stratton is a twenty-something waitress. She dreams of one day opening the world's first certifiably hygienic ball-pit bar, incorporating a Tinder-like entry program with approval based entirely on the creativity of written applications. Her favourite drink is a gin and tonic, and her favourite cuisine is Italian. Just FYI.

Rita Tognini is an Italian born Western Australian writer. She writes short fiction and is a published poet. Rita won the Peter Cowan Writers' Centre 2016 Trudy Graham-Julie Lewis Literary Award for Prose and gained second and third prizes in the OOTA Writers' Group, 2016 Spilt Ink Competition.

Lynette Washington is a short story writer, editor and teacher of creative and professional writing. She holds a PhD in Creative Writing from the University of Adelaide. Her stories have been published widely and in 2014 she edited the short story collection, *Breaking Beauty*. Her debut collection, *Plane Tree Drive*, will be published in 2017. Facebook: Lynette Washington – Author. Twitter: @LynneTashi

MidnightSun Publishing

We are a small, independent publisher based in Adelaide, South Australia. Since publishing our first novel, Anna Solding's *The Hum of Concrete* in 2012, MidnightSun has gone from strength to strength.

We create books that are beautifully produced, unusual, sexy, funny and poignant. Books that challenge, excite, enrage and overwhelm. When readers tell us they have lost themselves in our stories, we rejoice in a job well done.

MidnightSun Publishing aims to reach new readers every year by consistently publishing excellent books. Welcome to the family!

midnightsunpublishing.com

MidnightSun *Publishing Brilliance*

www.ingramcontent.com/pod-product-compliance
Lightning Source LLC
Chambersburg PA
CBHW031003190726
48285CB00004BB/1453